you have a match

ALSO BY EMMA LORD

tweet cute

you have a match

WITHDRAWN

Emma Lord

WEDNESDAY BOOKS

NEW YORK

First published in the United States by Wednesday Books, an imprint of St. Martin's Publishing Group

www.wednesdaybooks.com

Designed by Anna Gorovoy

The Library of Congress Cataloging-in-Publication Data is available upon request.

ISBN 978-1-250-23730-9 (hardcover)
ISBN 978-1-250-81301-5 (international, sold outside the U.S., subject to rights availability)

ISBN 978-1-250-23731-6 (ebook)

Our books may be purchased in bulk for promotional, educational, or business use. Please contact your local bookseller or the Macmillan Corporate and Premium Sales Department at 1-800-221-7945, extension 5442, or by email at MacmillanSpecialMarkets@macmillan.com.

First U.S. Edition: 2021
First International Edition: 2021

10 9 8 7 6 5 4 3 2 1

For Evan and Maddie and Lily, the stone-cold pack of dweebs I am grateful to be part of every day of my human life

you have a match

one

It starts with a bet.

"Abby, I'm one hundred percent more Irish than you are," begins said bet, when Connie—who, admittedly, is about as ginger as they come—challenges me at the lunch table.

"Having red hair is not the be-all end-all of Irish-ness," I point out through a mouthful of Flamin' Hot Cheetos. "And my grandparents on my dad's side were like, so Irish they bled potatoes."

"Yet between you and all three of the gremlins you call little brothers, not one ginger," Connie points out, narrowly avoiding slopping her chili on the mountain of study guides she has propped on the lunch table.

"Dodged a bullet there, huh?" I tease her.

Connie lightly kicks my foot. I'd feel worse about it if she weren't so staggeringly beautiful that she has been mistaken for the actress who plays Sansa Stark more times than I can count on one hand, an especially impressive feat considering we live in a suburb of Seattle some bajillion miles away from any famous person who isn't Bill Gates.

"Not that I support this Anglo-Saxon nonsense—"

I flinch, and then Connie's chili *is* on Connie's pile of study guides. It is a testament to how committed she is to pretending things aren't awkward between me and Leo that she wipes the beans off the one loudly titled "AP FUCKING GOV! IS! YOUR! BITCH!!" without one threat to murder me.

"—but I'm doing one of those send-away DNA test things," Leo finishes in a mumble, planting himself and his lunchbox down next to Connie.

"Oh yeah?" I ask, leaning across the table and making deliberate eye contact with him.

Leo, the anchor of our trio, has known us both since we were little—me because we live in the same neighborhood, Connie through youth soccer. So we've both known him long enough to understand that this is kind of a big deal. Leo and his sister were both adopted from the Philippines and know next to nothing about their birth parents or their backgrounds, and up until now, he didn't seem to have any interest in looking into it.

But we're all taking Honors Anthropology and are right in the thick of a project where we're learning the proper way to track and denote lineage in our family trees. Hence, the Irish-off that Connie and I are currently engaged in, and probably Leo's new curiosity about tracing his roots.

Leo shrugs. "Yeah. I mean, I guess I'm more curious about the health stuff it'll tell you than anything else."

We both know that's only a half truth, but Connie pokes at it so I don't have to. "Health stuff?"

"It can also connect you to other biological family members if they've taken the test," Leo says quickly, more to his massive Tupperware of jambalaya than to us. Before we can ask any follow-up questions, he adds quickly, "Anyway, there's a discount if you buy more than one. If you're in, I can buy yours with mine and you guys can pay me back."

Connie moves Mount Study Guides off the table to make room for the rest of Leo's lunch, a bunch of delicious mismatched leftovers from his weekend culinary adventures. "You know what, I've got some money saved up from the ice-cream shop."

I wrinkle my nose. We all know I have money saved from babysitting aforementioned "gremlin" brothers during my parents' Friday date nights, but I also have my eye on a new lens for Kitty, my camera, that I'm obsessively tracking the price of online.

Except Leo's eyes find mine and linger in this way they haven't really in the last few months. At least, not since the Big Embarrassing Incident—more colloquially known as the BEI—I am still actively trying to scrub from my brain. Whatever it is in his gaze cuts right past it, and I understand at once that it isn't about the discount.

"Yeah. Yeah, let's do it."

Connie grins. "Loser has to make the other one soda bread."

Leo, the only one of us who can actually cook, perks up at this. "I'll help the loser."

Connie and I shake on it, and Leo starts talking about some soda bread fusion with cherries and chocolate and cinnamon, and the bet is finalized by the time the bell rings to end lunch.

To be honest, hours after we all spit into tubes and send off our kits, I forget about the whole thing. There are perilously low grades to juggle, endless tutoring sessions to endure, and worried but well-meaning parents to dodge. Plus with Leo focused on graduation and Connie focused on more extracurriculars than I have fingers and toes to count on, all three of us are basically spun out onto different planets.

But there it is, a month later: an email in my inbox, directing me to a website that apparently knows more about me than my sixteen years of knowing myself.

I scroll down, morbidly fascinated by the details. It tells me I'm most likely brunette (check), have curly hair (aggressive check), and am prone to getting a unibrow (rude, but also check). It tells me I'm probably not lactose intolerant and probably don't have issues with sleep, and that I am more likely than others to flush when drinking alcohol (noted, for future college endeavors). It also tells me I'm 35.6 percent Irish, a fact I immediately tuck away to rub in Connie's face when the time comes.

But whatever else it knows about me is abruptly cut off by the hum of my phone. It's from Leo, texting the group chat: DNA results came in. Big fat nothing.

It's the kind of text that I don't even have to wait for anyone to respond to in order to know we're all going to head over to Leo's. Still, I wait a few minutes, putting Kitty in her case and popping some gum in my mouth, giving Connie a chance to catch up to me so we'll get there at the same time.

"Where are you headed, kiddo?"

Allow me to clarify, because in the last few months of him shifting into working from home more often, I've become semi-fluent in Dad. In this case, *Where are you headed, kiddo?* loosely translates to *I'm pretty sure you haven't finished rewriting that English essay you tanked, and I'm 100 percent using this as a loving, yet still deeply passive-aggressive way to bring it up.*

I tighten my grip on my helmet, keeping my eyeballs as still as I possibly can even though resisting an eye roll right now might actually be pressurizing something in my brain.

"Leo's."

My dad pulls one of those affable, apologetic smiles of his, and I brace for the usual segue into the routine he and my mom have been perfecting since the start of junior year, when my GPA first took a swan dive.

"How's the old Abby Agenda?"

Ah, yes. The infamous "Abby Agenda." This chipper turn of phrase includes, and is not limited to, all the exhaustive tutoring sessions my parents signed me up for, the student-run test prep meetup for the SATs they keep making me attend, and a giant running list of all my homework assignments put on a whiteboard in the kitchen (or as I like to call it, the Board of Shame). I will give them points for creativity, if not subtlety.

"Dad. There are like, five days before summer vacation. I'm good to go."

He raises his eyebrows, and just as he intended, there's a fresh wave of guilt—not because I care all that much about anything on Abby's Annoyingly Alliterative Agenda, but because he looks straight-up exhausted.

"I'll *be* good to go," I correct myself. "But it's Saturday. And it's illegal to talk about homework on Saturdays."

"Says the kid with two lawyer parents." His smile is wry, but not enough to let me know I'm off the hook.

I blow a stray strand of hair out of my face. "I've got another draft ready, okay? I spent half the day on it. Now can I please go look at the sun before it swallows up the earth?"

He nods appreciatively. "We'll take a look at it when you get home."

I'm so relieved by my successful jailbreak that I basically tear holes into the street with my skateboard on my way to Leo's. It's only after I roll to a stop and shake the helmet head out of my mass of curls that I see the text from Connie, who is yet again held up at a Student Government Association meetup, and has essentially left me for dead.

"Well, shit."

If this were a few months ago, hanging out with Leo one-on-one would have been just another Saturday afternoon. But this isn't a few months ago. This is right the heck now, and I am standing like an idiot in his driveway, the shadow of the BEI creeping over me like an extremely humiliating, pheromone-ridden ghost.

Before I can decide what to do, Leo spots me and opens the front door.

"That'll be the Day," he says.

In lieu of nicknames, Leo's greetings of choice include any and all idioms about the word *Day*, which happens to be my last name. I start to roll my eyes like I usually do but pause at the sight of him in the doorway—the sun is starting to set, casting warm colors on his face, honeying the brown in his eyes and gleaming in his dark hair. I'm itching to know what it might look like through my camera lens, an itch I'm not so familiar with. I almost never photograph people.

Actually, these days my parents keep me so busy I barely photograph anything at all.

Leo's expression starts to shift, probably because I've been staring too long. I look away sharply and pop a wheelie on the way up to his front porch.

"Show-off," he says.

I prop my skateboard by the door and stick my tongue out at him. It's a relief to be on teasing terms again, but it's immediately punctured by what he says next.

"Where's Connie?"

He winces as soon as he asks, but I do what I do best and walk it off.

"Busy with last-minute details for tomorrow's Keyboard Wash for the junior class fundraiser."

"Keyboard Wash?" Leo's a senior, along with his non-Connie-and-Abby friends, so he's out of the loop on half of our goings-on. "Like a car wash for keyboards?"

"I've watched you use yours as a dinner plate, so I'll pencil you in."

I follow him into his house, inhaling warm butter and burnt cheese and, as always, the faint waft of cinnamon. Leo flicks on the front hall light, which exposes the precarious tower of pans, pots, and miscellaneous ingredients crammed into the small bit of counter real estate he has in his kitchen. His laptop is propped up on the table, open and exposed enough that I figure his parents and his sister, Carla, must be out.

I'm about to ask about the DNA test results displayed, but he puts a plate in front of my face first.

"Lasagna ball?"

I pull a wrapper out of my pocket and spit my gum in it. "Hell yeah."

"Careful, they're—hot," Leo says with a sigh, seeing I've already blatantly ignored his warning by popping it into my mouth.

The roof of my mouth instantly burns, but not enough that I don't appreciate how absurdly delicious it is—the legendary lasagna balls, one of Leo's many workarounds to actually cook in his house. He's become something of an oven snob and doesn't trust his to stay at a steady temperature, so he got himself a high-end toaster oven—hence, a lot of bite-size, dollhouse recipes, so I always feel like I'm in some fancy culinary pop-up when I'm just as stuck as I always am in the depths of Seattle suburbia.

"Are you okay?" he asks, with his usual mingling of exasperation and concern.

"You could've come over," I say, the ricotta legitimately steaming out of my mouth.

This is part of the reason Leo has been essentially absorbed by the Day family—our kitchen is humungous. And while we appreciate all that extra counter space for laying out several boxes of Domino's pizza during a feeding frenzy, nobody in our family actually cooks. Leo, on the other hand, is basically the Ina Garten of our high school and needs the space to fully manifest his Food Network dreams (plus, if we're being real, the ego boost of the Day brothers hollering about his six-cheese pizza at the top of their tiny lungs).

Not that Leo comes over much these days. We're not so great at being alone like this anymore. And as supportive as I want to be, I can't help the way my eyes keep skirting to the door, the way I keep waiting in the beat of silence that Connie usually fills.

"Is that Kitty?" Leo asks, looking at my camera case.

There it is again—that squeezing cycle of panic and relief. The teetering line between *are we okay?* and *we're okay enough.*

"And all nine of her lives."

"She's probably down to about six by now," says Leo. He would know—he's the one who gave the camera her name, after she survived more than a few harrowing drops, near plunges into bodies of water, and that time I thought it'd be cool to hang upside down from a jungle gym to get the sunset through the metal bars and ended up with a mouthful of playground rubber.

"You mind?" he asks.

I tuck my chin to my chest, hiding my smile as I pull Kitty out of her carrier. Leo reaches over my head into the cabinet to grab his mom's nice white plates, and I start arranging the lasagna balls on them. For a bit we're so locked into the easy quiet of this old pattern that I almost forget to wish Connie were here: I take a few shots of Leo's creations with Kitty, he uploads and posts them on his Instagram, and I promptly eat all the spoils.

He has a habit of uploading all my other photos, too. I'm not expecting him to today, though, until he surprises me by holding a hand out for Kitty. I try not to watch him as he clicks through views from the top of my mom's office building in Seattle, a sweeping, pre-dusk skyline punctured by the Space Needle, the clouds stark and heavy in the air.

I stand on my tiptoes, peering at the screen. My head barely clears his shoulder, forcing me close enough to him that the heady smell of cinnamon is thick in the air, warm in my lungs.

That's Leo's calling card—sneaking cinnamon into everything. Muffins, burritos, pudding, grilled cheese. Even when it's not supposed to work, he'll find a way to do it. Ever since we were kids he's always smelled like he was rolling around in the display case of a Cinnabon.

He stops on an image, tilting the camera so I get a better view. Leo claims not to know jack about photography, but of the dozen or so pictures I took, he still chose my favorite—the one where the shadows are a little harsher, right as the sun was gearing up to poke out from behind a cloud.

I glance up to nod my approval, but he's already watching me. Our eyes meet and there's something soft in his that holds me there—and without warning, the warmth of his knuckles skims under my jaw. My breath hovers somewhere unhelpfully in my chest, suspending me in the moment, into something brewing in Leo's eyes.

"You, uh—there was some cheese," he says. "On your . . ."

I touch the spot where his hand met my face. It feels like it has its own pulse.

"Oh."

"So, um, post it?"

I try to meet his eyes again, and when I do all I see is that familiar honey brown. You'd think I would have enough experience with my camera to know when something is only a trick of the light, but I can't ignore the tug of disappointment I know better than to feel.

"Yeah, if you wanna," I say, shrugging myself away from him and his autumnal smell and over to the table.

Leo clears his throat. "Sweet."

For a while he's been uploading these photos on a separate Instagram he made for me, even though the idea makes me feel a little topsy-turvy. He keeps saying it will be good to get a following, to have some kind of portfolio and a way to connect with other photographers, like he and some friend of his from summer camp have been doing with their own Instagram accounts. But the truth is, I viscerally dread the idea of sharing my photos with anyone. The thought of people out there seeing my work makes me feel so weirdly naked that I don't even look at the account.

Plus, if anyone's actually following it, I'm sure they're bored out of their skull—most of my pictures from the last year are the same places over and over, since the academic leash I'm kept on gets tighter by the day. And even if it weren't, I haven't been out as much lately. Photography was my *thing* with Poppy. It's been harder to go anywhere outside my element without my partner in crime.

A zillion hashtags and one masterfully shot blob of cheese and noodle later, Leo's lasagna ball Instagram is posted, and a large percentage of them are in my stomach. Leo sits on the couch, watching the likes trickle in, and I sit on the arm, hesitating before letting myself slide down with a *plunk* into the worn cushions beside him.

"So are we going to keep putting cheese in our faces, or talk about this DNA test thing?"

I'm not so good with the whole art of segueing. None of us are, really. I'm too blunt, Leo's too honest, and Connie—well, Connie just plain doesn't have the time. So Leo's fully expecting the question, the anticipation easing out of him with a sigh.

There's a silence, and this wobbly, uncertain moment when I think he might try to blow the whole thing off, and I won't know how to not take it personally. But then he turns to me with more frankness than he has in months.

"It's— I don't know. Like, how you know that statistically speaking, the odds that there isn't some other form of life in the universe are like, zilch." He picks at a seam in his jeans that hasn't quite come loose yet but is on its way. "But why the quiet? Do they not want to know us? Or can they just not reach us yet?"

I nudge Leo's shoulder with mine, tentative at first, but then he sags some of his weight into me. The relief is almost embarrassing. I hate that it takes one of us being upset for things to feel okay between us.

"My family tree is the Fermi paradox."

I wait in case he wants to elaborate. That's the thing with Leo, though. I always understand more about him in the beats after he says something than when he says it.

"Well, whatever that means—I'm sure it's that they can't reach you," I tell him. "I can't imagine anyone not wanting to know you."

Leo bristles. I take some of the edge off, because we both need it: "Even if you are kind of a dork."

This earns me a sharp laugh. "*Hey.*"

"Facts are facts."

He bops me on the knee with the palm of his hand, his skin touching mine where my jeans are ripped. His eyes linger on an old scar, just above my kneecap. I have no memory of what it's from, but Leo does. He always keeps score of that kind of thing, like it's some personal failing of his—ever since we were little, I've been the daredevil, and he's been the safety net. Me climbing and jumping and shimmying into places I shouldn't, and Leo a few feet behind, warning and worrying and probably developing Abby-shaped ulcers in every one of his organs along the way.

Before he can comment on it I rest my head on his shoulder, like when we were kids and napped on each other on the bus—one of the few times I was ever still for more than a few moments. Only it doesn't feel quite like it did. There's a new firmness to him, and he's so tall now that my head doesn't fall in the same place. It presses us closer, me trying to find some purchase on him, him scooting to let me fit.

I really shouldn't do this. I know better. But it feels like I am playing a game of chicken with the universe—like I can make this whole thing feel normal, even when it actively is not.

Because normal isn't my heart beating in my fingertips and in the skin of my cheek on his T-shirt sleeve. Normal isn't noticing the way that cinnamon smell of his has gone from grounding to dizzying, taking on something sweeter and too innate in me to name. Normal isn't having a big, stupid, ridiculous crush on one of my best friends, especially when he most certainly doesn't have one on me.

And there it is: the BEI bubbling its way back to the surface and popping all over again. My brain is so into reliving it that sometimes I'm almost glad my parents keep me busy—the more time I sink into trying to keep up at school, the less time I have to think about how I colossally messed things up with Leo and almost took down our whole little trio with it.

I take my head off his shoulder, turning to face him. "And you know, the database on this thing updates all the time," I press on. "You could check in a few months and maybe someone related to you *will* have taken the test. This isn't game over."

Leo lets this sink in. "I don't know if I want to be like, waiting on that, you know?"

"So give me your password and I'll check on it for you."

He huffs out a laugh that's equal parts appreciative and dismissive. "I'd still be waiting on it."

I hop off his couch, reaching for his laptop. "Then I'll change your password. Write it down on a teensy piece of paper and eat it."

"You're ridiculous," he says.

"I'm serious," I tell him, poised to type. "Minus the eating part."

"What would the eating part even have accomplished?"

We're veering off course, but I can tell he hasn't fully gotten this off his chest yet. And even though he's not going to tonight, and it will likely manifest into another one of his cooking and/ or baking frenzies that will keep me and Connie fed at lunch for the next week, we can at least try.

I glance back at him, waiting.

"I don't even really think about it that much. I mean, I didn't, until recently. But I always kind of figured if I wanted to know, I could."

"You can't ask your parents?"

Leo glances at the driveway, as if one of them is going to jump out from under the porch window. "Well—the adoption was closed, so . . ."

"You don't think they'd be chill with you looking?"

"No, no, they—of course they would," he says, his eyes lingering on the front of the house.

The most Leo thing about Leo is this: he's always putting other people's feelings before his, always trying to keep the peace. Someone nearly ran him over in Pike Place Market running a red, and when the driver immediately burst into hysterics, Leo apologized to *her*. It's like he's a barometer for human emotion, and anytime someone is out of whack he feels obligated to tip the scale back in their favor.

This is somewhat mitigated, at least, by the fact that Leo's parents are both psychology-majors-turned-teachers and knew this about him before he even started forming full sentences. They're both pretty busy with work, but they make up for it with enough family game nights, weekend outings, and infinite parental empathy to make the parents from *The Brady Bunch* look like chumps. If anyone is prepared to handle their kid asking questions like the ones Leo has, it's them.

But that doesn't mean Leo won't talk himself out of it anyway, for everyone's sake but his own.

"It's just, there's really no wikiHow page on how to tell your white parents you're looking for the family that actually, y'know, looks like you." He pauses before adding, "That, and Carla doesn't want to know."

Ah. Carla and Leo were adopted together and are full-blooded siblings so close in age they're mistaken for twins more often than not. But that's all either of them has ever known about the adoption—that they came as a pair, when Leo was a year old and Carla was brand-spanking new.

"I guess that's fair," I say cautiously.

"Yeah. But it's—I don't know. I've never been good at . . . not knowing things."

Leo and I may be different in a lot of ways, but here we are too alike: the "latch" factor.

Leo's *knowing* thing goes as far back as I remember him. He's always trying to understand how stuff works, whether it's whatever paradox Fermi's dealing with or the precise amount of time it takes to use a mixer on egg whites for the perfect cloud eggs. As early as preschool he was driving every teacher he had up the wall, ending every explanation anyone gave him for anything with "But why?" To this day, his mom still mimics his piping little voice—"But why? But why? But why?"—a teasing glint in her eye.

For me, though, it's a *doing* thing. While Leo's been busy asking questions, I've been busy not asking enough of them. An idea pops into my brain and I can't talk myself out of it: Cut my hair to see if it would grow back overnight. Hop past the NO TRESPASSING sign on a trail to get a better view. Commit to whatever the hell was going through my head during the infamous BEI.

Maybe it's why we've always kind of gravitated to each other. I pull Leo off the ledges of his thought spirals. He pulls me off literal ledges. We've got each other's backs.

"Here," I say, pulling up my results. "Show me how to get to the ancestry part so I can hack into your account later."

Leo goes rigid. A van decked out with soaped-up words in our school colors loudly idles in front of Leo's place and comes to a stop, and Carla hops out and waves to the other cheerleaders in her carpool. Leo stands up from the couch so fast someone might have electrocuted him.

Then his shoulders slump, like something he's held together too long is starting to fold up inside him.

"It's, uh—it's pretty straightforward," he mumbles. "Just tap the 'Relations' thing under 'Ancestry.'"

Carla spots me through the window and picks up the pace, her backpack bouncing on her shoulders and her ponytail bobbing. I wave at her, waiting for the page to load, and Leo lets out a sigh.

"It's probably better to drop the whole thing," says Leo. "It might just be a waste of time, and I should be focusing on my future, you know?"

He says something else that gets drowned out by the words on my phone screen, which are somehow impossibly loud.

"Abby?"

I'm on my feet so fast that I trip on the carpet. Leo grabs me before I pitch forward, and there's this momentary shock of his warm hands on my skin. Before I'm totally paralyzed by it, we're interrupted by the clatter of my phone bouncing off the carpet and onto the faded hardwood.

"Uh—am I interrupting something?" asks Carla, looking between me and Leo with a faint smirk.

Leo releases me so abruptly that I feel like a balloon someone accidentally lost hold of—I'm untethered. Aimless. Unsure of where to go, except that I need to get out of here *fast*, away from walls and words on a screen and the way Leo is looking at me, like he's already ten minutes ahead anticipating whatever stupid thing I'm about to do next.

"I have to—I just realized—I have tutoring," I blurt.

Leo reaches down to pick up my phone, but I dive for it, grabbing it before he can. He tries to make eye contact with me, but I can't, or it's all going to spill out of me before I even know what it means.

"Abby, what's . . ."

"On a Saturday?" Carla asks, scowling.

"For, uh—" They're both staring at me. I try to think of a single school subject I'm taking or even one passable word in the English language I can use to excuse myself, but there's only room for one thought in my brain right now, and it's swelling like a balloon. "I just have to—I gotta—I'll text you later."

Leo follows me to the door, but I'm too fast for him. Within seconds I've yanked my helmet onto my head, grabbed Kitty, shoved my phone into my back pocket, and torn onto the sidewalk faster than my rickety old skateboard has ever gone. Halfway home, the stupid thing Leo no doubt predicted happens: I roll right into a crack in the pavement, end up flying like a crash test dummy, and find myself a few mortifying seconds later on my very bruised butt with my skateboard lying in the grass of someone's front yard.

I sit there, my heart beating in my ears, my mouth tasting like pennies from biting down on my tongue. I do a quick body-check and discover that, while the embarrassment may be lethal, the rest of me remains relatively unscathed.

Only after I pull myself up does my phone slip out of my back pocket, revealing one majorly cracked screen. I cringe, but that doesn't stop the phone from unlocking, or opening to the page that's been burned into my eyes ever since I saw it—a message request from a girl named Savannah Tully that reads, Hey. I know this is super weird. But do you want to meet up?

A message request from a girl named Savannah Tully, who the DNA site identifies as my full-blooded sister.

two

When you find out your parents have harbored a secret older sibling from you for all the sixteen years you've inhabited the Earth, the last thing you should probably do is suck in a mouthful of air and yell, *"Mom!"*

But I walk through the front door and do exactly that.

It takes her approximately ten seconds to reach me, and they are simultaneously the longest and shortest ten seconds of my life. Long enough to understand that what happened is going to fundamentally change me forever; short enough to decide I don't want it to just yet.

"What happened?" she asks, her eyes widening at my knees. I look down and only then notice the matching bloodstains around the holes in my jeans, which have now ripped so wide they look like I'm trying to send my legs to another dimension.

I open my mouth. "I . . ."

Her arm is streaked with green paint from one of my brothers' art projects, her wild brown hair yanked into a high bun, and she's balancing a laundry basket on one hip and a large folder of depositions on the other. She stands there in all her *my mom*–ness, her brow furrowed and her teeth biting her lower lip, and suddenly the whole thing is absurd.

This is a person who tells me grisly, ridiculously personal details about her cases, knowing I won't make a peep. This is a person who very frankly explained sex to me in the third grade when I interrupted one of her and my dad's movie nights during the fogged-up car window scene in *Titanic*. This is a person who *cried* when she told me about Santa Claus, because she felt so bad for lying.

This is not a person who keeps secrets, and especially not from me.

"I—fell on my skateboard."

"Are you okay?" Her eyes are already edging toward the first aid kit, which, between me and my three brothers, is stocked more regularly than any of our lunch boxes.

I wave her off, not looking her in the eye. "Fine. Great!" Which may have had a chance of sounding believable if I didn't follow it up by nearly tripping over the mountain of Velcro and light-up boy shoes haphazardly piled at the door as I attempt to sprint toward my room.

"You sure?"

"Yup!"

A beat passes, one of those stretched-out ones like she's going to call me out on something. I hover at the door of my room, bracing myself for it: *I know you know the thing I didn't want you to know!* Like she saw it on my face as soon as I walked in, and only just put the pieces together with her uncanny psychic mom powers.

Instead she says, "Well, I left some of those flyers on your bed, if you get a chance to—"

"Thanks!" I cut her off, and close my door swiftly behind me.

I beeline for my laptop, as if opening a new screen will make the thing I saw on the other one go away. But to get to it I have to shove off the pile of aforementioned glossy, painfully colorful flyers propped on top of it, along with a Post-it Note that says "Looks fun!!" stuck on top.

They're all for Camp Reynolds, this new summer program

the school guidance counselor told my parents about. He tried to sell me on it too, cheerfully telling me over the human-head-size candy bowl he keeps in his office that it's perfect for "kids like me"—a.k.a. kids whose college prospects are dwindling with every lost decimal of their GPA. It's supposed to get students up to speed with the SATs and college application prep and all the other stuff that I'm going to be shoved into the cross fire of next year.

Until two hours ago, my life's mission was getting out of it. But whatever sense of linear order my life has just got blown to pieces.

I shove the flyers onto the mattress, drumming my fingers on the keyboard as I wait for the laptop to wake up. Whoever this *Savannah* is, she can't really be my sister. They swapped my spit out for someone else's, or sent me the wrong results. I mean, the thing said I'm more likely than others to match musical pitches, and I'm so tone-deaf my brother Brandon—arguably the most agreeable kid to ever live—screamed bloody murder when I tried to sing to him as a baby. These are some other slightly Irish, unibrow-prone girl's DNA results that got bungled with mine, and in a few hours we'll all sit at the dinner table and laugh about the whole thing.

But I glance at the "Relations" page anyway so I can do my due diligence when I make a customer complaint. *Savannah Tully*, says the name on the top of the list.

And then my heart wrings like a sponge in my chest. *Georgia Day*, it reads. *We predict Georgia Day is your first cousin.*

And the next one: *Lisa McGinnis. We predict Lisa McGinnis is your second to third cousin.*

The names below it—second, third, even fifth cousins—are unfamiliar. But Georgia and I were born in the same month, and even though she lives in San Francisco, we're in loose touch, tagging each other in the occasional Tumblr meme and texting whenever the body count gets a little preposterous on *Riverdale*. And Lisa definitely friended me on Facebook within an hour of Poppy's funeral last summer.

Which can only mean . . .

"Oh my *god*."

I don't realize I've yelled it until I hear a knock and my dad's head pops in. "What is it?"

I slam the laptop shut. "I thought I saw a spider."

My voice is just loud enough to carry to the boys' room, where an instant commotion is set off.

"*Spider?* Where?" pipes Brandon, who is notoriously afraid of them.

"Spider? *Where?*" demands Mason, who is going through an aggressive Spider-Man phase.

Before anyone can get a word in edgewise, a pan clatters from the kitchen, which can only be Asher trying to take macaroni-related matters into his own hands again. Dad winces, and Mom yells, "I got it!" in the same exasperated way she always does, and so begins an extremely familiar number in the soundtrack of Day family chaos.

"You got that draft ready to rumble?"

I can hear how tired his voice is before he's even fully in the room, the kind that's way past "parent of three boys and one very stubborn teenager" levels of tired. Ever since Poppy died, it sort of seems like he and my mom are never not in motion. My dad gets to his office at the crack of dawn and my mom gets home at about a bajillion o'clock at night, the two of them desperately trying to make sure someone's always home or home adjacent to keep track of us now that my grandpa can't.

Which is why I feel extra bad that I am teetering the line between a solid C and high D in English, and extra *extra* bad that he's not even mad about it the way a normal parent would be, and is instead reading the umpteenth draft on this essay I have written about why Benvolio from *Romeo and Juliet* is a total buzzkill for constantly nagging his friends.

Okay, the thesis is slightly more academic than that, but the point stands. English isn't exactly my strong suit. It's not that I don't like reading, or that I'm a bad student—actually, up until this year, I was doing okay in the land of academia—but my vendetta against English in particular is that I hate arguing, and arguing is like 90 percent of any English class you take. Sure, it's organized, nerdy arguing, but arguing nonetheless—about a thesis statement, or some character's motivation, or what some author did or didn't mean to say.

And I'm about as Type B as they come. I have no interest in arguing, or confrontation in general. Give me the wrong scoop of ice cream? I'll eat it. Sneak into my room and cut the sleeves off my red sweater for your Spider-Man costume? Shit happens.

Lie to my face about a sister who lives a few suburbs away for sixteen years?

Well.

"Yeah," I say, like the cowardly coward that I am. I pull it off the printer and hand it to him.

My dad frowns. "What's got your gourd?"

"Nothing."

My phone buzzes, and a picture of Connie pretending to lick the display case at Yellow Leaf Cupcake Co. pops up on my screen. Nobody in their right mind calls on a phone anymore, but Connie's so busy with her chronic overachieving that she claims she doesn't have the time to type.

"I know it's a drag, but it gets a little better each time, right?" says my dad, holding the essay up.

Not in the slightest. I pick up the phone and my dad waves himself out with a flourish, taking the fifth draft of my godforsaken essay with him.

"Yo. Put Leo on. I've got a pep talk ready."

"I'm not at Leo's."

"You're not?"

There's something almost accusatory in the way she asks, and I think maybe she'll bring it up—the weirdness we've all been semidancing around since the BEI. But she cuts through the tension before I can even decide if it's real or not, saying, "In that case, 31.8 percent, *sucker.*"

I am so far removed from reality that I genuinely have no idea what she's talking about.

"You owe me soda bread. And no cheating, you can't have Leo do the whole thing for you," she tells me.

"Uh . . ."

"Anyway, I'll just call Leo's phone, is he still around?"

"Yeah."

Connie pauses. "Why do you sound weird?"

My mouth is open, but the airflow between my lungs and the outside world seems to have stopped, like I'm breathing into a plastic bag.

Savannah Tully.

"Um."

I can't seem to get past monosyllables. It's like my tongue is too thick for my mouth, as if I've become some whole other person since my ill-fated skateboard ride back from Leo's, and I'm not sure how she's supposed to act, what she's supposed to say.

"Oh shit. Are you more Irish than I am after all? You're like, Saoirse Ronan's secret twin—"

"No. I mean, I am more Irish, but—"

"Is it one of the health things? Oh man, I've put my foot in it, haven't I? If it makes you feel better, I totally got flagged on the celiac gene—"

"It's not that."

The words come out a snap, which stuns both of us into silence. I'm never short with Connie, or anybody, really. I get riled, sure, and impatient, but never with anyone but myself.

I'm not even sure what I am right now, though.

"Abs?"

I can't. If I tell her, it'll be real. And I'll have to do something about it. Okay, I won't *have* to, but that's the thing with me—it's the "latch" factor. If I let myself get in too deep on this, I won't be able to let it go, even if I wish more than anything that I could.

I won't let myself latch on to this. I *can't.*

"It's not—I mean, yeah, I'm more Irish than you." Even in the midst of what might be my First Ever Existential Crisis, I can't help but rub it in. "But I . . ."

Maybe I'll regret saying it, but it feels like there is some kind of pressure building up in me that might explode if I don't let it out.

I spring out of my chair and shut the door to my room again as slowly as I can, muffling the *click.* That's twice now I've shut my door in a span of ten minutes. I almost never close it—my brothers are in and out so often that it's basically a second living room—so I'll have to make this fast.

"It says I have a sister."

Connie is dead silent, and then: "Huh?"

"Like, a full-blooded sister. Some girl named Savannah Tully who *lives a half hour from us,* in *Medina.*"

"Whoa, like rich-person Medina?"

She is missing the point here. "Like, full-blooded as in *we have the same parents.* Like, the parents that I have made some other person before me who I don't know about. And get this—it says she's *eighteen.*"

Another silence, and then: "Oh my god."

"What?"

"Abby . . . she looks like you."

"She what? How did you—how are you—"

"She's got like, half a million followers on Instagram."

"Okay, how do you even know it's—"

"Because she legit looks like you. I'm sending you a link."

Don't, I almost tell her, but it's too late. I've latched. I've freaking latched, and I have to know.

I pull the phone away from my ear and tap the link, landing on an Instagram account with the handle @howtostaysavvy. The bio reads, "wellness dweeb, nutrition nerd, wannabe mermaid. all about staying savvy."

Connie wasn't exaggerating—her follower count is obscene.

I scroll down and see the first few images. A beaming girl jumping on a rocky beach, her limbs splayed out in a strappy bikini, the water of the Puget Sound gleaming in the background. Another of her at a white table outside of some restaurant, chestnut brown hair blowing in the wind and tongue stuck out playfully, her fork poised above a colorful salad. A selfie with a Labrador retriever, close enough to see the dusting of freckles on her scrunched nose, the white of her teeth in her open, mid-laugh smile, the poreless perfection of her skin.

I close the app, my hands shaking.

"She doesn't look anything like me."

"Bull*shit*." And then: "So what are you going to do? Can you message her?"

"She already messaged me."

"Way to bury the lede," Connie exclaims. "Saying *what?*"

I pull it back up and tell her, pacing across the room as if I can get farther away from the words on the screen even though the phone is still in my hand.

"Are you gonna message her back?"

No. Yes. "I don't know." I end up doing what I usually do when faced with a difficult choice: pull a Carrie Underwood and let Connie take the wheel. "What would *you* do?"

Thirteen-year-old Connie would have told me, along with a twelve-step action plan in a shared Excel sheet so aggressively color-coded that the Lucky Charms leprechaun would have shuddered at the sight. Seventeen-year-old Connie is, unfortunately, too wise for that.

"Let's make a pros and Connies list," she offers instead.

I groan, both at the pun that Connie will never let die and the prospect of making said list. A "pros and Connies" list is different from a typical pros and cons list, not just because it makes everyone's eyes roll into the backs of their heads, but because instead of framing the question as, "What would happen if I did this?" Connie insists on writing the list as, "What would happen if I *didn't* do this?" That way, she insists, the cons aren't negatives, but cold truths. Connies, if you will. Fitting, I guess, because Connie is nothing if not brutally honest.

The first pro is so immediate that there's no point in writing it down: I wouldn't make my parents mad. I'm assuming they'd be mad. Right? Like, whatever this is, it's not only super weird, but they must have gone to some pretty extreme lengths to hide it from me.

And I'm not exactly in a great position to go around upsetting my parents. Between shuffling me to tutors, constantly replacing my broken phone screens, and fielding calls from concerned neighbors every other day saying they saw me climb something I wasn't supposed to, having me for a kid seems baseline exhausting.

Yet something else knocks all that guilt aside: the idea of an ally. Someone I could talk to about things I can't share with my parents or even Connie—things like the BEI. Or how I am sometimes so overwhelmed by all the scrutiny on my grades that if anything, it makes the situation worse. Or how I have no idea how I'm supposed to fit into the world after high school, if there's even a proper place for me to fit at all.

Someone who might be to me what Poppy was, before he died. Someone who understood me well enough that I never felt self-conscious telling him about the embarrassing stuff, or even sharing my photos. I come from a family of worrywarts and planners, but he was the one who was always like me—he loved a good adventure, was every bit as impulsive, had embarrassing stories to tell that rivaled mine. I could tell him the truthiest truths of me—the good, the bad, and the "I'm pretty sure I threw away my retainer and it's somewhere in the sixty bags of garbage behind the school gym" levels of ugly—without ever getting the sense that I might disappoint him.

There it is. The "Connie." Maybe I can find a person who understands me the way nobody else can. If I don't do this, I'll never have the chance.

"Hey, Abby? I've got some notes!" my dad calls.

I close my eyes. "I gotta go. But—don't tell anyone about this, okay?"

"'Course not." Before I can hang up, Connie asks, "Wait, not even Leo?"

"I'll tell him, I just want to . . ."

Scream into my pillow? Bust into my parents' bedroom and yell "I KNOW THE TRUTH!" like I live in a comic and there's a speech bubble over my head? Run away, join the circus, and never think about any of this ever again?

"Got it. Godspeed." There's a beat. "Also, is it weird if I follow her?"

"Connie."

"What? She's goals. She can do those crazy handstand yoga poses. And I'm obsessed with Rufus."

"Who?"

"Her dog."

"Good*bye*."

I hang up and take the kind of breath that is less of a breath and more of a decision. One that, pros and Connies aside, I couldn't unmake if I tried.

I open up the app and type back: **Are you free tomorrow?**

three

I know the drive from my house to Green Lake so well that it feels less like visualizing a map of roads than a map of myself. As a kid I'd wake up every Saturday at the crack of dawn, waiting, waiting, waiting for Poppy to come pick me up and take me to Bean Well, the little coffee shop he had started with Gammy, who died before I was born. My parents would spend their weekends catching up on their law school reading, and I'd spend them munching on chocolate-chip scones, coloring endless pages of dragons and unicorns, and fiddling with the buttons of Poppy's beaten-up old Nikon camera.

My dad pulls up to Bean Well with an almost apologetic sigh. "You don't want to pop in?"

I do. I miss Marianne, the manager, who has taken over since Poppy died last year. I miss the sugar crunch on top of the scones and the regulars marveling at me being "so grown up" and Mrs. Leary's dog, who loves the place so much that sometimes he wanders over on his own to whine for free dog treats.

I miss taking this place for granted, because now I can't. Marianne is retiring and my parents are selling the place, and a big old chunk of my childhood right along with it.

I wrench my eyes away from the lit-up Bean Well sign above the door, to Ellie the barista with her Cindy Lou Who–high topknot laughing at someone's joke at the register.

"Maybe later," I say. "I heard there was a bald eagle popping in and out of the park, thought I might try to get a shot."

A lie wrapped inside of a lie that just jump-vaulted off a cliff into another lie, but not one that my dad will question. The thing is, Green Lake is almost exactly halfway between Shoreline and Medina, which Savannah and I figured out in our brief exchange last night before planning to meet here.

"Sounds good, kiddo. I'll text when I'm done with the realtor."

I step out of the car and into the humid June fog, feeling the frizz of my curls start to rise like they've become sentient. I start to pat them down but stop myself. If Savannah really is my sister, I have no reason to impress her. We're made up of all the same weird stuff, aren't we?

Which somehow has not stopped me from stress-chewing my way through an entire pack of gum and changing my socks three times, as if putting on the striped ones would have made this catastrophically strange thing any less strange.

A shiver runs up my spine as I cross the street to the park, keeping my eyes peeled. I'm a few minutes late, but it's not like I could tell my dad to step on it because I have a date with my own personal reality show. I'm assuming I'll find Savvy by the benches, but they're full of kids with sticky ice-cream fingers and joggers stretching their limbs.

I squint, and there, beyond the benches, toward one of the massive trees that borders the lake, is a girl in pale pink capri workout leggings and a pristine white top posing with a water bottle, her hair mounted in a slick, shiny ponytail without a single strand out of place.

"Can you see the label on the bottle?" she's asking. "They're gonna make us redo it if—"

"Yup, label's fine, it's just the weird shadows from the leaves," says a girl with her. "Maybe if we . . ."

I can only see the back of her, but there's no mistaking it. I hesitate, trying to think up an opening line. Something other than *Hey, may I just be the first to say, what the actual fuck?*

Before I can get close enough, the biggest, fluffiest Labrador retriever to ever exist comes barreling at me, paws up and pouncing on me like my bones are held up with kibble. I squeal, letting him bowl me over into the grass—*Rufus*, I remember, from the deep dive I took on Savannah's Instagram account last night—and he yelps his approval, a bottle of sunscreen falling out of his mouth.

"I got him, I got him," says someone—the one with the camera, an Asian girl with two long French braids and a broad smile. Either I am extremely concussed from Rufus, or she is rocking a full sleeve of punk Disney princess tattoos on her left arm and various Harry Potter–related ones on her right. "Whose even *is* this, you furry little thief?" she asks, seeing the sunscreen at our feet. Now that she's closer I can see the edges of the tattoos are temporary, all bright and gleaming in the sun. She turns back to me. "Sorry," she says sheepishly, "he only ever does this to—"

Her mouth drops open. She looks me up and down, or at least as much of me as she can with Rufus on top of me.

"Savvy," she says. She clears her throat, taking a step back like I've spooked her, while Rufus continues to lick my face like it's a lollipop.

"Um," I manage, "are you . . . ?"

Another hand comes into view, offering me a lift up. I take it—colder than mine, but not cold enough to cancel out the immediate eeriness. I feel like I've been displaced in time.

"Hey. I'm Savvy."

Poppy had this thing he always said when we were out with our cameras. He'd show me how different lenses captured different perspectives, and how no two photos of the same thing were ever alike, simply because of the person taking them. *If you learn to capture a feeling,* he told me, *it'll always be louder than words.*

Sometimes I can still hear the way he said it. The low, gravelly sound of his voice, with that bare hint of a smirk in it. I always clung to it, growing up. He was right. Feelings were always easier in the abstract, like the breathless moment the skateboard tilted down the big hill in my neighborhood, or the reassuring way Connie squeezed my hand between our desks before a big test. Words always fell short. Made the feeling cheap. Some things, I think, there weren't supposed to be words for at all.

Everywhere I go I have those words tucked somewhere in my heart, but right now they're pulsing through me like a drumbeat that somehow led me here, a few short miles and a hop across a familiar street, to the loudest feeling I've ever felt.

"Abby," I introduce myself.

I stare at her staring at me and the resemblance is so uncanny I'm not sure if I'm staring at a person or a bunch of people all at once. I guess, having little brothers, it's hard to see the parts of them that look like my parents and the parts that don't—they're still mostly sticky and hyper and un-fully-formed. I've only ever noticed the parts of me that look like them because I grew up with everyone telling me.

But there is something about seeing Savvy, with my mom's dainty nose and my dad's high forehead, Asher's and Brandon's full cheeks, and Mason's distinctive cowlick in the crown of her hair, that seems less like genetic inevitability and more like science fiction. Like she was conjured here, all the people I love smushed into one very short, extremely chic person.

Her hair, though—even with all the product she's used, it's starting to come undone in the heat, and it's all mine, all my mom's. Wild and untamed, the kind that curls in some places

and frizzes in others, so it never once does us the favor of looking the same from one day to the next.

"Wow. It's like Alternate Dimension Savvy. One where you're
taller and wear actual clothes instead of athleisure all day," the
other girl mutters, peering at us in turn. Even Rufus seems uneasy, his furry head bobbing from me to Savvy and back, letting
out a low, confused whine.

Savannah—Savvy—clears her throat. "Well—I mean—I sup-
pose we do look a little alike."

Her eyes graze me. It only takes a second, but I see the places
she lingers. My ratty shoelaces. The widened rips in my jeans
from yesterday. The gum in my mouth. The tiny scar that interrupts my left eyebrow. The slump of my limp ponytail, held
together with a glittery scrunchie of Connie's that doesn't match
anything I've ever touched, let alone owned.

I try not to bristle, but when her eyes meet mine, almost
clinical in the way she's accounting for the pieces of me, my
eyes are narrowed. I do a once-over of her but can't find a single
flaw. She looks like she fell out of a Lululemon ad.

"Yeah," I concede. "A little."

There's an awkward beat where the three of us stand there,
looking and not looking. Maybe there's a word for the feeling
after all. Maybe it's disappointment.

"I'm Mickey," says her friend, extending her hand to shake.
"Er, McKayla. But everyone calls me Mickey, on account of—
well," she says, showing me her left arm, which also features a
rainbow gradient version of Cinderella's Castle in the Magic
Kingdom smack-dab in the middle of all the Disney characters.
"Bit of a thing."

I take her hand, wishing Connie could have come with me.
I even start to wish Leo were here. People who define the little
borders of my world in a way that plain old me in my beaten-up

Adidas and sudden inability to string words into sentences can't on their own.

"Oh," I realize, seeing the rings stacked on Mickey's middle finger as she pulls her hand away. "You're the girlfriend."

Mickey's entire face blooms red, starting at her neck and ending somewhere at the tips of her ears. "Well, not *the* girlfriend," I backtrack, wondering if that was rude. "Savvy's, I mean. From Instagram?"

Savvy's mentioned the girl she's dating in a few of her posts, but they all have a distinct "my girlfriend in Canada" vibe. Beyond a few artfully staged shots of their hands or captions alluding to her, she never actually makes an appearance. The rings, though, I remember seeing just off frame in a shot of some bougie vegan place Savvy ate at in Bell Square last month.

"Oh," says Savvy, looking flustered. "She's not . . ."

Mickey only gets redder. "No, no, we're just friends. Best friends! Since like, the beginning of time," she says, "but—"

"Sorry," I blurt. "I—saw the rings, on Instagram, and thought—"

"You're thinking of Jo. She's interning at some fancy office downtown," says Mickey, whose turnaround on social recovery is way higher than mine or, apparently, Savvy's, who offers a "Yeah" to confirm.

There's another silence. I nudge some dirt in the wet grass with my foot, right as Savvy looks down and does the same. It's unnerving. It's why, I realize, we've been dancing around the thing we came here to do—we are both breaking a rule by being here. An unspoken one. A rule buried so deep in our past that our parents never even told us it existed. It has strange power over us even now, standing right in front of each other with the proof that we're both real.

"I, uh—my dad's gonna text soon. He's finishing up some stuff down the street."

I wince as soon as I say it: *my dad.* Because he's not *my* dad, is he? Technically he's *our* dad. And only then does the weirdness feel less abstract and more solid, like some barrier in between us we can both touch.

Savvy nods. "Do you want to sit?"

I eye the bench, knowing if I let that happen the ringing in my brain is going to go full scream. "We could walk on the path around the lake?"

Savvy seems relieved. "Yeah."

"I'll kick it here with Rufus," says Mickey, with a wink. "Try to figure out who the heck he robbed of their SPF sixty."

I've known Mickey for all of two seconds, but as we take off on the overly crowded gravel path, I somehow genuinely miss her. My throat feels drier than the griptape on top of my skateboard, my palms sweaty enough that I might have just emerged like some creature from the algae overgrowth in the lake. I feel—not myself. Not the person I usually am, whoever she is. I've never had to think about it before, never had anything to measure myself by, and now there's this walking, talking, Instagram of a measuring stick, some new way to define myself that there's never been before.

We're quiet as we put some distance between us and the rest of the people on the path. She leads like it's second nature, but when she checks back to make sure I'm still behind her, the unease brewing in her is clear. I wonder if it's the same for her as it is for me—the strangeness of feeling like I'm looking at some other version of myself, and the sudden dread that I'm not sure I like it much at all.

four

"So," Savvy starts.

I laugh this nervous laugh I've never laughed before. "So."

I can't look at her, but I'm also looking right *at* her. My eyes are on her and around her, everywhere and nowhere at once. The me and the not-me of her. I can't decide what's weirder, the parts of her I recognize or the parts that I don't.

She diverts off the path unexpectedly, grabbing someone's mucked-up, abandoned water bottle, and stalks off to the recycling can. I stand there, not sure if I was meant to follow, but she doesn't look back.

"That was going to bother me," she says by way of explanation when she gets back.

Even in this short amount of time I am starting to get a taste for Savvy's world—or at least, the world as Savvy makes it. Clean. Precise. Controlled. A lot of things that I most certainly am not.

"I'll start," she says, with the air of someone used to taking charge of situations. "I guess I should say that I've always known I was adopted."

We're walking, but her eyes are steady on me, making it clear I have her full and undivided attention. Just from her three seconds of prolonged eye contact it's clear she is not a person who does anything in halves—when she's focused on me, she is *focused*,

YOU HAVE A MATCH 37

only pausing to get out of the way of cyclists and kids on Razor scooters.

"I guess I should say . . . I had no idea you existed."

I'm afraid she might take that the wrong way, but she only nods. "You either. My parents always told me that my bios were really young and didn't stay together. But it looks like they had you."

Before I can think to soften it in some way, I blurt, "And like, three brothers."

Savannah's eyebrows shoot up. "You have three brothers?" Those are the words she says out loud. The ones I hear are, *We have three brothers?*

I'm surprised by the sudden flash of possessiveness I feel for these wild, ridiculous, gross boys of mine who learned all their wildest, most ridiculous, and grossest tricks from me. Not even because I think she'd want anything to do with them. More like I'm suddenly afraid that she wouldn't. Like maybe she'd think less of them, these little extensions of me, the chubby cheeks and grimy fingers and scabbed knees that make up my world.

When I finally look over at Savvy, though, there's this slight give between her brows. Like maybe she gets it. Like maybe all either of us can do is try.

"Could be four," I say, trying to keep it light. "Sometimes I lose count."

Savvy doesn't do that thing where she laughs at your joke to fill up space. A small part of me respects it, but most of me is itching in the quiet, not sure what I should or shouldn't say.

"I always assumed I was an accident," says Savvy.

"Me too, to be honest." It's the first time I've ever acknowledged the thought out loud. I mean, my parents had me during law school, which I know from Connie's biannual viewing of *Legally Blonde* is no easy feat. That, and they didn't bother with the big white wedding. As far as I know, a family friend did the whole "do you take this human" bit and sent them on their merry way.

"But you're—what, sixteen?" Savvy asks.

I nod. A year and a half younger than her, according to the picture she posted posing with a bunch of rainbow balloons on her eighteenth birthday in December. It had more than a hundred thousand likes.

"You know what's crazy? I didn't even mean to take the test," she says. "It was a formality. We did a sponsored post with the DNA site—for Instagram, I mean," she says, waving it off like she already knows that I know about it, and doesn't want to get into it. "I did it for the health section. And yeah, I thought *maybe* one of my—one of your parents might pop up, which, whatever. I've always known it would be easy to find them if I looked into it. But I never imagined . . ."

Her eyes sweep up to mine in question, like I might know something she doesn't. It sets me even further on edge. I wonder where my loyalties are supposed to lie, or if there are loyalties to be had at all. There's this unhelpful knee-jerk reaction to defend my parents, and an even less unhelpful knee-jerk reaction to tell her whatever I can think of, anything to throw them under the bus after they lied to me all these years.

"I keep thinking someone snuck a hallucinogenic into my McFlurry," I say, skirting the issue entirely. A strategy pulled right out of what Connie calls "the Abby Day playbook on chronic conflict avoidance" and Leo has dubbed "making a Day of it."

Savvy lets it slide. "Tell me about it. When that email came in—"

"QUACK, quack, quaaacckkk!"

We look up with a jolt and see two little girls, obviously sisters, crouching at the edge of the lake and quacking. Their matching shoes and leggings are all muddied up, their identically red hair spilling out of pigtails. The smaller one is pushing the older one forward, echoing her quacking noises.

Savvy and I both follow the direction of their quacks out to the lake, and she surprises me by letting out a short laugh. It softens her for a second, and I see something familiar in her that isn't just my face.

"Duck Island," she says, shaking her head fondly at the little patch of land in the middle of the lake. It's a bird sanctuary, so overgrown with trees that even as small as it is, you can't see through it to the edge of the lake on the other side.

I almost don't say it. I'm oddly self-conscious around her, like I can feel her taking stock of me, of things I haven't even examined myself. But the quiet is more overwhelming than the noise of my own blathering, so I tell her, "When I was little, I thought Duck Island meant it was like, some kind of kingdom run by ducks."

I'm not ready for the incredulous smile on her face when she turns back around. "So did I," she says. "Since people aren't supposed to go there. Like it was some secret duck world, right?"

It's the first time she's looked really, fully human to me. Everything about her—her uncanny posture, the discerning look in her eyes, the thoughtful pauses she takes before she speaks—has seemed so deliberate and planned, like we're living in her Instagram feed and every moment of it is being documented, up for the world's judgment.

But she turns around to look at me with a grin that's right on the verge of a laugh, and it's like someone pulled up a veil between us, opening up a depth of her where I couldn't not see myself if I tried.

Maybe that's why I suddenly feel compelled to blurt, "I've been there."

The grin falters. "On Duck Island?"

I nod, maybe too vigorously, trying to get it back. "My friend Connie and I, we—we took a kayak over there once. Just to see."

Savvy appraises me, her "I'm legally an adult and you're not" face back in full force. "You're really not supposed to do that."

She's right. Given the island's status as a sanctuary, there's a big old human ban slapped on signs all over the park. But kids and kayakers are roaming around it all the time. If Green Lake has any kind of authoritative body stopping people from doing it, I sure as heck have never seen them.

"I know," I say quickly. "But we were super careful. Barely even got off the boat."

"Then what's the point?"

I lift up Poppy's old camera, which I've swapped out for Kitty today. I don't do it often, given my less-than-stellar track record for keeping things intact, but sometimes I need a piece of him with me. It feels like a talisman, the weight of it steadying me when it's around my neck.

"The view," I tell her sheepishly, because it feels slightly less dorky than *I wanted to stalk some birds.*

Her lips form a tight line and it looks so much like a face my dad makes that I'm bracing myself for a lecture, but she holds out her hand. "Can I see?"

"Huh?"

Savvy juts her chin toward the mass of trees in the middle of the lake. "Duck Island."

"Oh. I don't . . ."

Show people my photos, I almost say. But as embarrassed as I am about someone seeing my photos, I am somehow more embarrassed about confessing it.

She tilts her head at me, misinterpreting my hesitation. "You didn't post them?"

"Oh," I say, to stall for time. Time to figure out how I'm going to gracefully tell her that she may be allowed to share all my DNA, but she is not allowed to see photos I took on my camera. "Maybe."

She gestures impatiently for me to hand my phone over, and I'm too overwhelmed not to. Besides, this is what I wanted, wasn't it? Someone I could trust with this kind of thing. And even though Savvy is a lot of things I didn't expect, she could still be that someone, if I give her the chance.

"Hold on. It's, uh . . ."

I try to remember the Instagram handle Leo gave me. He was so proud of the pun. Something about saving things. Something about my last name. Something about . . .

The words aren't there, but Leo's face is—the way he was beaming on my fifteenth birthday, that August afternoon when he'd finally gotten back from camp and Connie had gotten back from a trip and we were all sweating profusely and slurping our Big League Milkshake Mashes from our perch at Richmond Beach. He took my phone from me, his dark eyes trained on mine, a rare sliver of sun poking through the fog and lighting up the bronze of his face.

"It's not a real gift. It's kinda dumb. Anyway—you can change the username, if you want—"

"Just *show* her already, you dope," said Connie, yanking the phone from him and putting it in my hands.

"Right. So. You know how some of my camp friends made Instagrams for our stuff? Don't be creeped out, but I took some photos off your camera. I wanted to find a way to save them, and . . ."

There it is, unearthed from somewhere in my brain: @savingtheabbyday.

I pull it up and hand it to Savvy without looking at it. She thumbs the screen and her eyebrows lift, looking genuinely impressed.

"You took these?"

Maybe I should be offended by the surprise in her voice, but I'm too busy being humiliated that my Instagram probably looks like a bird-watching society threw up on it. "Yeah."

"These are really great," she says, lingering on one of my favorites—a sparrow with its beak open, mid-crow, its wings poised in the second right before it took flight. I practically had to stop breathing for a full minute to get that shot, anticipating every shudder of her little bird body, waiting for the perfect moment. "You could monetize this."

I nearly choke on my own spit trying not to laugh. "Nah," I say, taking the phone back from her.

"No, really," Savvy pushes. "This is the kind of stuff you could sell to local papers, to gift shops, the whole nine yards. Why not look into it? What've you got to lose?"

Everything, I almost say, even though it's bordering on melodramatic and definitely veering into teenage cliché. Even if I weren't mortally terrified at the idea of people looking through my lens, photography is the only thing that's *mine*. No teacher telling me I'm doing it the wrong way, no parents asking about it while exchanging super unsubtle glances at the dinner table. Nobody calling the figurative or literal shots but me.

"I couldn't . . . I don't want to be like that," I say, which is easier than saying *I'm scared.*

"Like what?" she asks sharply.

"Like—I don't know." She's watching me with her eyes narrowed, and just like that I'm sweating again. Not only my hands, but my entire stupid body, like a one-girl geyser. "I—I don't really care about Instagram or all the other noise. I do this for fun."

Holy Duck Island, do I need to shut up. She goes stiff, and it's clear I haven't just put my foot in my mouth, but swallowed it. The more she stares, the more the circuits in my brain start to fire unhelpfully, trying to fix the stupid words I said with *more* stupid words, like I'm piling up a stupid word sandwich.

"I think monetizing it might wreck it."

Savvy takes a breath and chooses her answer carefully. "I'm not miserable just because I'm making money."

There it is—the thing that's been irking me under the surface since I first got here. That she never even bothered to explain her whole Instagram hustle, because she already knows that I know. Because she already assumes I've sunk time into her, clicking on her Purina spon con, zooming in on her earth bowls, staring at her mountain of birthday balloons.

And worst of all, because she's exactly right.

She turns away from me, back toward the lake. "You'll have to make a living eventually," she says, shrugging like she isn't as bothered as she clearly is. "Shouldn't you be doing what you love?"

Jesus. I came here looking for an ally, and instead I managed to find the least-teenagery teenage girl in all of Seattle. My eyes are stinging like some dumb little kid's, the disappointment so misplaced in me that I don't know how to let it out, except—

"You love posing with water bottles in a bunch of spandex?"

Shit.

Her mouth forms a tight line once more, her head whipping toward me so fast that her ponytail makes a little *snap*, whipping in the muggy air. I freeze, not sure which one of us is more stunned by it, her or me.

I open my mouth to apologize, but Savvy turns away before I can, looking back at the quacking toddlers. Their squawks have reached a fever pitch, the kind of frenzy that I know from way too much experience with my brothers is going to end in either a fit of giggles or one of them in tears.

"So, no secret duck kingdom?" Savvy asks, as if the last minute didn't even happen.

My relief makes my limbs feel heavy, makes me want to sit in the grass or maybe just shove my face into it and stop myself from saying anything that might muck it up again. I'm not used to the back-and-forth of meeting someone new, of trying to suss each other out. I've gone to school with the same kids and been best friends with the same two people my whole life. This would be weird even if she didn't share all my DNA.

"Not even a duck dynasty," I say, which earns me a groan.

"Shame," she says, glancing over. "My mom always told me there was a whole duck kingdom. Like with its own government and a ruler and everything. She called her—"

"Queen Quack," we say at the same time.

I blink at her, at the question in her eyes. "That's what my mom told me," I say.

Savvy considers this. "I always thought that was something my mom made up."

My voice is small when I answer. "Me too."

Savvy blows out a breath, and the two of us stare out at the cluster of trees in the middle of the lake, sharing the same pace but remembering a different time.

"This is weird," says Savvy. "But do you think our parents knew each other?"

I frown. One "Queen Quack" does not a conspiracy theory make. "I mean . . ."

But as I stare out at the water, the slight breeze lapping it to the edges of the lake, I realize it's the only part of this senseless-ness that makes sense. It may be near impossible to imagine my parents giving up a kid born only a year and a half before I was, but it's even harder to imagine them giving her to strangers.

Savvy pulls out her phone and in an instant has a photo pulled up. It's from a holiday card, taken in front of the giant Christmas tree in Bell Square, shoppers milling all around them. Hugging Savvy between them are a man and a woman with pristine posture but kind eyes and warm smiles, dressed in sleek khakis and cashmere knits. They look like a Hallmark card, but in a good way. In a way that you just kind of know if they invited you over for dinner they'd put more food on your plate without asking and hug you extra hard at the door.

"That's us," says Savvy.

I'm about to say something dumb—a comment about how she looks like them that is guaranteed to wreck the moment—but then I take the screen from her, zooming in on her mom.

"Wait. I've seen her."

"She teaches art classes. Maybe—"

"No, in photos. Wait. Hold on. Hold on."

Savvy takes her phone from me and rocks back on her heels, as if to say, *Where else am I gonna go?*

It takes me a second to figure out how to access the Dropbox where we've been dumping the files for our big end-of-semester Honors Anthropology project. The one that nudged Leo into taking the DNA test, that pulled us all into it with him and led to this.

I found a photo of my parents' wedding in a shoebox tucked into the basement closet. The picture I took of it loads on my phone, and there they are, my parents in all their late-nineties glory. My mom is in a plain white dress with hair large enough for small objects to get caught in its orbit, and my dad is in a suit beaming and so bony that he looks more like a kid than someone who's about to be a parent.

And there, in the middle, is the family friend who officiated the ceremony.

I look over at Savvy to ask the obvious question, but her eyes have bugged out looking at my phone screen. It's her mom.

"The year," she says, seeing the date in the corner of the photo. "That's before *either* of us was born."

My heart feels like it's beating in my throat. Our eyes connect with such immediacy that the force of it is like a thunderclap. Even as every part of me is trying to reject the truth, the two of us stare at each other with a sudden understanding: Something big happened here. Something much bigger than we could have imagined.

Something so big that my parents have made a conscious effort to lie to me about it every day for the last sixteen years.

My phone buzzes in my hand, and I give a little jump. The word *Dad* comes up, and Savvy looks away sharply, like she's seen something she isn't allowed to see.

Where r u? Just finished up

"Crap." I spring away from her, like he's going to jump out of the bushes. "He's probably headed over."

"We've got to figure out what happened."

"Uh, *yeah*." I close my eyes, thoughts coming too fast. "I mean, my parents keep me pretty busy, but if you're around next Sunday, maybe—"

"Next Sunday I leave for summer camp." Savvy starts backing away from me, the two of us looking like extremely anxious repelling magnets. "Bad service and like, one shared computer for the junior staff. Barely enough Wi-Fi to Skype."

"Yikes."

Now that I know about this I'm not sure if I can go the full summer *not* knowing. We both felt it in that thunderclap of a feeling, the echo of it still humming in between us.

"Even if you were here, I'm gonna be slumming it in the community center getting SAT prep questions beaten into my skull."

"Come to camp with me."

It's not a demand, but not a request, either. She says it the way Connie might—with the weight of shared history, and the expectation that I'll say yes.

The laugh that bubbles in my chest is borderline hysterical, but it only makes Savvy all the more persistent.

"It's called Camp Reynolds. You can take an academic track.

Half studying, half regular camp. They just started the program this year."

My mouth drops open. The flyers on my bed. *Camp Reynolds*. It's the same one the counselor's been pushing on me all semester—only the brochure was full of aggressively cheerful stock photo students laughing at their calculators. It looked like nerd jail. Certainly nobody said anything about being let outside.

Savvy falters, mistaking my reaction. For a moment, she isn't Savannah Tully, Bona Fide Instagram Star With a Bossy Streak, but Savvy, a person who looks every bit as clueless and freaked out as I am.

"Is that ridiculous?" she asks.

It occurs to me that she has a much bigger stake in getting to the bottom of this than I do. If I walk away, nothing in my life has to change. I could pretend I never met her. Go on living this carefully preserved lie that my parents must have had reasons for telling, for guarding all these years.

But even if I could pretend everything was normal, there is something else I can't shake. One look at that picture of my parents beaming with Savvy's mom is all it takes to see they must have been closer than just friends—the kind of close I am with Connie and Leo. That inseparable, all-encompassing, ride-or-die kind of close. Which means whatever happened, it must have been catastrophic.

I don't want to think that could happen to me and Leo and Connie. It's my worst nightmare come to life.

And there's that latch again—the need to see it through. To figure out what happened. If not for our parents' sake, then for my own, because even imagining a world where I don't speak to Connie and Leo for eighteen years leaves an ache no amount of time could ever heal.

"No more ridiculous than the rest of this."

Before either of us can overthink it, we swap numbers and dart in opposite directions of the park. My dad, it turns out, is right where I left him, standing in front of Bean Well and looking over some paperwork with his eyebrows puckered. I watch him, trying to find some way to still the tornado in me—the adrenaline thumping in my bones and the sudden guilt that feels like it might crush them.

"Get any good shots?" he asks.

There's a breath where I think about telling him everything, spilling my guts, if only to get this feeling out of my body and put it somewhere else.

But trying to imagine how that conversation would go just leads to a massive mental roadblock, one that suddenly has Savvy's face. I don't know what she is to me, really. At least aside from the literal, biological sense. But whatever it is has taken root in me and is tangled deep.

Then a slithering voice comes unbidden in the back of my head: *They lied to me first.* If they're allowed to keep this kind of secret from me my whole life, I sure as hell should be allowed to keep one from them.

"A few," I tell him.

I worry that he might ask to see them, but he's uncharacteristically distracted, tucking the paperwork back into a folder and heading toward the car. It occurs to me that my mom should probably be handling the sale—it was her dad's place, after all—and it reminds me, not without an extra shot of shame in my churning guilt latte, that I'm not the only one who misses Poppy. Nobody *wants* to sell this place. But there are some things in life you don't have a choice about.

I wonder what that choice was eighteen years ago.

I feel marginally less like the world's worst daughter when I mention, on the car ride home, that I've been looking into Camp Reynolds and have decided I'm interested in going. My

YOU HAVE A MATCH   49

dad perks up and looks so pleased with himself that my guilt only seems to get bigger, like every time I try to kill a cell of it, it divides and gets twice as big as it was before.

"It really does sound fun," says my dad, glancing over.

I don't say anything, and he starts going into some variation of the "we'll always be right here to come get you if you need it" spiel, which I tune out when I see a new text on my phone from a 425 number. I am right on the verge of rolling my eyes, certain it's a pushy reminder to get my parents on board. Instead, it's a link to Savvy's latest Instagram post, along with the caption: "do what u love, especially if what u love is posing with a water bottle in a bunch of spandex."

I snort.

"What's shaking?" my dad asks.

"Nothing," I say, exiting out of my texts just as another notification comes in, and the smirk wilts right off my face. It's an email from the school, with a subject line so aggressive it feels like our principal is shouting it right into my eardrums: MANDATORY SUMMER SCHOOL—SIGN-UP INSTRUCTIONS WITHIN.

Shit.

five

There are several things my parents are unaware of when they drop me off at the ferry dock, where I am, at the mercy of the entire universe, somehow escaping to Camp Reynolds for the summer.

The first of those things is, obviously, Savvy.

The second is that I deleted the email about me failing English and having to go to summer school. And then I used our Netflix password to hack into both of my parents' emails and delete it from theirs, listing all emails from the school district as spam while I was at it. And after, I sprinted home between school and tutoring sessions to check our home voicemail and intercept every message left by the power-hungry twenty-something who runs the attendance office and feasts on the misery of all the students whose parents he calls in the middle of the day.

The third is that when my mom asked if I'd made my bed and cleaned my room I said yes, even though the floor is more clothes than carpet and it'd be a miracle if someone *found* the bed right now, let alone made it.

To be fair, I haven't exactly been rolling in spare time. Last week was finals, plus Connie was packing for her big Europe trip with her cousins, and Leo was prepping for a summer job in the kitchen at Camp Evergreen (or, as I dubbed it when we were kids, "Camp Whatevergreen"), and I was more than a little preoccupied leading my new super hip double life as Abby Who Doesn't Lie To Her Parents and Abby The Lying Liar. We were planning to meet up to see a movie or something before we all took off, but I guess it slipped through the cracks.

The last of the cars start filing onto the ferry, so walk-on passengers have to get on or get left. My dad hugs me first.

"Take care of yourself," he says. "If a bear tries to eat you, punch it in the nose."

My mom swats at him. "There are no bears on that island." At my look, she sighs and admits, "I checked."

My dad and I both laugh at her, and she swoops in and hugs me tight. I squeeze back, hard, like I can squeeze out the competing waves of guilt and anger that just crushed me, followed by a trickle of something else. Something uneasy and unfamiliar. I've been so distracted by "Operation Stealth Sister," as Connie has started calling it, that it didn't occur to me until now that I'm leaving for a full month. I've never been away from my parents for more than a few days in my whole life.

Before I can do something dumb like blubber all over them in front of several dozen ferry commuters, all three of my brothers pipe up at once, and I'm smushed with two hugs that are arguably more violent than not and one lick to my face, courtesy of Asher.

I wipe my face with my sleeve and give them all noogies, and the three of them spin out back toward the car, growling and hissing and taking on their "monster" personas for whenever I mess up their hair. My dad follows them before they end up monstering themselves off a ledge into the Puget Sound, and my mom hugs me one last time.

"We're leaving to see your uncle in Portland in a few days, but we're only there for a week," she reminds me. "But if you need anything, let us know."

I hug her back, feeling like a bigger monster than all three of my brothers combined.

The ferry ride is a short one, a jaunt across the water to where Camp Reynolds sits on the edge of one of the islands that surround the Seattle area and beyond. I'm about to fully let myself lean into my impending panic spiral, but I look out the window and see the day is so stark clear that for once you can actually see Mount Rainier in its full glory, peeking out over the suburbs in the distance. With all the fog in this city, that damn mountain is basically my white whale. I pull Kitty out, glad she has the long-range lens on her already, and am about to head out to the front of the boat when—

"Abby?"

I know who it is before I turn around, before my brain even consciously thinks his name. I know from the two swoops, the one that plummets in my stomach and the one that goes up my spine, the full second of my body fighting itself that I've gotten used to feeling any time he takes me by surprise.

But this isn't surprise. This has skipped right past surprise and straight to *what in the legitimate fuck*.

"Leo?"

I haven't seen him in a few days, which has inconveniently only heightened the things about him I've been trying diligently not to notice. Read: the way he's grown out his hair a bit, too short to tuck behind his ear but long enough that my fingers are twitching to try. Read also: the way the sun is streaming in from the ferry window, lighting up the amber of his eyes on his aforementioned face. Still reading: the way he is smiling, a full-body smile, the kind that might have started in his lips but clearly goes all the way down to his toes.

"What are you *doing* here?" he asks.

Before I can ask what *he's* doing here, the guilt I was already coated in gets a fresh new layer of more guilt painted right on it.

Because here's the thing: I haven't told Leo about any of this. I could blame being busy, or say that I wanted to tread carefully about finding Savvy when Leo didn't find anyone. But while both are true, neither are truer than this: the Big Embarrassing Incident is somehow still bigger than us both.

"I'm—uh—going to camp?"

"I can't believe it," he says.

And, of all things, he crosses the space of the waiting area and wraps his arms around me in a bear hug so firm I can see the popcorn he's holding spilling out in the periphery. It's a wave of warmth and cinnamon and home. I almost forget to hug him back, my heart beating somewhere in my throat instead of doing the one damn job it's supposed to do, my face so hot that I'm sure he can feel it where my cheek is pressed to his chest.

Jesus. I used to nap on top of him during movie nights when we were little. Now one second of prolonged contact is all it takes for my limbs to go wonkier than Connie's after the student government kids raided some parents' beer stash.

"Abby," he says, so earnest and stunned that for once there's not even a pun to accompany it. "This is the *best* surprise."

I blink into his chest, and he lets me go, beaming like someone just shoved stardust down his throat.

"First I score a summer job at Camp Evergreen, and now you're going to be there, too?"

I know the name well. It's the camp Leo and Carla have spent every summer at since we were little kids, since their parents used to work on the staff. He'd come back with all these stories about misadventures with camp friends around the same time Connie would come back from traveling with stories about her cousins, and I'd nod and only half listen so the jealousy wouldn't eat me alive.

"No, I'm going to Camp Reynolds," I correct him.

"Oh, yeah," he says with a derisive snort. "I forgot they renamed the place when Victoria took over and they collab'd with that academic thing."

"Oh," I say, and in my head, a slower, deeper, phenomenally more screwed *Oh*.

He tilts his head, and something in my chest aches at the sight. How that head tilt is so familiar to me, so familiarly *mine*, and how it's been so long since I've seen it. Long enough that I realize he's grown even taller in the last few months, and I've been so busy keeping my head down around him, I missed it.

Leo's head untilts, and it dawns on me that Leo thinks I *followed* him here. And he seems ridiculously happy I did.

I stare back out the window, at the view of Mount Rainier passing us by, trying to recover from the whiplash. I should be relieved, shouldn't I? Maybe this is proof that the weirdness is over, and we've made it out the other side. Finally made the BEI our bitch and are better off for it.

But I guess if I'm being honest, the weirdness didn't start with the Big Embarrassing Incident. It's been brewing since last August, when he got back from camp. We hadn't seen him in a few months, and he'd had, as Connie put it, "an extreme glo up." Not only had Leo shot up several inches, but he seemed to have acquired a jawline and some major "I dragged kayaks back and forth across a wet beach every day for two months" biceps.

I mean, yeah, I noticed. Suddenly we couldn't swap hoodies anymore and other people in our class were asking me things like whether Leo was dating anyone or—most awkwardly of all—if he was dating me.

I rolled my eyes and waved everyone off, because it was all super dumb—until it wasn't. Until Connie went to visit her grandparents over Thanksgiving break, and Leo dragged me to a line outside Best Buy for some game release, and we spent an entire night huddled in the dark, sleep-deprived and delirious and probably judgment-impaired from all the cranberry sauce in our veins. Until right when the sky started to bleed pink, and I eyed the roof of Leo's dad's pickup truck, thinking that maybe from that height I might be able to get a shot of the sunrise over the mountains in the distance. Until the moment when, before I'd even so much as moved a muscle, Leo put a hand on my shoulder and said, "Don't you dare, Abby Day."

He'd said the words probably a thousand times. But this time was different, because this time when I looked at him—eyes bright, cheeks flushed, with that knowing smile pressed into his lips—it seemed far more ridiculous not to kiss him than to kiss him. As if it was something that wasn't just inevitable, but long overdue.

So I leaned in. And I closed my eyes. And then—

And then both of our phones pinged at the same time.

It was the ping we'd set specifically for Connie. I pulled back, my heart hammering. It was maybe the first time in my life I actually managed to stop myself from doing something impulsive. Of all the things in the world I could never compromise, chief among them are my friendships with Connie and Leo.

And with that almost-kiss, I could have torpedoed fourteen years of our trio's dynamic straight into the sky.

"Sorry." I wasn't sure what I was sorry for—initiating it, or stopping it, or all the moments in between.

Leo stared at me like I was a stranger. "Don't be," he said.

But we hardly spoke for the half hour left waiting in line, or the drive home. And when I finally called Connie and confessed what almost happened and how bad I felt about it, I found out why.

"So I actually asked Leo a few weeks ago if he thought of you that way, since everyone was asking about it," she told me. She said it matter-of-factly, the way she had just finished telling me about her cousin clogging the drain with potato skins a few minutes before. "Don't worry. He doesn't."

Don't worry. I should have asked why "everyone" was talking about us. Should have asked what exactly Leo said, or why Connie brought it up. Anything to give me a point of reference other than *Don't worry,* which is all I've done since.

"And thank God. Can you even imagine how weird the group text would get?" Connie laughed. And I was grateful, but too gutted to say anything myself, and so stunned to even be gutted that it felt like I was unearthing all these hidden parts of myself, little faults in the crust of me slipping and knocking into each other all at once.

"So weird," I eventually managed to say.

If that was baseline bad, it was about to get worse. After hearing that I just pretended the almost-kiss never happened, for everyone's sake. And I shoved as much crap as I could into the cracks of those faults, enough so when Leo asked when we got back to school if I wanted to talk that I was able to say, "What about?" without missing a beat.

Leo nodded. Opened his mouth to say something— apologize, maybe, even though there was nothing for him to be sorry about—and said instead, "I don't want what happened to change anything."

I'd never tried to fake a smile before, but I could only guess from the look on Leo's face that I was pretty bad at it. "'Course not."

"Friends?"

The word seemed cheap, with or without the BEI. It was never going to fully describe what we were to each other. But that wasn't what the word was doing right then. It wasn't a definition; it was a boundary. One I needed to accept.

"Friends."

It's been months. *Months.* And I've basically spent every waking moment actively beating my feelings for Leo out of my brain. He must know that. There's no way he doesn't.

So why is he one glitter toss away from giddy that I'm here, when really, if it is what he thinks it is, he should be more than a little wigged out?

"I'm going to be in the kitchens most of the day, so we can't really hang out a ton," says Leo apologetically. "But the head chef said Mickey and I have full run of the place at night, if you want to come hang."

"Mickey Reyes?" I blurt, without thinking. I only know her last name because she very enthusiastically friended me on all social media since Savvy and I were holding off so our parents wouldn't spot it and ask questions. It's been a week of endless pictures of Rufus with his tongue lolling out and massive sauce-pans full of food, which seems to be Mickey's Instagram MO.

"You know Mickey?" asks Leo, bewilderment dimming some of the wattage in his grin.

I'd better mention her now, before we get there and Leo ends up confused as hell when Savvy and I link up. "Yeah—through, uh, Savannah."

"You know *Savvy*?"

At that, every thought racing in my head stops at once, stumbling into one another like a car crash: Leo's been going to this camp his whole life, and Savvy's been going to this camp her whole life, which means *Leo has known my secret sister for their whole lives.*

"Not well," I say. "We—uh—I met her . . ."

"At those photography meetups, right?" says Leo, finally noticing Kitty in my hands. "She told me she was thinking about starting something in the area."

It all comes rushing into my brain at once, like there was a bubble where Camp Leo lived separately from Regular Leo and someone just took a knife to it. He's mentioned a Savvy before. A Mickey, too. I try to reconcile them—these blurry faces he's been having camp adventures with versus the two girls I met in the park—but it's all so scrambled that I can't pull it apart.

"Well . . ."

I want to tell him. I'm *going* to tell him. But it's so rare that I get quality time with him like this that some selfish part of me wants it for the rest of the ferry ride, one last hit of Leo before he realizes I did not, in fact, come here for him, but for my own selfish and incredibly bizarre agenda.

He puts his phone in my face, a picture on the screen. I've seen it before. It's Leo with a cluster of his camp friends, all of them beaming and soaking wet from the pool, an oversize towel wrapped around four pairs of shoulders. Mickey, whose mouth is wide open in a laugh, her arms bare of her signature temporary tattoos and her shoes missing. Some boy with big, wet curls that I don't know, his cheeks ballooned out as he makes a face, leaning so far into Mickey that she looks precariously close to tipping over. A skinnier, ninth-grade version of Leo, who's not even looking at the camera, grinning broadly and clearly anticipating the fall. And on his other side is Savvy, or some younger, less composed version of her. Her damp hair is frizzy and curled like mine, and she's wearing a one-piece with little cartoon fish on it, sticking her tongue out so far it gives Rufus a run for his money.

She looks so genuinely happy that I almost don't recognize her.

"You know Savvy has this super popular Instagram account, right?" asks Leo. "She's the reason I started ours. She helped me with all the hashtagging in the beginning, too."

This discovery doesn't know how to settle in me. A few days ago I had no idea Savvy existed. Now I feel like she's been slowly leaking into my life for years, lurking in places I never thought to look—apparently even in places I already did.

Leo's eyes flit to the front of the ferry, where a few people are clustered outside for the view. He nods toward them and says, "Camp Ever—er, *Reynolds*, I guess—it's got tons of awesome views. And all this wildlife. Birds and deer, even *orcas*, if you're lucky. I bet we can get at least one good shot of some before the summer's out."

I lean against the ferry window, temporarily distracted from my shock. Half of me is here, but half of me already living in that moment—in the adrenaline rush of seeing something magical and knowing you only have a small window to capture that magic, sometimes only a fraction of a second. It's why I love photographing nature and landscapes most. You never know exactly when the magic is going to happen. There's nothing quite like the rush of getting to hold that magic still and keep it forever—allowing something so big to feel so intimate and personal because a part of you belongs to it, and a part of it belongs to you.

"It's a good thing you know Savvy," he says. "She's got a really good knack for spotting them."

I bristle. "We don't . . . I mean, I know more *of* her than actually know her."

This, at least, is not a lie. Despite spending the whole week texting back and forth with her to square away details—the stuff we were both bringing, from photographs to marriage records we found online to actual printouts of our DNA relative lists—I don't know that much about her. I mean, aside from the stuff that half a million literal other people know about her, courtesy of Instagram.

"Huh. Well, small world," says Leo. "Anyway, I'm glad you're looking into the Instagram stuff. I keep telling you there are all kinds of opportunities—"

"Yeah, yeah," I say. It smacks way too much of Savvy's little pseudolecture last week, especially since my existence on Instagram might even be her fault. Leo lowers his head a bit, looking back out over the water at the view of the mountains. "But you . . . know Savvy pretty well?"

Leo laughs, the kind of ambiguous, open-ended laugh you do when you know someone well but have no idea how to explain them to other people. I feel an unwelcome pang as it tapers off. I'd call it jealousy, but first I'd have to figure out what for: that Leo knows Savvy, or that Savvy knows Leo. Or maybe just the inevitability of those facts, which is that right now, they're probably both closer to each other than either of them are with me.

"She's great," says Leo. He thinks on this, like he's not having trouble describing her, but describing her specifically to me. "I mean—she's like, your polar opposite—"

"Hey!"

My tone is teasing, but the hurt is real, hitting fresh and sharp like it does when you didn't think to ready yourself for it.

"Oof," says Leo, dodging my attempt to elbow him, anticipating it before my muscles can even twitch. "Bad phrasing, especially if I want to live another Day—"

"Now you're legit toast."

"Aw, come on. I just mean—she's big on rules, and you kind of make your own." He lowers his gaze to mine. "Truth is, nobody's like you. There can only be one Abigail Eugenia Day."

I pivot from him, lowering my arm. It is a true testament to how far gone I am and how impossible it's going to be to come back that he's managed to make the name "Eugenia" sound sexy. I can practically *hear* his smirk behind me.

He bumps the back of my shoulder with his, a gentle, cloying nudge to prompt me to turn around. When I do the smirk is entirely gone, softened into something that makes my ribs feel fluttery.

"I'm really glad you're doing this."

I don't mean to sound like a record scratch in the middle of what is arguably the most normal conversation we've had in eons, but I can't help it. If I don't ask, I'm going to spend the whole summer waiting for some other shoe to drop.

"You are?"

Leo's smile flickers. "Why wouldn't I be?"

"Because . . ."

Leo's closer to me than before and I'm not sure whose fault it is, his or mine. He lowers his voice, the words a gentle prod. "Because what, Abby?"

I lose the words as fast as they come, and I'm not even sure who to blame, my brain or my mouth or every synapse in between. Maybe an entire lifetime of avoiding conversations like this—the big scary ones that have power over every conversation that happens after them.

It's the kind of thing I haven't had to worry about too much. I may be bad at fighting my own battles, but that's what I have Connie for. But this isn't a battle, and Connie's nowhere in sight.

Leo's voice is still soft when he speaks again, the rumble of it feeling more like it came from somewhere in me than from him.

"That morning—"

"Thanksgiving break," I bleat out.

Leo's mouth opens, surprised. "You remember."

Even if my knees weren't threatening to knock into each other, I wouldn't know how to respond to that. I *remember?* Every excruciating second of it is tattooed so permanently to my consciousness that I'm pretty sure it's the last thing I'll see before I die.

"Uh, yeah."

"When we almost—"

"When I almost—"

"Sorry," we both blurt. I try to take a step back and the stupid boat lurches and I stumble forward. Leo reaches out in case he has to catch me, and when he doesn't my eyes fly up right into his and snap like a key fitting into a lock.

"It's okay. That was back in the Day," he says, trying to be cheeky. "I got over it."

I blink at him, but the spell is already broken. "You . . . got over it?"

He reaches up and scratches the back of his head, sheepish. "I mean—we both did, right?" he says, the words coming too fast.

"Right," I whisper.

But nothing feels right, not with the words *I got over it* pinballing all over my brain. Did he mean the embarrassment? Or could he have meant something else?

I pivot toward the doors that lead to the front of the boat. I turn my head, nodding for him to follow, and when I catch his eye it hitches some part of me and holds me there. The Leo-shaped ache in me I have tried every way I can think of to ignore, humming louder than ever, pushing me to open my mouth and *say* something.

But even if Leo liked me at one point, he *liked* me, past tense. As in, not anymore. And if that were true, it would mean Connie deliberately lied to me.

No. Connie wouldn't lie to me, especially not about something as important as this.

"Did you know there was this baby orca, like years and years ago, that got separated from its pod and just followed the ferries around all day? They named her Springer."

Leo is starting to talk really fast in that way he does just before what Connie calls one of Leo's "information dumps," which is basically when he shakes his brain and an encyclopedia falls out. Except this time, it's less Leo geeking out and more Leo freaking out, desperate to fill the awkwardness with something else.

So I listen. The wind is whipping at our faces, blowing my curls out in every direction and into my mouth, tousling Leo's hair over his face. Soon the boat slows to a crawl, and I close my eyes and make a promise to myself. No matter what happens, by the end of this summer, I am going to get over Leo. I am going to learn to be just his friend again, for Leo's sake, and for Connie's, but most of all, for mine. What Savvy and I are doing may have us in way over our heads, but this I can manage.

I turn to face him, buoyed with resolve, almost relieved. It'll be like exposure therapy—Leo on Leo on Leo until I'm so sick of him that it'll be like that week we ate leftovers of the Number Twelve from Spiro's every day for two weeks and never wanted to look at a pineapple on a pizza again. By the end of camp, Leo will be pineapples, and I will be free.

"Where's Springer now?" I ask.

"She has two calves, and she's chilling with a pod in Vancouver," says Leo, his cheeks flushed, either from relief or the wind. "You'll have to settle for a shot of a less famous orca this summer."

Leo searches my face, an anxious almost-smile on his. I smile back and push the back of my shoulder into his chest. "Unless you tell anyone my middle name is Eugenia. Then I won't be taking photos, I'll be feeding you to them."

Leo tweaks me on the side, hard enough that I yelp and end up stumbling straight back into him. There is this arresting moment of heat, his front against my back, some *want* that rises up in me faster than the waves lapping against the shore. I turn my head to meet his eye, but he grabs me by both shoulders and whips me around so fast that I gasp out a laugh, one he meets with a smile inches from my face, close enough that it feels like a current shocked us both.

It's lighting up his eyes, and when he leans in, they are the only thing I see. "I wouldn't expect anything less."

I don't know what game Leo is trying to play here, but I'd kill for some pineapple right now.

six

Camp Reynolds is a scam.

And for the record, so is Savvy.

It starts out okay, if awkward. After the ferry lets us off, Leo heads into a van with other staff members, and a counselor helps the rest of us smush ourselves onto a bus. It becomes evident in the first ten seconds of being on said bus that of the actual campers, I might be the oldest one here. While I knew it was going to be rising sophomores, juniors, and seniors, from here it just looks like a bunch of babies.

Like a bunch of painfully smart babies.

Like, "look at this cool thing I just programmed my graphing calculator to do" levels of smart babies, which is a thing happening in the front row of this bus that has attracted so much attention that the driver tells everyone to sit back down before the nerdy mosh pit tilts us into a ditch.

I tell myself to relax. I probably won't be in sessions with them. There are different tracks in the "Reynolds method"— kids prepping for AP classes next year like these probably are, and kids like me who are prepping for the SATs. With any luck, they're hiding around here somewhere or ended up on a different, much less math-inclined bus.

Things get marginally better once we get to the camp. The bus starts winding down, down, down to the shore from the main elevation of the island, where we are suddenly surrounded by trees so large that it'll be a miracle if Leo doesn't call them Ents by the end of the summer. The air is thick with pine through the bus's open windows, and rare sunlight is streaming in through the branches, and when I peer out the stretch of trees goes so deep into the ground below the main road that it feels endless in all directions—a bottomless and sideways infinity of green and light.

Eventually we reach the main ground, and it is straight out of a cliché camp dream: wooden cabins all named after constellations, a rocky shore with worn kayaks in bright colors lined up along the edge, a giant signpost with pointers in all directions for the mess hall and firepit and tennis courts. I've been so worked up about getting to camp that I didn't actually let it sink in that I'm going to *camp*. That for the first time in my life, I'm sort-of-but-not-really, enough-that-it-is-still-embarrassingly-thrilling *free*.

Mickey's the first one to spot me when I get off the bus—or at least I think she is, until Rufus barrels his way through the campers with his tongue lapping out of his mouth. He jumps up on me with so much unabashed puppy love that between the force of him and the weight of my backpack on my shoulders, I immediately start to tip over.

Someone deftly grabs my elbow right before I end up introducing my butt to the mud.

"Rufus, *manners*?" says a voice I don't know.

I turn around and could almost blow a kiss at the sky with gratitude—a camper who actually seems to be my age, with messy curls and a smirk that he aims at me without an ounce of self-consciousness. He must be a veteran of Camp Whatever It's Actually Called, too.

Not just a veteran, but the other boy in Leo's picture.

"Thanks," I say. "Uh . . . ?"

Instead of giving me his name, he salutes me, leans down to pet Rufus, and then disappears into the throng. By the time I look up to find Mickey, Leo's beaten me to her.

"Your hair!" she exclaims, reaching up to mess with it.

"Your *sleeve*," he says, grabbing her other arm by the wrist and examining it. "I thought you decided you were a Hufflepuff."

"Yeah, but a Gryffindor *rising*," says Mickey, justifying the latest iteration of her temporary tattoo sleeve. "Anyway, my mom made too many of them and let me snag a few before I left for camp, so—Abby! Hey! You should meet Leo."

Leo turns to me, his eyes bright with mischief. "Pleased to make your acquaintance," he says, offering his hand.

I take it, squeezing it hard. "Likewise—Liam, was it?"

"Leo," says Mickey helpfully.

"Oh, *Leon*," I correct myself, without breaking eye contact with Leo. He's trying to play along, but laughter is starting to creep into his smile.

"Actually, my legal full name is Keep This Up And You Won't Get A Single Lasagna Ball Out Of Me This Entire Summer—"

"You guys know each other?" Mickey cuts in, delighted.

"Yeah. Leo's been talking up this camp for years," I say, turning to her with meaningful eye contact. Well, eye contact I hope is meaningful enough to say, *Please for the love of God give Savvy the heads-up about this before she shows up.*

Leo wraps an arm around my shoulders and squeezes, displaying me like a kid sister. "Must have said something right, if it finally got her to come."

Mickey's eyes widen for a split second, enough for me to know she got the message to *not* blow my cover loud and clear. "Well—wow—that's great!" she says. "Well—Leo, you should probably go check in."

"On it," he says, saluting us both as he goes and tossing me a wink, one that Mickey definitely doesn't miss.

She raises her eyebrows at me, looking gleeful. "Okay, I have zero time to yell about how much I ship this, because apparently the whole camp computer system crashed and it's all hands on deck."

I dismiss the comment, waffling between her and Leo, feeling like it's the first day of kindergarten all over again and I'm about to lose both my chaperones. "Should I just . . . go to orientation then?"

"Yeah," says Mickey, pointing in the general direction of where the other campers are moving. "Savvy's down in the pit running the show while we try to un-fuck-up all the class rosters. Never a dull moment!"

I hesitate, looking at the curved, elevated rows of benches around the pit full of unfamiliar faces. Even the boy from before seems to have disappeared into the ether, but thankfully a blond girl in neon colorblock leggings beckons me over to sit with her and a few others on the left side.

"Psst—hey! We've got a spare seat!"

The girls on either side of her scoot to make room for me, nodding to acknowledge me as one of them moans, "I can't believe my parents signed me up for the SAT prep portion. I'm not even *going* to college. I already have a whole plan!"

"Ugh, same. I have a 1560 and they *still* enrolled me in those stupid sessions. Like, I'm already set on premed, haven't I already filled the quota for parental bragging rights?" the other girl groans. "They're lucky I'm too lazy to incite any kind of legit teenage rebellion, or they'd be screwed."

They pause, giving me space to do the sociable thing like agree with them or at the very least introduce myself, but I'm struck by sudden and decidedly unwelcome panic at the words "whole plan" and "already set on." It's not like senior year is a surprise or anything. I guess it's just a surprise that I still don't have any kind of scope for what comes after it.

"Seriously," says the girl who beckoned me over, "parents are so competitive now, all the school districts here have gotten out of control."

I'm about to nod in agreement when we all cringe at the crackle and whine of a cheap microphone coming to life.

"Hey, Camp Ev—Reynolds!"

It's Savvy, standing on the little elevated stage just beyond the middle of the pit. Despite the perpetually damp air, her hair and makeup are as immaculate as ever, but now she's wearing a tank top with the camp's name on it tucked into a pair of high-waisted khaki shorts and rocking sleek black sneakers. A hush falls over the campers, save for the group of girls next to me, who all start whispering at once.

"Oh my god, that's *her*."

"Those shorts are so cute."

"She's shorter than I expected!"

"But *so* much prettier in real—"

"Shh," one of the other junior counselors hushes them as the gears start clicking together in my brain and I realize that I accidentally planted myself next to an entire Savannah Tully fan club. I peer at them out of the corner of my eye and see three high ponytails and three pairs of identical black sneakers and immediately pull out another piece of gum to stress chew.

"As you know, we had a bit of a revamp this year," says Savvy. "Some of the pieces are still moving, so we appreciate you bearing with us. But we're proud to announce the first official camp session of Camp Reynolds and thrilled to have you here."

I'm expecting the unrepentantly half-hearted cheers I'm used to hearing at school, but the volume ramps up all at once—kids whistling and whooping and clapping their hands. When it doesn't die down, I realize it isn't only Savvy hype. A lot of the kids have been here before. I'm the unenthused outsider.

I try to make eye contact with Savvy, but she looks away quickly when our eyes meet. Mine dart away too slow, and I feel like a total loser in the aftermath.

"If we could, uh, start with everyone grouping themselves together based on the camp track you're on?" says Savvy to the group, seeming to go out of her way to point her face in any direction other than mine. "SAT prep here in the middle, AP prep to my left, and general campers on my right."

The girls start to get up with reluctant sighs, but I grab the elbow of 1560, and the other two pause.

"Hold on," I whisper. "I heard they messed up the rosters. Maybe if we don't move they won't know we were enrolled in the SAT thing."

"I Already Have a Whole Plan" narrows her eyes. "Wait, seriously?"

"Just—sit tight for a second," I say. "If we get busted we can pretend we got confused."

We go silent, letting the crowd of general campers swallow us up until we're standing in the middle of the pack. I'm so sure we're going to get caught that I start chewing my gum with violence.

"Oh," says the girl who beckoned me over in the first place. "We're really not supposed to—"

The same junior counselor from before shushes us, and we all clap our mouths shut and face front, jumpy that we're about to get caught playing SAT prep hooky.

"As for what to expect . . . I really appreciate you reading up on the new rules in advance, and pre-appreciate you respecting them during your session here. It might have seemed like a lot, but it's all pretty simple really—"

I pop a bubble, and Savvy stops dead at the sound, finally

turning to look at me. I'm so stunned that it takes me a second to realize the entire pit of campers has turned, too. I lick the deflated bubble goo off my lips and stare back, wondering if there's some kind of stray insect climbing up my face and nobody wants to tell me.

"Uh." It's Savvy, talking to me. Talking to *me*. I take a step back, wondering if she's lost her goddamn mind when she adds, "Sorry, but . . . I'm going to have to give you a demerit."

I blink at her, and everyone seems to lean in like they're passing a fender bender on the road and want to get a better view. "Wait. What?"

The girl next to me brushes my elbow, her voice small and tentative. "Um, the camp banned gum?" she says. To her credit, she sounds every bit as miserable giving the news as I am to receive it.

This has got to be a prank, but when I look around, not a single camper looks fazed. Before whatever part of my brain is responsible for common sense kicks in, I blurt out, "Are you *shitting* me?"

"Excuse me."

The voice behind me is way too old to be a junior counselor, or even a head one. It has an authority to it that makes me extremely certain I'm done for before I even turn around.

Sure enough, it's a woman with a clipboard and a name tag that reads VICTORIA REYNOLDS. She has steely gray hair and matching steely eyes, which are focused on me in a way that makes me want to stare down at myself and make sure I haven't burst into flames.

"Sorry for the interruption," she says to the others. And to me: "Young lady, you can follow me."

I open my mouth to protest, but one subtle, single shake of her head is all I need to think better of it. Instead I turn to Savvy, hoping I might catch some twinge of remorse, some hint of apology on her face, but she won't even look at me. It's like I am nobody to her. Like I don't even exist.

So I turn and leave the firepit, my head held high and my mouth chewing the offending gum hard enough to snap my jaw, and don't look back.

seven

"Who taught you how to wash dishes, the Hulk?"

I pause in the admittedly hostile washing of the plate in my hand and turn my head one begrudging fraction of an inch. It's the boy from this afternoon, the exact same smirk on his face, as if it's been there this whole time.

"Well," he says when I don't answer, "if the whole dish-washing thing doesn't work out, at least you'll have a solid career replacing the kid mascot for Dubble Bubble."

So he's a chatty type. Too bad. Whatever curiosity I had for him before is every bit as shoved down the drain as the leftover chili I've been washing off these mucked-up plates.

He leans against the sink, watching me in my vigorous routine of wash, dry, stack. "I'm Finn, by the way."

I offer him a tight smile. He takes it in and lets out an exaggerated sigh.

"Fine," he says. "I'll help you. But only because you look kind of pathetic." A pause. "And also cuz I got assigned kitchen duty, too."

"What did *you* do?"

He waves me off. "What didn't I do? Can't get away with anything under the new regime," he says. "It's like they've all gotta be *shitting* me, if you know what I mean."

I pause, the sink still running piping hot water into the soapy basin. "I didn't see you at the pit," I accuse.

"Ah, so you were looking for me?"

Ordinarily I'd be embarrassed, but I don't care what this Finn guy thinks of me. I'm too angry to care what anyone thinks, really. A week of after-dinner kitchen duty assigned by a sixty-year-old woman with a whistle hanging around her neck will do that to you.

"I was there. Preoccupied, maybe, by the 'Camp Reynolds' sign I was defacing, but definitely there."

I sigh, handing him the scalding-hot wet dish in my hands. He takes it so cheerfully that I can only guess he was hoping to get saddled with kitchen duty.

"You planning on telling me your name, or should I just give you one?"

I ignore him, handing over another dish. The thing is, Savvy's been avoiding me. After Victoria assigned me kitchen duty and gave me a stern talking-to about "language" and a printout of the foot-long list of rules she didn't care that I didn't know about, she was nowhere in sight. And when I finally cornered her outside the cabins hours later, she had the nerve to think I was coming to apologize to *her*.

"What was I supposed to do?" she hissed under her breath. "It's my first day as a junior counselor. The youngest one we've ever had, by the way, because Victoria *trusts* me. And then you come blazing in and deliberately test my authority in front of everyone—"

"I'm sorry, since when is what I put in my mouth part of your *authority*?"

"Did you not even bother to read the rules?" Before I could answer, she let out a huff and stepped back from me in faint disgust. "Of course you didn't."

"What's that supposed to mean?"

She took a breath and glanced around the edge of the building—making sure nobody saw her with her delinquent blood match, I could only guess—and said, "Listen, let's forget about this. We've got bigger things to worry about. Come to the rec room during the free hour before curfew."

"I can't," I told her. "Thanks to you, I have kitchen duty after dinner for a week."

It was almost worth the punishment to get to drop that little bomb on her and watch her mouth form an inadvertent "oh" of surprise. Savvy, I'd already learned, was not a person who adjusted well to people messing with her master plans.

Then her brows furrowed, and she pointed at me. *Pointed* at me. Like we were in an after-school special, and she was the Extra-Disappointed Teacher. "You've got nobody to thank for that but yourself."

I thought that was going to be it, because she whipped around to head back to the camp. But I let out a laugh that was more of a scoff, this ugly noise I'd never heard myself make before. I was almost proud of myself—hidden talent unlocked— until it prompted Savvy to turn back and say, "If you're just going to make a bunch of trouble, why'd you bother to come at all?"

She said it fast, without even looking at me, but it still landed hard enough to sting. And just like that, all the anger I was trying to work up was knocked right out of me, and I was more puddle than person. I'd been someone's little sister for less than a week, and I already screwed the whole thing up.

"Dubble Bubble girl it is," says Finn, shaking me out of my thoughts and back to the plates I'd been mauling with the sponge. "Unless your parents gave you a better one."

"Doesn't matter," I tell him. "I'm out of here tomorrow."

"Uh, come again?"

"I'm leaving."

"Huh," says Finn, propping himself up on the counter and taking his sweet time with the whole dish-drying thing. "So what's the plan, then? Hike up the two-mile-long hill to the main road and stick your thumb out until a local takes pity on you? Or swim back to the mainland and hitch a ride on a fish?"

I only tell him because I'm still working up the nerve to go through with it. Saying it out loud makes it less terrifying. "I'm calling my parents."

"Yowza. That bad?" he asks. "Listen, Savvy's all bark and no bite, so if that's what's got your Camp Reynolds hoodie in a twist—"

"I didn't even want to be here in the first place."

Only now that I've said it do I realize how true it is. Even before I accidentally blew up my own spot and earned myself top billing on Savvy's shit list, I haven't been able to squash my uneasiness—the sense that so many things I thought I knew are falling apart, and I'm not even there to watch them crash. My parents have been lying to me about Savvy. Connie might have lied to me about Leo. And the distance between me and them only seems to magnify the weirdness of it ten times more than if I were home.

It would be easier to leave. To pretend the last twenty-four hours never happened. Nobody would have to get angry, nobody would get hurt.

"What brought you here, then?" Finn asks. "Are you one of those SAT score chasers, the Stanford-or-bust type?"

"Exact opposite."

"So you're a Savvy stan?"

I wrinkle my nose. "She wishes."

Finn manages to finish drying exactly one dish. I go ahead and hold my applause. "Gotta say, I'm impressed—usually it takes a lot longer than three seconds to get under Savvy's skin."

"Guess I'm an overachiever after all."

"You know, it'd be a shame if you left now."

I'm supposed to ask him why, but I really, really don't care what he has to say. The only thing I care about is doing these dishes, finding Leo to explain this whole mess, and doing whatever I can to get the first ferry off this island in the morning.

"It's just that, without Wi-Fi decent enough to stream more than twenty seconds of Netflix, your little spat is the closest thing to binge-worthy entertainment we've got."

I roll my eyes.

"What makes it funnier is you guys *weirdly* look alike. More than any of her Savanatics." Finn pauses, somehow making even less progress drying his second plate. At this rate we'll be here all night. "I mean, it's uncanny. Even that 'shut up, Finn, you're driving me nuts' face you're making right now is spot-on Sav—"

"Of course it is," I blurt. "She's my stupid sister."

I maybe had half a chance of playing that off as a bad joke if I hadn't punctuated it by accidentally dropping the plate in my hands, freezing as it bounces off the rubber part of the kitchen floor and cracks on the tiles under the sink. I lean down to pick it up, and when I rise, Finn is staring at me with his mouth wide open.

"Holy shit."

I turn away from him to put the broken plate pieces in the trash. It doesn't matter. It's not like Savvy and I pinky-swore or made some kind of blood oath that we wouldn't tell anyone.

"Okay, okay, back up, Bubbles. Savvy's adopted."

Ignore him. Ignore him and he'll go away.

"So you're, what? Her half sister?"

"I'm *leaving* tomorrow, is what I am."

"How'd you find her? Did you stalk her here?" His eyes are alight, loving every minute of this. He's on board with the weirdness that is my family so fast I'm struggling to keep up, and it's my damn life. "Are you single white female–ing your own flesh and blood?"

That earns him a snort, only because I couldn't want to be less like Savvy and her stupid rules if I tried.

Finn prattles on like he's writing the next great book-turned-HBO-murder-mystery-miniseries. "You *are*. And she doesn't even know you're here, does she? She's just minding her business, Instagramming her juices, and there you are lurking in the—"

"She *asked* me to come here." I round on him so unexpectedly that he takes an exaggerated, comical step back, putting his hands up in surrender. "She's my full-blooded sister, by the way, and she reached out to *me*. She's the one who wants to figure out why our parents didn't tell us about each other, and *she's* the one who dragged me into this SAT soul-sucking, bubble-gum-banning bullshit in the first place." I take a breath, firming the resolve that's been working its way up in me since this endless dish duty began. "So yeah, I'm leaving. I have no interest in spending the summer feeling like an idiot."

It's almost satisfying to see the smug amusement get knocked right off Finn's face. That is, until I hear the *whoosh* of the kitchen doors opening and turn to see Leo walking in. He has clearly heard everything. He stands there, his apron in one hand and something wrapped in aluminum foil in the other, and looks at me like I've grown an extra limb.

"Leo," I bleat. He's supposed to be done for the night. "What are you doing here?"

"Hey, man," says Finn, talking over me. Well, not really. My voice is so small I can barely hear it. "How's it—"

"What did you just . . ." He stops, seeing the look on my face, and recalibrates. Even in this moment, when he has full license to be mad, he's thinking of my feelings instead of his own—but he can't keep it out of his voice, a hurt so quiet and deep that it breaks my heart. "You came here because of Savvy."

His eyes lock on mine, with an intensity that makes it feel like every living thing in the cafeteria has crushed to a halt. Even Finn's mouth snaps shut, and he takes a step back like he's trying to get out of the way of whatever is happening in the ten feet of space between us.

"And now you're leaving?"

"I was going to come find you and explain," I say in a rush.

I brace myself for Leo to ask for an explanation, but what happens instead is worse. He just kind of deflates, and his eyes wander away from mine, toward the back exit.

"Leo, wait."

He doesn't. Finn cocks his head toward the door, a silent *Go*.

I don't hesitate, running through the kitchens even though I was explicitly told not to run through the kitchen, along with approximately one bajillion other rules that Victoria warned me about before dinner. But when I stumble out into the campground, a thick fog has rolled over the island, just barely broken up by the guiding lights between the cabins overhead. The back of the kitchens spits me right out into a main fork diverging in five different directions, and I don't see the back of Leo in a single one.

I want to pick one and run down it, on the off chance that I'll pick the right one and catch him, but that's the thing. I can outrun him, maybe, but I can't outrun whatever just happened back there. At this point I don't even know if I can keep up with myself.

eight

"Uh, Abs, not that it isn't great to hear from you . . . but it's almost two o'clock in Italy, and according to math, that makes it the buttcrack of dawn in Seattle."

I cringe, holding the phone closer to my ear and shifting to avoid the gaze of the camp employee who reluctantly let me into the main office after I stood outside it like a lost dog. "It's five in the morning," I tell Connie sheepishly.

"That's just unholy. What have they done to you?"

The truth is, I was calling with every intention of asking her about Leo and dissecting the conversation she had with him all those months ago. But as soon as I hear her voice on the other end, the rest comes spilling out of me too fast for the question to catch up.

"Connie, you're not gonna believe this. But *Leo's* here. Apparently this is Camp Evergreen with some new name. I ran into him on the freaking ferry."

"Wait, what?"

"He's known Savvy his whole life—"

"Wait, *what*?"

"—except now he's furious with me—"

"Uh, back up here—"

"Not that it even matters, because I'm busting out of here as soon as it's late enough for me to call my parents. Eight in the morning is probably the sweet spot—"

"Abby. *Abby.* Hold on. I'm going to . . . take a very large bite of this sfogliatelle," she says, in perfect Italian because it is, after all, Connie, who achieved near fluency for kicks over the past semester. "Then I am going to chew and process everything you just said."

After several seconds of chewing, she clears her throat and says, "Okay, first of all, extreme jealousy that you guys get to spend the summer together without me aside, please explain why Leo is mad? I didn't think he had a barometer for anger much higher than a puppy."

I blow out a breath and watch it fog up the office window. "I . . . might have forgotten to tell him about Savvy."

A moment passes. "You forgot?"

Which is to say, she's not buying it, the same way Leo probably won't either.

"I'm a jerk," I say, so I won't have to go into it.

"You're not a jerk. A cautionary tale on conflict avoidance, maybe, but not a jerk."

"No, I am." I sink into one of the chairs and prop my head on the back of it. "Even Savvy hates me. I've pissed off one of my best friends *and* my secret sister, and I haven't even been here a full day. I'm going home."

"Wait a minute. So you're telling me you hacked into every form of communication your parents own and came all the way out there, and now you're just gonna give up?"

Oh boy. Here comes one of Connie's famous pep talks. I brace myself, even though I expected one. I wouldn't have called if I hadn't.

"I mean . . . I wanted to know what happened with our parents. But not enough to torture myself for the next four weeks."

"First of all, forget your parents," says Connie, without missing a beat. "That girl is your damn sister. Do you know how much I've always wanted one of those?"

Connie spent most of our childhood asking her parents for a sibling, pleas that usually reached a fever pitch whenever another one of my brothers was born. Whenever someone mistook us for sisters it was the highlight of her week. As soon as we were allowed to roam the mall by ourselves Connie was always trying to play the sister card—*Can I get a dressing room next to my sister?* or *My sister's saving us seats over there.* It was fun, both because it was a game and because Connie really *is* like a sister to me. But to Connie it was less of a game and more like wishful thinking.

"And the universe just gave you one on a silver platter. You're telling me you don't want to get to know her?"

"I don't think *she* wants to get to know *me*," I deflect.

"And are you really torturing yourself? Didn't your bring your camera? Aren't you making new friends?"

I want to say no, for the sake of justifying the leaving. But that's the problem—or the three problems, I guess. Finn's "Savanatics."

I walked back to Phoenix Cabin last night feeling like scum on the bottom of someone's shoe, but opened the door a decorated war hero—it turns out they were all waiting for me, and the instant I opened the door the cabin erupted in cheers. Once I realized the noise was for me and not because someone's sleeping bag was on fire, they told me that all three of them had successfully signed up for recreational activities during the SAT prep block tomorrow, and no one suspected a thing.

"You're a lifesaver, Abby," said Cameron, the one who had waved me over at the pit. She'd already changed into another pair of matching neon leggings and tank top since my arrival, her smile as bright as the fabric.

"An angel," echoed Jemmy of Team Not Going To College, hopping on her bunk bed to grab the Goldfish she'd somehow snuck into the place and offering me some.

Izzy, aka 1560, swung a towel around my neck like a decorative sash and declared, "A liberator of SAT prep hostages everywhere."

After, we spent a lot of time chatting, bonding over our mutual dread of penning college admissions essays, counting one another's already alarmingly large number of mosquito bites in the dark, and breaking into the giant twelve-pack of gum I had stashed in my suitcase. I don't remember ever stopping—we all just conked out midconversation. The next thing I knew it was nearing daylight, and I was sneaking out to talk to Connie.

"I . . . guess people are nice here."

"See?"

"Trouble is, they all think Savvy is infinitely cooler than I am."

"You know what, Abby? I think this scares you. This new place and new person you have to deal with. And that's why this is good for you. I think you should find a way to ride this out."

She's not wrong. I am scared. I don't even think I've let myself fully feel how deep it goes until I'm hearing her say it, and now it feels like some kind of well in me, something I've been trying to fill up long before Savvy or camp ever came into the picture.

"Besides, I'm infinitely cool and you've never had any trouble hanging out with me, right?"

My laugh gets stuck in my throat. "I wish you were here," I say softly. My life might feel like chaos, but it's never reached a level where one conversation with Connie couldn't bring it back into focus.

Connie lets out a sad little hum. "I wish you were *here*." Before I can answer, she asserts, "But hey, at least we're getting back around the same time."

Neither of us misses the very bold assumption that I will be staying at camp. But that's Connie for you—when she wants to will something to happen, nine out of ten times she'll get her way, and the tenth time she'll double back when you least suspect it. Terrifying for our teachers, but extremely helpful in a best friend.

"Tell me about Italy."

"Oh, it's whatever. Only the best food I've ever tasted and breathtaking views and fascinating ancient history around every corner. I'll put some of my stunning pictures in the Dropbox so you can see just how over it I am."

I grin into the receiver. "You poor thing."

"Hey," says Connie. "When we get back, can we maybe . . . have some 'us' time? I know I saw you like every day at school, but it feels like I haven't actually *seen* you in ages, you know?"

"Yeah. I know what you mean."

"We can borrow my mom's car. Have a picnic at Richmond Beach."

Connie's the realist between us, so I hate that I'm the one who will have to remind her what's going to happen in August. I'm inevitably going to be in the second summer school session, and she'll be nose-deep in the mountain of required reading for AP classes, and our window of time for seeing each other will shrink from there.

But we have to try. I'll stick a foot in the window and jam it open, if I have to. Connie might be right about staying, but if she is, it's only because she knows me better than I know myself—and there's no better person to take advice from about my sister than the sister I already have.

"Assuming you haven't been swept off your feet by a hot Italian and ridden a moped into the sunset by then? Sounds like a plan."

We talk for another ten minutes or so, and only after I've ducked out of the way of the still wary camp employee and out into the eerie quiet of the empty camp do I realize I never asked her about Leo. I had plenty of time and still managed to swerve around it like it was oncoming traffic. I couldn't think of a way to ask Connie without implying that she might have lied.

But the farther I get from the office, the more I think that maybe this is different than my usual "conflict avoidance." This is plain old self-preservation. Connie wouldn't lie, which means I already know Leo doesn't like me—the same way I know it's going to break my heart if I have to hear it again.

nine

Before I can decide whether to go rogue and call my parents anyway, I run smack into Cameron, who drags me to the mess hall to eat. I try to duck out by lying about going to the bathroom, but Jemmy braves the line for the giant vat of Nutella and presents us all with our own globs of it, beaming. After we devour them, Izzy just about pins me to a chair to do my hair up in a high ponytail to match theirs, with enough determination that I figured it was either be her personal Barbie or suffer her personal wrath.

I touch it when she's done, knowing it's the Savvy ponytail, or at least as close to it as my frizzy hair can get. Same as their Savvy stud earrings and their Savvy sneakers and their Savvy-inspired breakfast bowls—some mix of oatmeal, yogurt, sliced fruit, nuts, and drizzled almond butter they fashioned for themselves, straight out of one of Savvy's Instagram stories from last week. It's unnerving, but at least we're also enjoying Leo and Mickey's French toast and omelet bakes, even if they aren't fit for the 'gram.

I ache at the thought of Leo. I haven't seen him since he ducked out into the fog last night, but one bite of French toast is all I need to know he's here. Nobody in my whole life has ever come close to getting the ratio of egginess and bread in

YOU HAVE A MATCH   87

French toast as well as Leo, and someone *definitely* snuck some cinnamon into the omelet bake, a Leo power move if there ever was one.

"Okay, one more of them together, and then we eat?" asks Jemmy, pushing all their bowls toward the center as Cameron hovers above it with her phone.

It really does make for a stunning photo, soothing and colorful. I wish my life could be as orderly as their oatmeal aesthetic, but it's a hell of a lot more like whatever remains of the poor Nutella vat half the camp is abusing in the corner.

"Well, look who's still here."

The rest of Phoenix Cabin raise their eyebrows curiously at the newcomer, who props a leg up on the empty chair next to me but doesn't sit. I don't bother holding in my sigh, only half looking up to acknowledge Finn.

"I thought you'd be halfway to the mainland," he says.

Isabelle's mouth pops open. "Really, Abby? We only just got here!"

"I mean, I know that kinda sucked yesterday, but it was a misunderstanding," says Jemmy, spooning more almond butter into her oatmeal.

"Besides, you're probably feeling better about it today, right?" asks Cameron.

I glance around the table at their earnest faces, both embarrassed and pleased at the idea of them caring whether I stay.

"Don't you worry, ladies," says Finn, kicking his leg off the chair. "The committee for camp deserters is on the case."

He offers me his elbow.

"We can't leave," I say flatly. "It's against the rules."

"Rules only count if you get caught." He flashes a shit-eating grin. "And with me you won't get caught."

"Two hours of kitchen duty last night begs to differ." I turn away from knockoff Han Solo and back to my plate. "And you still haven't given me one compelling reason to abandon this French toast."

"We'll save it for you," says Jemmy, nodding at Finn with conspiratorial eyes.

And yeah, it occurs to me that, objectively, Finn is not bad-looking. He's even cute, in that scruffy, mischievous puppy way.

But he's not Leo, and right now Leo is taking up about 90 percent of the real estate in my brain.

I glance toward the doors to the kitchen. The lengths he is going to to avoid me are getting absurd. It's not like I wanted any of this to happen. And yes, ideally I would have told him on the ferry, but can I be blamed for dropping the ball when his *I got over it* dropped an iceberg?

"Listen, I've got a foolproof way to solve all your problems," says Finn. His gaze has followed mine to the kitchen, making it clear he knows exactly which problem in particular I'm stuck on.

I narrow my eyes, but of all the people in this mess hall, he might actually be the most equipped to help. At least, the most-equipped person whose name I know. He's clearly in with the kids who have been coming here their whole lives, Savvy and Leo included.

"It'll take like five minutes," he says, most definitely fibbing. "Ten tops."

I look away from the kitchen doors, shoving another bite of omelet bake into my mouth. "Fine."

ten

Finn's whole *follow me* bit might be more charming if he didn't proceed to lead me directly to the edge of the woods, so thick and muggy they're basically begging to become the set of a true crime documentary. Which, to be fair, can be said for all the edges of the woods around the camp.

"Oh, great," I deadpan. "Another rule I can get lectured for breaking."

I'm not actually sure what the rule is re: sneaking off during breakfast into some murder woods, but Finn's eye roll seems to confirm it.

"They're gonna have to loosen up on those. Most of us have been around here since way before those stupid rules and we're all in one piece, aren't we? Give or take a few secret sisters popping out of the ether?"

I deflect, not entirely certain we're out of earshot yet. "Sounds like you don't really want to be here, either."

For once in my short time of knowing him, Finn goes quiet.

"Well, Camp Not-So-Evergreen-After-All sucks, but it's not like I had anywhere else to be," he says after a pause, in a tone that's a little too casual. "Besides, I was clearly meant to come here and unravel this nonsense for you."

We've reached the end of the campgrounds. I turn back, but

nobody's watching us. I take the opportunity to pull a pack of gum out of my back pocket and shove a stick of it in my mouth.

"How good are you at climbing trees?" Finn asks.

I think of all the things I have scaled in my lifetime, from trees to the electrician's van to the literal roof of our school, all in pursuit of a good angle for a shot. "Too good. Why?"

"Because we have to climb one if we're going to talk to the ghost."

This is probably the part where I should turn around and leave Finn and his minor league delusions to himself.

"Plus, sick view," he says, making a camera gesture with his fingers and a clicking noise with his tongue. He must have seen me fiddling with Kitty at breakfast. "Bet you haven't gotten a good shot since you got here."

Okay, he's got me on that. Even if we get busted, at least I might get a few good landscapes of the island and the water before they toss us out. I pat my backpack, checking to make sure Kitty's relatively secure, and let Finn lead the way.

"So basically, some girl bit it at camp in like, the fifties or something. Don't google it, it definitely happened. She was climbing a tree and fell and broke like, all of her bones."

"I thought you were going to solve my problems, not make more of them."

"We're not going to the tree she fell off of; they chopped it down. We're going to the one next to where it used to be. The Wishing Tree. You climb it and make a wish and—"

"Fall to your untimely death?"

"Gaby, the ghost who haunts the camp, makes it come true."

He says this matter-of-factly, leading us through the thick, root-tangled path that spits out to a clearing before I can wonder too much if he's really a serial killer disguised as an overgrown Labrador. Sure enough, there's a tree in the middle of it—thick trunked and squat, bursting with solid branches, looking about as climbable as a tree can look. For a second I forget about everything else, itching to get my hands on the rough bark, to see how fast and high I can climb.

"Well, my only wish is to get out of here."

"Nah. You came here for a reason," says Finn, touching the tree. "And I brought you here because I'm bored and I want to know the reason."

"I told you." Not by any means intentionally, of course.

"Yeah, I'm going to need a heck of a lot more to go on than that."

Instead of answering I start to climb, reaching out for a thick branch and curling my fingers around the damp bark, losing myself in the satisfaction of pulling myself up and up and up. The tree is so well-traveled that I can almost feel the grooves of where other campers must have climbed. Sure enough, the higher we get, the more we see little carvings faded into the bark: sets of initials, little sentiments, tiny shapes. And at the top, a miniature, paint-chipped signpost nailed to the tree with three fading words: MAKE A WISH.

I settle there and breathe in the view—layers on layers of wilderness, thick trees that give way to rocky beach then the pale blue of the water, the heavy white of the fog. Finn is talking as he works his way up, more cautious than I am, but I can't hear him over the endless sky.

Eventually he's close enough that I hear him say, "Told you. Stick with me this summer, Bubbles, and I'll get you the best views this place has to offer."

I'm already peering through Kitty when he says it, holding her lens cap between my teeth and using my other arm to brace myself to the tree. I take a few shots that may or may not turn out—I may have about as much regard for my mortality as a Looney Tune, but even I'm not stupid enough to test my luck by scrolling through or trying to adjust the lens.

"Guess the photography thing runs in the family, huh?" he asks.

I hum to acknowledge him, taking a few more shots. "I like to be behind the camera, not in front of it."

Finn lets out a soft laugh. One that makes me wonder if, for all his goading about this tree, he might not be so great with heights.

"Must be weird to see someone get famous with your own face, huh?"

I wrinkle my nose. "She looks nothing like me."

"Eh, you might not be clones, but you're definitely Savvy-esque. And look, I don't know how long you've actually known her, but she's chill. You know, under the whole compulsive-goody-two-shoes, aggressive-hashtagging, pulling-the-ugly-leaf-out-of-her-salad-so-it-photographs-well bit."

He waits, like I'm going to talk over him. The truth is, I don't know enough about her to try.

"But she's also like, not only the friend you call at midnight when your car tire blows. She's the friend you call when someone Matt Damons you and leaves you in a war zone or on Mars. She'd do anything for people she cares about."

It's not that I don't believe him. I do. Savvy is as intense as they come, and I can easily see that bleeding into the way she takes care of her friends.

The trouble is, I don't think I'll ever be one of them.

"Also, you know her parents are 'donated a building to the Seattle Center' level of rich, right? Most of the profits from her Instagram go to charity. She's out there doing the most because she really wants to help people. Even considering the obscene amount of green juice she has thrust on me, you gotta respect that hustle."

I have this impulse to defend myself, but I guess Finn is

Savvy's friend, not mine. I swallow it down and say, "So you've known her a long time."

"Since the beginning, basically," says Finn, leaning farther into the tree trunk to be a little closer to me. "Me, Savvy, Mickey, and Leo."

It's weird hearing Leo's name tacked on to theirs. I try to think of all the times Leo may have casually mentioned Savvy, but it's too eerie. Our shared DNA aside, there's this sense Savvy and I have been on parallel paths—living in the same area, dragging our cameras everywhere, sharing Leo—but even now, having met her and knowing what we know, it still feels impossible for our worlds to touch.

"You're Abby, right? Of Abby-and-Connie lore?"

"What makes you so sure I'm Abby and not Connie?"

"Cuz he tags an 'Abby' to credit all those pictures you take for his foodie Instagram." He glances down at the ground, this little pulse of nervousness, and back at me. "Also he was super upset when—well, you were the one whose grandpa died last summer, right?"

My face is so red I pull my camera away from it like my cheeks might set it on fire. "Yeah?"

"Sorry," says Finn, forgetting for a second to be terrified of the height. "I mean—it sounded like you were close, the way Leo was talking about it."

"We were."

I don't know what it is about being up this high that makes the ache come back, somehow even fresher than it was in the weeks after he died. Maybe because it was around this time last year that my parents started preparing us to lose him. I'd known he was getting weaker—we spent so much time together that I probably understood how much before my parents did—but last summer it was this blur of visiting hospitals and murmuring about pneumonia and my uncle coming into town. This summer I can look clearly back on it and it's not a blur, but a definitive line. A world where Poppy was here, and a world where he isn't.

It's selfish to think I lost more of him than everyone else, but I *had* more of him. I had his stories about traveling the world after serving in Vietnam, getting into hijinks across Europe and taking pictures of everything along the way. I had that settled, thoughtful quiet of his, the kind too many people mistook for disinterest, but I knew always had some valuable thought on the other side of it if I only waited long enough. I had full rein of him in a way my brothers, or even, I think, my mom never did—I don't think I ever asked him a question he didn't have an answer for.

I wish more than anything I could ask him something now. I was prepared to lose him, maybe. But I wasn't prepared for what happens after the losing.

"Sorry, I didn't mean to—"

I wave him off. "It's fine. Really."

The two of us sit there, breathing in the damp morning air.

"Anyway, that's my two cents on Sav, take it or leave it," Finn finally says. He taps the little sign at the top of the tree. "But we came up here for a reason."

With that, he closes his eyes, abruptly ending the conversation. I stare at him, waiting for the punch line, but he seems like he's seriously projecting wishes at some dead girl who apparently won't take receipts unless you're more than twenty feet above sea level.

I let out a sigh, popping my camera lens back on. I'm all the way up here. It's not like I've got anything better to do.

I close my eyes, feeling stupid, trying to think of a wish. *I wish I hadn't come here.* Unhelpful, but true. *I wish Savvy liked me.* I open my eyes, mad at myself for even thinking it, and they immediately sting and tear up. Even more unhelpful, but also true. *I wish . . .*

My throat aches, and I stare out at the fog, at the place in the distance where I should be able to see the suburbs beyond it. Most of the things I could wish for I can't have. It's big stuff, like how I wish Poppy were still here and we weren't selling Bean Well. Or medium stuff, like I didn't worry so much about where I stand with Leo and Connie, or I wasn't one ping in my parents' inbox away from get busted for skipping out on summer school. Or stuff that wells up in me from some place I can usually keep quiet—I wish I were old enough to do whatever I wanted, to go out and take photographs all over the world instead of the same sleepy suburb over and over and over again.

I wish I didn't feel like a problem my parents had to solve.

And, reluctantly, something that is maybe less of a wish and more of a confession: I wish I knew why they never told me about Savvy. I wish I knew why they lied. I wish I didn't care, like I've been telling myself I don't since our spat, because caring will make it that much harder to walk away from.

I hide my face behind the camera's viewfinder. That's enough wishing for the day. Otherwise the ghost is going to shove me off the tree for whining and I'll have to pick my own part of the woods to haunt.

"What are you wishing for?" I ask instead.

Finn cracks an eye open. "Things to be less fucked up, I guess."

"What things?"

He gestures vaguely with his free hand. "The things."

Whatever those *things* are, he doesn't get a chance to elaborate, because of the particular *thing* that brings our communion with the camp ghost to a crushing halt: Savvy, yelling at us from the ground.

"What the *hell* do you think you're doing?"

Finn leans over, popping his head down to look at her. I don't bother. I already know the exact crease of her scowl, the precise angle of her fists propped on her hips.

"G'morning, Sav," Finn calls down.

"Seriously? You too? What the hell is the matter with you both?" And in the blink of an eye Finn's attempt at smoothing things over between me and the sentient spon con is null and void.

"Coming, O grand junior counselor, crown princess of Camp Reynolds, ruler of hashtags—"

"Clam up, Finn," Savvy calls. "We both know you're too terrible at climbing trees to multitask."

"Okay, that was ten years ago. And I only fell, like, five feet."

"On top of me."

"But did you die?"

I follow Finn down, albeit slowly. His tree-climbing skills really are lacking at best. Watching him come down, I'm wondering how he got up in the first place. I focus on not tripping him up, which gives me plenty of time to think up something especially biting to say to Savvy—except when I reach the ground, I've got nothing.

"Literally the first rule," says Savvy, pacing like she's trying to build a moat around the tree. "Like, not even a Camp Reynolds rule, but a legitimate rule. *No more climbing this damn thing.*"

Finn brushes some dirt off his shoulder, walking over to her like he's expecting something. A hug or a fist bump or whatever it is they are to each other. But Savvy's too busy glaring at me to notice, and Finn stops short.

"Nice to see you, Finn," he says under his breath, in an uncanny imitation of Savvy's voice. "Been a long year, what's going on in your life—"

"Is this how it's going to be?" Savvy interrupts, aiming every word at me. "You're just going to run around this place and rack up demerits like carnival prizes?"

"Wait, you're giving us demerits?" Finn asks.

Savvy doesn't hear him, scowling at my mouth with enough rage to pop a vein. "Spit that out."

I scowl right back. "It's a piece of *gum*, not cocaine—"

"Spit. It. Out."

I look her right in the eyes and spit it into my open palm, offering her the big saliva-soaked blob as she reels back in disgust.

"Savvy's got a thing about germs—"

"*Not helping*, Finn," Savvy snaps.

Finn's face goes beet red and he takes a step back, kicking some dirt. "They give you a shiny junior counselor lanyard and you get to be the boss of us all, huh, Sav?"

This rattles her enough that I see something I'd rather not. This moment of recognition reflected back at me in her face. It's not even something I can see, but something I feel. It's not my mom or my dad or my brothers. It's me. My own confusion, my own fear. She could look like a stranger to me, and I'd still feel it as plainly.

She sucks in a breath and says, "You are both getting demerits, and when we get back to camp, you are emptying your suitcases of any more contraband."

I grind my heel into the dirt. "Fine. Take anything you want. I'm leaving."

It's almost satisfying, watching the way her eyebrows fly up. "You're not going anywhere. You promised—"

"I didn't *promise* anything."

She takes a sharp step toward me, taking the last card in her deck and playing it ruthlessly. "You're supposed to be my sister."

I open my mouth to say something I'm going to regret, but Finn beats me to it. "And you're supposed to be my *friend*," he says.

"Finn, what are you—"

"But I guess you're all too busy to be friends with me now that I'm just a camper and you're all running the damn place," he says.

"That's not true. I didn't—" An alarm goes off on Savvy's phone. "Shit. I have to go. I'm leading a yoga class."

Finn scoffs. "Naturally."

"We'll talk," she tells him, leaning forward to pull him into a quick hug. It happens too fast for him to react, so fast that I'm not expecting the heat of her eyes on me in the next instant. "And you—I'll be seeing you this afternoon. The gum has to go. Seriously. If another counselor catches you, they'll be a lot less lenient."

She takes off down the path without waiting to see if we've followed. I stand there, stunned, the gum in my palm and my mouth wide open.

"Lenient?" I repeat, dumbfounded. "Also, did she . . . not hear the part where I very explicitly said, within one foot of her human ears, that I am leaving?"

Finn shakes his head ruefully. "Guess she's got more important things to worry about these days than her best friends or blood relations." He sighs. "We should head back to the camp before she rats us out to Victoria."

I feel a twinge of sympathy for him, even more pronounced than my annoyance with Savvy. He spent the last ten minutes defending her upside down and backward, and she came here and tore him a new one. He may be the one who dragged me out here, yet I can't help but feel responsible that it happened.

"Wanna go chew twelve packs of gum in four hours before Savvy comes to collect?" I ask, attempting to perk him up.

Finn looks at me, his eyes bright with mischief. "Actually, yeah. But only if you're on board with a super gross idea."

"I think I've reached my questionable-Finn-ideas limit for today."

"Even one that will get you even with Savvy?"

I should not entertain this. She's already pissed off enough.

Trouble is, so am I.

"Only if we can do it before I get my parents to take me home tomorrow."

Finn's smirk deepens. "Deal."

eleven

"I need a jaw transplant."

I shoot Finn a look, or at least as defined of a "look" as a person can give when there are somewhere between seven and ten sticks of gum wedged between their teeth. "Don't wuss out on me now. This was your idea."

"You have like, sixteen years of pro gum chewing under your belt, Bubbles," Finn moans through his gum wad. "I'm a mere mortal. My teeth are going to fall out of my—"

"Less talking, more chewing. We're running out of time."

Finn cradles the lower half of his face as if he were clocked with The Rock's fist instead of subjected to a half hour of non-stop gum chewing. "What time is it, anyway?" he asks, a sliver of drool dribbling down his mouth.

I snort at the sight and almost choke on the virtual planet of Juicy Fruit in my mouth. It sets Finn laughing, until we make enough noise that we actively sabotage our already doomed plan, prompting the door to the junior camp counselors' cabin to open and reveal Mickey on the other side.

Finn and I freeze midchew. Mickey beams and throws her arms around him. Finn's cheeks bulge in an effort not to expel the gum as she squeezes him, and I have to lean on the side of the cabin not to double over from laughing.

"Finn! You're real!"

Finn nods, giving her a mumbled "Mm-hmm" without opening his mouth.

"And I see you've met Abby," says Mickey, reaching out a fist to bump me on the shoulder.

I relax, grateful Mickey doesn't help hold Savvy's grudges for her. Finn spits his gum into his hand while Mickey's back is turned and cracks his jaw.

"Yeah, Bubbles and I are besties," says Finn. "Since everyone else is too cool for me now."

Mickey's smile softens, and she reaches up the absurd height between her and Finn to ruffle his hair. "Yeah," she says. "I want to catch up. Maybe tonight in the kitchens, after dinner?"

Finn nods.

"My mom told me what happened. I'm sorry about—"

"Leo told me about your girlfriend," Finn interrupts, loud enough that Rufus comes scampering out of the cabin, woofing expectantly. Mickey and Finn both seem a little too grateful for the interruption—that is, until Rufus starts sniffing at Finn's fist, which must be oozing with prechewed gum.

"Oh, yeah, well—I broke up with her, so."

"Really?" Finn asks. "But I thought—"

Mickey has the same "help me" eyes that Finn did a second ago, so I make myself useful and interrupt before they put each other through the paces of something neither wants me to overhear.

"We're here to clean the cabins," I say, gesturing at the cleaning supplies Finn pilfered from one of the rec room closets.

"Oh. Right. Part of our demerit punishments," says Finn, remembering our not-so-carefully crafted lie.

Mickey's nose wrinkles. "Yikes. Well. Have at it. I'm heading down to start dinner prep." Before she heads off, she squeezes Finn's arm, holding him there for a bit. "It's really good to see you. We'll talk."

Something wobbles in Finn's expression as she heads off, Rufus in tow, but before I can decide whether to ask him about it, he charges into the cabin, prying the gum from his hand like it's precious cargo instead of the least-appetizing wet blob either of us has ever laid eyes on.

We scan the room and stop at the sight of the bed outfitted with a Himalayan salt lamp, a book titled *Spring Cleaning for Your Brain*, and an inordinate amount of Rufus-colored dog hair at the foot.

"Ah," I deadpan, "but however will we know which bunk is Savvy's?"

Finn doesn't hesitate. "I'll go first. You watch the door."

"Well, if I didn't feel like a criminal before, I sure do now."

"Don't go soft on me, Bubbles. Besides, all we're doing is sticking some gum on the bottom of the bunk above hers. It's not like we're putting cyanide in her acai bowl."

Finn begins separating his wad of gum into smaller pieces and squinting up at the space as he curates his gum masterpiece. I watch the door, letting the cool breeze of the afternoon lift my curls, settling into the first bout of quiet I've had all day and wishing Finn would fill it. From his silence, he's pulled himself somewhere far away, too.

"Okay, your turn," he says after a few minutes.

When I crouch into the space between Savvy's bed and the bunk above it, I feel a legit twinge of guilt for desecrating the "sanctity of the sleeping space"—Savvy's words from a recent Instagram story, not mine—but then I remember she sentenced me to peeling hardened nacho cheese off camp dinner plates with my fingernails for two weeks, and just like that, my head is back in the (admittedly disgusting) game.

Finn has fashioned his gum into a giant *F*, so I follow suit and leave an *A* in front of it. As in "disgusting AF," I guess. Finn comes over to survey our germ-infested calling card when I'm done and clicks his tongue in satisfaction.

"Art in its highest form. We should open an Etsy shop and sell gummed-up goods."

"We should get the heck out of here is what we should do," I say, so nervous that—of all the ironies—I wish I had some gum to chew on.

Finn does a little skip on the way out the door. If nothing else, he's a lot more chipper than he was this morning after Savvy blew him off. Even if Savvy wants to throw us off a dock and feed us to the rather entitled ducks that hang out on the fringes of the camp for this, I think that might make her happy, too.

"So," he says, once we're a safe distance away from the cabin. "I promised you good views, and I have a few in mind."

I raise my eyebrows. "How many of them involve breaking a camp rule?"

"Only all of them." He must assume whatever face I'm making is answer enough, because he starts heading for the docks with a merry "Let's go."

twelve

The end of the day sneaks up on me so fast that I have no choice but to corner Leo in his element by showing up to kitchen duty early. From the door I can hear his back-and-forth with Mickey as they prep for tomorrow's breakfast in the middle of a lively debate about whether jackfruit is better in savory or sweet dishes.

"I'm just saying, there's a *reason* all the chain restaurants here are suddenly using it as a meat substitute," says Leo. "The texture really lends itself to—"

"Almost everything. Jackfruit is the party animal of the cooking world; this country was just slow on the uptake. Anyway, try my turon and you'll never doubt its proper place in dessert again."

"Nothing against your turon, but—"

Leo spots me first, pausing at the counter. I freeze, and we stare at each other the way dumbfounded deer do when they stumble on your path in the woods.

I clear my throat and say a silent prayer to whatever gods are in charge of puns to forgive me for my sins. "I know you probably don't want to give me the time of Day right now . . ."

Leo groans, but it works—he's got the beginnings of a smile and is only halfway trying to hide it. Mickey tweaks him on the arm and winks at me. "I'm gonna go meet up with Finn, since we're wrapped up here. Your blasphemous jackfruit opinions aside."

Then Mickey's gone, and the kitchen is completely silent, save my awkward shuffling on the tiled floor and Leo fiddling with his apron ties.

"Wanna go outside?" he asks finally.

I nod, figuring the only person to bust me for not doing kitchen duty is probably Leo himself.

The air is unusually muggy, even for June. It puts a heaviness in our steps, in the space between us, making me more aware of him than the baseline of all-too-aware that I already am. The slight sheen of sweat where his shirt collar meets his chest. The faint scent of cinnamon, plus whatever spices were in tonight's sweet potato bake. The warmth of him, so familiar to me that I don't even need to be near him to feel it. I can conjure it all too easily, even when he's nowhere near.

We sit on a bench that looks out at the water, to the stretch of the mainland and hints of mountaintops beyond. The sky is all deep purples and blues, moody and mystic. I've always wanted to take photographs of it like this but still haven't quite mastered what it takes to get good images at night.

We settle in, neither of us looking at each other, staring at the lazy lap of the water on the pebbled shore. I'm so relieved to be near him that at first it's too overwhelming to speak.

"I should probably explain," I start.

Leo shakes his head. "Mickey filled me in earlier."

"Oh." I imagined most of this conversation would be me giving the recap to the soap opera of my life and figuring out a place to apologize on the way. Without that to guide me, all that comes out is a graceless, blurted "I'm sorry."

"To be clear—that is why you're here, right? For Savvy?"

There's no graceful way to say it, so I don't. "I'm glad you're here, too."

He's not looking at me, staring straight ahead at the water even as I will him to turn his head, to see how much I mean it.

"I thought we told each other everything," he says quietly.

I close my eyes for a moment. I've been looking at all this through the lens of my own embarrassment, without thinking of how he sees it—not as me trying to keep things normal after the BEI, but as a friend who compromised his trust.

"I mean . . . I told you why I was taking the test. And I told you what I found out." He says the words slowly and deliberately, like they've been weighing on him all day. "And you—you must have found out about this in my living room, and you didn't say a word."

"I was in shock at first. And then—it all happened so fast, and . . ."

"Did you think I'd be upset or something? That you found family and I didn't?"

I wince. The truth is, I have felt guilty about it. He took this test to find people, and now I have this sister I'm not even sure I want. This thing Leo and Connie both want so badly in their own ways is something that threw a massive wrench into my world, and I've been too wrapped up in what it means for me to let myself fully acknowledge what it means for him.

"Well—yeah," I admit. "I guess that was part of it."

"And the rest?"

He's looking at me now, with the same patience he always has. He gives me too much room sometimes. Enough to say whatever I need to say, even if it's something I shouldn't.

"When I saw you on the ferry, I was going to tell you. But we got distracted, and . . ."

Distracted may not be the right word. But I never know what the right word is when it comes to my feelings about Leo— it's equal parts hopeful and disappointed, these mismatched moments where I'm so certain he might want me too that are punctured in an instant by the ones where I'm sure he doesn't. I've gone over that conversation we had on the ferry at least a hundred times since it happened, picked it apart from every angle, either trying to find reasons to keep hoping or to shut it all down.

I let the sentence hang there, worried he'll press the point. Worried, but also a little bit eager. Like it'll open a door I'm too scared to open myself. Instead he takes my hand and squeezes it briefly, a quiet forgiveness, and lets it go.

"Not gonna lie," says Leo. "This is a weird one to wrap my head around."

I slouch into the bench, trying not to read anything into the way Leo leans over so I'm mostly slouching against him. "You're telling me."

Leo reaches forward, plucking one of the gloves hanging out of my apron's front pocket. "So . . . do I even want to know how this happened?"

"Probably not," I say, taking it back from him. "This place isn't exactly what I expected."

Leo snorts. "Me neither. At least everything's the same in the kitchen. Dunno if I'd want to be a camper under—what's Finn calling it?—the 'Reynolds Regime.'"

"Eh, today wasn't so bad, I guess. I even made some friends."

I smile to myself. Once Finn and I wrapped up our DIY home decor project in Savvy's bunk and he snuck me over to the neighboring camp to get a picture from their high dive, I spent the rest of the day with the girls from Phoenix Cabin—kayaking, hiking around the trails, even playing a game of capture the flag that got us so muddy we had to shower before dinner. We were so busy I kept missing chances to call my parents, and then it was late enough that I figured I'd better put it off until tomorrow, when it wouldn't freak them out as much.

Leo catches the tail end of the smile with a hesitant one of his own. I nudge my shoulder with his. "How have *you* been?"

Leo shrugs. "We're settling in. Catching up with everyone.

So far it's mostly just me and Mickey, showing off all the new cooking tricks in our arsenals."

"Please tell me the macadamia fried grilled cheese balls are in the mix," I say, thinking back to when Connie came back from Christmas break in Hawaii with so many tins of macadamia nuts that I'm surprised the plane could take off.

"I've got that one up my sleeve for later. I'll need a ringer for later this week. She's been hoarding leftover ingredients in a corner of the fridge and I've done just enough sleuthing to think a four-meat pochero is coming."

"So basically this kitchen turns into the set of *MasterChef* after dark."

"Except Mickey's only made me cry, like, twice." He shifts on the bench, his legs absurdly long when splayed out next to mine. Absurdly long and absurdly close—one of his nudges mine in a way that might be accidental, but when I don't move, it stays there in a way that definitely isn't. "But yeah, the head chef pretty much gives us free rein of the place after dinner as long as we clean up."

I'm about to make some crack about showing up to the kitchen to be fed every night like the stray cat I am, but I pause. Leo's lips are tight. He's going to say something but isn't quite sure how to say it yet.

"And I think . . . well, Mickey's dad and her aunts run their own restaurant up by the UW and she's—it's always been a big part of her life, you know? So I thought maybe—since being here has kind of put the brakes on the whole looking-into-my-roots thing—well, I'm gonna ask Mickey to teach me more about the Filipino dishes she's always making."

"Yeah?"

Leo nods, his eyes tentative and not quite meeting mine. He clears his throat and adds, "I mean, only after our annual week of cooking battles is done and I've established myself the clear victor."

"So crush her emotionally with your PB&J cinnamon rolls, and then ask her for a favor."

"Exactly."

The laughter tapers off, and both of our smiles soften with it. He's staring at me like he's waiting to hear what I think. Like maybe he's been waiting to hear what I think all day. And even if I know it doesn't really matter what I think, it feels nice that he wants to hear it.

"That's a really cool idea."

Leo falls into a satisfied quiet, then nudges me with his elbow. "And if you think that sneaky bid to get yourself some PB&J cinnamon rolls went unnoticed, you're wrong."

"They're your secret weapon."

"Weapon? With Mickey, those would be like showing up to a gunfight with a pool noodle."

"You're still cutting out. Hold on. Sometimes I get service down by the water."

Leo and I turn toward the voice to see Savvy, pacing far enough away that she can't see us, but close enough that we can hear nearly every word she's saying.

"No, you said you'd come *here* after two weeks, and two weeks after that I'd visit you. I literally sent you a Gcal invite. I checked on it an hour ago when I was going through parent emails to the camp staff. 'Jo visits Savvy.' And two weeks after that, 'Savvy visits Jo.'"

Right. Jo. The elusive girlfriend I've only ever seen in the edges of Instagram pictures or heard laughing in the background of an Instagram story. Last week we got as much as her full forearm and hand.

"I can't switch. I have to be here the whole monthlong

session, I only get the one window to leave before the second one starts. We *did* talk about this, at your graduation party, remember? Like, exhaustively. Hence the Gcal invites."

I cringe. My own attempt at a love life may have spent the last few months circling the drain, but even I draw the line at romance via G Suite.

"That's . . . wow. Okay. Maybe I don't, but it's important to me. Okay? Just because I'm not spending my whole summer rubbing elbows with people in power suits doesn't mean— wait, what?" Savvy's voice switches from annoyed to near livid. "Mickey literally has nothing to do with—shoot, I can't hear you. Hold on, I'll try the break room again . . ."

She wanders off without noticing us. We both shift awkwardly in her wake. I want to ask, and it feels like I should be able to, as if as her full-blooded whatever I am to her that I have some built-in right. But I don't, really. And in all my years of firsthand experience of being Leo's friend, I know he'd never talk about someone else's business.

"You know what's wild," says Leo in a hushed voice—not like he's worried Savvy's going to come back, but like he doesn't want to interrupt the stillness. We've migrated even closer to each other on the bench, his bare knee brushing mine, sending tingles up my skin. "I mean, aside from how your parents kept this massive secret from you. Somehow, even though I've known you both forever and you're basically carbon copies of each other, it never once crossed my mind."

"Uh, because we are of a different species?"

I'm prepared for Leo to say a lot of things, but not for him to defend Savvy. "The two of you just need to try to put yourself in each other's shoes," he says, all the confirmation I need that Mickey has filled him in on our running spat. "And maybe go easy on Savvy."

"Whoa. Whose team are you on here?"

"I'm not on a team," says Leo. "You're both way too important to me for that."

I know it's irrational, but that's the last thing I want to hear. Especially when I'm out of my element, surrounded on all sides by Savvy's friends and Savvy's fan club, not just immersed but fully dunked into Savvy's world.

"And you have more in common than you think."

I snort. "I've never been less like anyone in my life. You said it yourself on the ferry, didn't you?" I say, pointing out toward the water. It's turned an eerie, unusual magenta in the time we've been talking, the sky thick with color and clouds. "She's so high-strung. Obsessed with her rules and her schedules. She's basically running around on anxiety fumes. We're nothing alike."

"Uh, Abby, you're like, one of the most anxious people I know."

I raise my eyebrows. A lot can been said about me, maybe, but certainly not that. If anything, looking at my grades, I'm sure you could argue I'm not anxious *enough*. Leo doesn't back down, though, raising his eyebrow right back.

"I mean, you're my—we're best friends. I know Connie and I make jokes about you swerving away from dealing with stuff, but that's its own kind of anxiety, you know? I think sometimes you get overwhelmed and . . . avoid things. Bury them."

It stings, and he knows it. It's why he's saying it so gently, and why he's giving me the space to tell him he's wrong even though we both know he isn't. The proof is in a lot of things, but more than anything, in the distance between us—not the physical distance, but the distance I made all on my own.

Not telling Leo about Savvy. Not telling Leo about my feelings when I had them. Not telling Leo about them in all the months they've only gotten worse since.

"Connie said it was being a Hufflepuff," I remind him, trying to brush it off.

"Of course she did, she's a Slytherin. Plus she lives to fight your battles for you." Leo's eyes are on mine, a challenge. "You know we're always in your corner, right? But there are some things you gotta own up to yourself."

We both know, in the split second after he says it, he doesn't mean me lying about Savvy.

But this weirdness between me and Leo—I'm not avoiding it for my sake. I'm avoiding it for his. Because he's right, the way he was right to say it just after the BEI. We are best friends. And being someone's best friend comes with a responsibility, a lifetime of secrets and promises and shared moments, that were made with a certain understanding. A contract of sorts. *This is the person you are to me; these are the things I feel safe to tell you because of it.*

There are too many of them now, all scored into my heart. All these fragile, precious things shared between the three of us, years that have built themselves into something more concrete than time, but so precarious that it could all get knocked to the ground in the time it takes me to look over at Leo and tell him, *I think I'm in love with you.*

The thought is so loud that I flinch like someone screamed it in my ear. Leo watches it happen, and my heart's in my throat again, irrationally scared that he heard it. That it's as plain on my face as it is in my head.

"Abby . . ."

He's doing it again. Fighting my battles for me. Giving me an opening to say whatever needs to be said.

I take a breath. My chest feels swollen with the things this air might change if I use it to tell the truth. Because there are two possibilities here: Either Leo doesn't like me, and I'll humiliate myself. Or Leo *does* like me, which means Connie lied.

Either way, I lose. The only way to keep everything from falling to pieces is not to say anything at all.

I let the breath go.

Then the sky erupts, a flash of lightning streaking across the water, branched and forked in so many pieces that it looks like the earth shattered. It's far from us, and the rumble follows after a few long seconds, hungry in the ground, but deep and resonant, crackling in our bones.

"Holy shit," Leo marvels.

I let out a low hum of agreement. I can count on one hand the number of times I remember it thunderstorming in Seattle. Another streak of lightning makes the sky pink, divides it into infinite pieces, and I know I could live another hundred years and never witness something as breathtaking as this.

We both settle back into the bench, my heart still thudding like a drum, as if it's connected to the rumble in the ground beneath us. Leo moves closer to me, and I wait for him to start another one of his information dumps—something about storms and pressurization, or why Seattle gets them so rarely— but instead he wraps a steady arm around me, pulling me in. I relax into the warmth of him before I can second-guess myself, sinking into this stolen moment, into this strange, otherworldly sensation that makes the rest of them feel like they don't count.

"You should get your camera," he says lowly, into my hair.

I shake my head into his shoulder. We sit together, watching the lights pierce the dark and travel across the water, the two of us safe and dry in this twilight while the storm is far beyond us. I breathe in the sticky warmth of the air, the pine and the electricity and the ache of something deeper than I can name, knowing that no view I can capture will ever compare to this feeling—seeing it through my eyes while seeing it through his, letting us both bleed into a world where those two things can be the same.

thirteen

The next day I'm awake before dawn and tiptoeing out of Phoenix Cabin to get a shot of the sunrise, Poppy's old camera in hand. I end up picking the trail closest to our cabin, a short, steep one with a brutal five-minute uphill climb that leads to a minicliff looking out over the water. I'm so enamored with the hatched pattern of the endless clouds that it takes me a beat to realize I'm very much not alone.

"What are you doing here?" Savvy blurts.

I take a step back. "What are *you* doing here?"

Her whole face goes crimson, and only then do I see the tripod and a camera that must be set up on a self-timer. In fact, she looks way more put-together than anyone has any business being at an hour this unholy and was probably in the middle of posing in some Instagrammy way when I interrupted.

Another rustle comes up from behind me, and there's Rufus, wheezing excitedly with someone's badminton racket crushed in his jaw. He wags his tail and rubs his head all over my knees in hello.

"I . . . was taking a picture for Instagram," Savvy mutters to the grass.

I assess the situation, staring from the tripod to the skyline and back to where she won't quite meet my eye. We've got maybe thirty seconds before the sun starts to peek out. I may hate her a little bit, but I hate the idea of a missed photo op even more.

"Yoga pose?" I ask.

She cuts a wary glance at me and doesn't answer, which is to say *Yes*.

I walk over to her camera. I recognize the model—a pricey DSLR, but not nearly as expensive as the one she and Mickey were using out on Green Lake. I don't have a ton of experience with this one, but I remember reading on some woman's travel photography blog that the image stabilization goes to shit once it's on a tripod.

"I don't mind taking it."

Savvy narrows her eyes. "I don't think the gears will work if they're clogged with your gum."

I wince. Somehow in all my spinning post-thunderstorm thoughts about Leo, I'd forgotten about my antics with Finn entirely.

"Temporary truce?" I ask.

At first I think she'll blow me off, but something gives way in her body, some stiffness in her bones.

"Well," she says wryly, "seeing as we are on the edge of a very steep ledge right now, it seems unwise to say no."

I let out a laugh and pluck her camera off the tripod. I'm momentarily thrown off by the lack of viewfinder—I've been using Poppy's older model more often this past week.

"Say 'spon con.'"

Savvy looks a little miserable about it but turns and sees we're in the endgame of prime sunrise and doesn't waste any more time. In the second it takes for me to blink she's kicked up one graceful leg behind her, pulled it up with one arm, and extended her other out to the sky, like a lithe Fabletics-clad sky dancer. She's intentionally framed it so the sun will peek out in the circle she's made with the arm holding on to her leg, and so I lean a fraction of an inch down to get it dead center.

"That oughta do it," I say after a few shots.

"Thanks," she says sheepishly. I brace myself for her to go through the shots when I hand the camera back, but she doesn't. Like she trusts my ability. It feels nice—or at least it does until she turns and says, "Just so you know, this whole thing . . . being a junior counselor. I didn't think it would be this weird, or I would have said something."

I pause, holding my camera to my face, finger resting on the shutter. "Maybe you wouldn't have invited me, you mean?"

She clears her throat, taking a step back. "What I'm trying to say is, I'm not—I don't *like* bossing people around."

I pull my camera away from my face to raise my eyebrows at her, somewhat at my own peril. It earns me a slight smirk.

"Okay, *that* much," she amends. She shuffles her feet in the grass, still barefoot from the pose. Rufus is rolling around a few feet away with the black sneakers of Savanatics lore. "Look—I only want to do a good job. This place is important to me, and I . . . I want to do it justice."

"Fair enough," I say.

She accepts it with a nod, and we fall into an uneasy quiet. Now that we're actually talking we can't justify putting off what we came here to do—talk about our parents. I brace myself, and we stare at each other, playing a game of chicken over who will bring it up first. In the end, we both swerve.

"Your camera," she says. "I've never seen one like that before."

"It's old as hell, is probably why." I offer it to her, and she takes it, peering into the viewfinder. She seems so genuinely interested that before I can think the better of it, I add, "It was my grandpa's."

It's the first time it has crossed my mind that my grandparents were also biologically hers. Poppy probably knew about her. It wasn't just my parents lying to me—Poppy must have, too.

It hits me in an unexpected place, one I didn't even think could be hit. I almost wish I hadn't said anything. Or at least that I hadn't said it in the past tense.

She hands the camera back more carefully than she took it. "Is he the one who got you into photography?"

"Yeah," I say, relieved that she didn't bring it up. It's not that I don't want to share Poppy with her. I just don't know if I'd be able to do him justice. It's hard to describe someone when you feel less of what they were and more of what they aren't anymore. "We used to take little road trips. Go on hikes. Nothing too far from home." *Nothing like this*, I almost say, and feel like a traitor.

"That must have been nice."

She doesn't say it in that throwaway way you do to be polite, but like she means it. It makes me feel bold enough to ask a question of my own.

"How about you? How'd you get into . . ." I gesture at the sunrise, to the spot where her limbs went full Play-Doh in the name of social media influencing.

"Instagram?" she asks. "Oh, I don't know. I've always—I mean, my parents, they're pretty into, like, health stuff. Like, borderline paranoid."

I hold myself back from blurting, *You don't say.*

"So I guess I've just always been a part of the whole wellness world."

"Wellness?" I don't mean it to sound doubtful. I'm actually curious.

"You know. Nutrition. Yoga. Meditation," says Savvy, moving to sit in the grass next to Rufus. "Stuff I hated as a kid, but like, I get now. I think of it as a toolkit for dealing with stress, you know? And it's easier to understand, maybe—or at least a little more accessible to people—with Instagram making it pretty, breaking it down into easier steps. It doesn't seem as isolating or hard."

It's what Finn was trying to tell me. Savvy is legitimately into this whole scene to help people. And it's one thing to believe him, but it's another to see the proof in the way she talks about it—her words coming out a little faster, unintentional and unplanned.

"Anyway, that's what we're trying to do," Savvy adds. "Make it fun. Me and Mickey, I mean. It was her idea to turn it into an Instagram account in the first place. We started it here a few summers back."

She says it with this kind of wistfulness, like Mickey's far away instead of right down the trail, no doubt arguing with Leo over which fruit they're going to put into this morning's muffins. I think about the conversation we accidentally dropped a ton of eaves on last night—*Mickey literally has nothing to do with this.*

Maybe I'm not the only one with unresolved friend drama. Maybe Savvy and I really are more alike in the things that we can't see than the big, obvious one that we can.

"Helps that you both have an eye for photography."

"Well, Mickey's mom is an artist—she has a shop where she makes all those temporary tattoo designs and sells her other work—and my parents are big into art, too. Making it, but also, like, collecting."

"Ah, right. You didn't mention your parents are like . . . Tony Stark levels of rich."

Savvy doesn't blush or try to downplay it. "Yeah. Well, we live in Medina," she says, as if that explains the whole thing.

I freeze, realizing I accidentally walked into the topic of our parents like a bird flying into a glass window. But even I, the crown princess of putting things off, can't justify avoiding it any longer. I steel myself, walking over and sitting on Rufus's other side. He lolls his head over at me in acknowledgment, and Savvy watches me, expectant.

"The thing I can't figure out is how our parents knew each other in the first place," I say. "Like, they don't seem like people whose paths would cross, let alone be friends."

It isn't lost on me that the same thing could be said for us, sitting here in the muddy grass, the Instagram star and the English class flunkie. Briefly I worry she might take it the wrong way, but if there is one thing I can appreciate about Savvy, it's that she doesn't waste time beating around the bush.

"I've been wondering that, too," she says. "It seems to be the key. Like if we can just figure that part out, maybe the rest of it will make sense."

"Maybe they were in some kind of secret society. Something mega embarrassing. It was the nineties, right? What was embarrassing in the nineties?"

"Uh. Everything?"

"Maybe they were in one of those competitive Pokémon card game leagues."

So far I can count on one hand the number of times I've heard Savvy intentionally make a joke, so I almost don't know what to make of it when she adds, "Underground Beanie Baby fight club?"

I try not to let a beat pass, before whatever this is wears off her. "Honestly, maybe they were part of an emotional support group for people who watched too many movies about dogs where the dog dies. Is it just me or is it anytime your parents are like, 'Hey, let's watch this old movie from the nineties,' the dog totally bites it?"

"You know Mickey found a site that screens for that." Savvy shakes her head with a rueful grin, as if to say, *Only Mickey.* "It's legitimately called 'doesthedogdie.com.'"

I snap my fingers. "That was it! Their life's work. Their big contribution to society, and then . . ."

It's about as far as the joke can go, because what's on the other side of it isn't one. What's on the other side of it is Savvy and Abby, born one after the other but into entirely different worlds.

"And then," Savvy echoes, with a sigh.

We settle back into the damp grass, Rufus splayed out on both of us now, his butt on my legs and his head in Savvy's lap.

"Real talk, though. I went back down to our basement a few days ago, to look for photos," I tell her. "I didn't find any others of your parents."

"Same," says Savvy. "I even checked your parents' Facebooks from my parents' joint account. Not a single mutual friend. And my parents friend every breathing person they meet."

"So something definitely happened."

"You think so?" Savvy asks. "You don't think it was . . . I don't know. Something about the adoption? Like, the terms of it? Some birth parents aren't supposed to have access to the kid."

I don't say what I'm thinking, which is that I doubt my parents would have given up a child to a friend of theirs if they *weren't* planning on having access.

"Let's go back. See if we can find something in common." Even as I'm saying it, I know it might be a total dead end. I can list the things I have in common with Connie on one hand, and most of them are Leo. If someone tried to dissect our friendship it would only raise more questions than answers, and the deeper we dive into this the more their story seems the same. "Tell me about your parents."

Savvy blows out a breath, leaning back to stare at the horizon. "They're . . . normal."

"How'd they meet?"

"Rich parents with rich kids who met each other at a rich people thing, I'm guessing." She wrinkles her nose. "I'm making them sound like snobs. They're not. They're both kind of a little kooky, actually, which is probably how they found each other in rich people world."

The more Savvy talks about them, the more weirdly fascinated I am. Savvy's known about my parents her whole life, but to me, this is its own level of strange—seeing what happens when some-one with my exact same DNA ends up raised by someone else. The fact that Connie looked them up on Spokeo and found out they live in the kind of waterfront mansion that's basically porn for HGTV Dream Home nerds only adds fuel to my curiosity's fire.

"When did they get married?"

"Eighty-seven."

"So your parents are older than mine." Another thing that makes their friendship that much more unlikely.

"My parents always told me my bios were in their early twenties when they had me, so yeah. Probably by about ten years or so."

"Huh. What do they do for fun?"

"Aside from every wellness thing short of having an on-call astrologist?" Savvy gives a self-deprecating smile, like she hasn't just come to terms with her parents' little quirks, but owned them as a part of her. "They're really into the art scene. They're always sponsoring artists and own a bunch of galleries—Seattle, Portland, San Francisco. It's actually how I met Jo."

"Your girlfriend."

"Yeah. Her dad's an art dealer. They're friends with my par-ents, and I guess they talked about us so often they thought we might hit it off."

I frown down at the water. "Wait. Your parents set you up?"

Savvy sits up a little straighter. "What? I mean—no. It wasn't like that."

"It was, though." I don't know why this is so funny to me. No, I know exactly why—it's because she's turned a shade of red violent enough that cars might hit their brakes mistaking her for a stop sign. "Are you really so busy you let your parents pick your *girlfriend*?"

"Jo and I are both busy," Savvy defends herself. "It's one of the many things we have in common, and one of the many reasons why we're dating of our own free will, thank you very much. Our parents being friends is just convenient."

The sun has partially popped up through the clouds, filtering in streams of light across the water. The sky is opening up right as Savvy starts to close off, going quiet. I can practically hear her thinking up a graceful way to end the conversation. But suddenly I don't want to talk parents. I've scratched the surface of something, and I want to dig.

"*Convenient*," I repeat. She goes rigid, and I almost don't say it: "Now *there's* a sexy word."

Savvy pushes a palm to my shoulder, indignant. I pretend to topple over in the grass, and Rufus immediately takes the opportunity to pounce, and I fall over, taking him down in the mud with me.

"I don't see *you* dating anyone," Savvy points out, letting her dog clobber me.

"How is that possible when my boyfriend is literally on top of me right now?"

At this Savvy lets out a sharp laugh, and we push through the tension to a place where we can tease each other, hopefully without worrying about setting each other's admittedly fragile egos on fire. She pulls Rufus off me and chucks the slobbery badminton racket down the path.

"What does Jo think about this?" I ask, watching Rufus speed off.

"Think about what?"

"Uh . . . all five feet six inches of surprise sister that popped up in your inbox last week."

Savvy blinks. "I—shit." She goes rigid, like it's only occurring to her. "I didn't tell her."

It feels unproductive to get offended, but it's kind of hard not to be. Especially when she laughs again, this time in disbelief.

"I . . . wow. I can't—I mean, seriously—shit."

"Mood," I say, because I can only get one syllable out without the hurt slipping through.

Savvy notices, her eyes ticking over to mine. She looks like she's on the verge of apologizing, but what comes out is: "She's gonna be so pissed."

"Why?"

"Because I told Mickey, and she thinks—" Savvy shakes her head, cutting herself off abruptly. "It's got nothing to do with you." She shakes her head again, with more intention. "She probably would have said to tell my parents."

I pick at a stray piece of grass, breaking it apart with my fingers. I should probably think about whether it's really my place before I ask, but we're past that, maybe. "Why didn't you?"

She shrugs. "They had eighteen years to tell me, and didn't. So." It doesn't feel like the full answer, the rest hovering between us. I glance over at her, and it gives way. "Also, I have this weird feeling that . . . I don't know. Maybe things were supposed to shake out like this. Maybe we were supposed to find each other."

"Yeah."

My throat feels thick. Less from guilt of what we're doing and more out of this strange obligation I feel to Savvy—this feeling that neither of us set this in motion. Something carried us to this moment, some force that's been hovering so long in "if" that our meeting was always bound to be a "when." I've never once in my life felt like something was missing, but if I left right now, I'd be leaving a part of me here with her.

Savvy hugs her knees to her chest. "Ugh. It's been, like, two seconds. But I kind of miss them."

I know she means her parents, because suddenly I'm thinking of mine, too. About the pancakes Asher probably bullied our dad into making, about the coffee cup I usually steal swigs of from my mom. But it's deeper than the day-to-day. My brothers will be taller when I get back. They'll have enough time to make a whole new routine without me. The space I come back to, whether I want it to be or not, won't be Abby-shaped anymore—or maybe I won't be the shape of the Abby who left.

I take in a shaky breath and say, "Me too."

"It gets better," says Savvy, fiddling with the chain around her neck. "First week of camp is always kind of rough."

I watch as she pulls the chain out from under her shirt and stares down at the charm. I've gotten so used to the things that are the same about us—the color of our hair, the shape of our eyes, the way our voices both get a little high-pitched when we're mad—it takes a second to register that the charm wasn't something we were born with in common.

"Is that a magpie?"

"Wow," says Savvy, "you really are into birds. Most people think it's a—oh."

She falls silent, staring at the keychain I fished out of my denim shorts. Thicker, shorter chain. Same magpie charm.

Our eyes connect, both of us already knowing what we're going to say before we say it: "My mom gave it to me."

I swallow thickly, holding the charm in my fist. My mom gave it to me on my first day of kindergarten, with the emergency house key attached. I don't remember much about the conversation, only that even at five I could tell her hands had a different weight to them when she pressed the charm into mine and told me to keep it safe.

"I'm guessing yours never told you why, either."

"No," says Savvy. She pulls hers off her neck, and we hold them up to the light. "I've had it so long I can't remember *not* having it."

"Well, I guess we've got our first clue."

The two magpie charms dangle, glinting in the sunlight, identical in shape, but made different by time. Mine is nicked from falls, Savvy's worn at its edges from her rubbing it, the colors uniquely faded—but both still have that iridescent blue glimmering against black on white, two opposite extremes in one body, a bird at odds with itself.

"Maybe we make the truce a little . . . untemporary?" Savvy ventures. "That way you can stay. At least until we can figure this out."

I close my fist around my magpie charm, and she sets hers back against her neck. "Yeah," I agree. "Sounds like a plan."

fourteen

"My first theory is the obvious one: Savvy's parents used to be Seattle's most feared crime lords and Abby's parents owed Savvy's parents the kind of blood debt that could only be paid with a fresh baby, Rumpelstiltskin-style," says Finn, who managed to string all those words together through a mouthful of blueberry waffles at breakfast.

"You're getting closer," I deadpan into my yogurt. "I can feel it."

Savvy bonks him on the head with the name tag on her lanyard and goes back to artfully arranging the fruit on her waffle. Jemmy, Cam, and Izzy are less-than-subtly leaning over from a few tables away to watch. I gesture for them to join us, but the blood about drains from their faces and Jemmy lets out a self-conscious squeak that serves as my cue to drop the idea.

It's for the best. Savvy and I have only been getting along for about three minutes, and as nice as this bantering across the breakfast table has been, we should probably give it more time to gel before throwing more people into the mix.

"Maybe it's a full *Baby Mama*." Finn's been at this for twenty minutes, and apparently cannot be stopped. "Abby's mom was supposed to be the surrogate for Savvy's parents, but whoops! Your dad knocked up your mom with Savvy instead, and—"

"Finn," I beg. "I'm *eating*."

He looks at me soberly over his waffles. "Parents have sex,

Abby. Accept it. Internalize it. Because in your case, it's happened at *least* five times, if not—"

"One more word and I'll let Rufus use your pillow as a chew toy," Savvy warns, getting up to wave at Mickey and Leo across the mess hall.

"I'm being helpful," Finn protests. "Nobody's a better expert on fucked-up families than I am." Before I can look over to Savvy to glean what he means, he adds, "Besides, did you guys come here to figure out your whole secret sister drama or not?"

"Uh, you might want to keep your voice, like . . . way down," says Leo, reaching our table, Mickey at his side. He grabs a chair from another table and plants himself next to me, close enough that our knees knock into each other's. "I'm pretty sure they can hear you on the other side of the Sound."

Mickey loudly kisses her palm and sets it on Savvy's forehead. "Good morning, lady. I have not seen you in many moons. How did this morning's selfie turn out without my expertise?"

Savvy beams up at her, taking Mickey's hand off her forehead and squeezing it. "Abby took care of it."

"Did she?" asks Mickey, nudging my chair with her foot. "I hope you got her good side. She's convinced her left cheek is *slightly* different than the—"

"*Mickey.*"

As this is happening Finn holds out his fist for Leo to bump, which devolves into a complicated pattern of nonsense gestures that takes place over my lap and is arguably more of an interpretive dance than a secret handshake. Leo ends it with a flourish, then reaches into his back pocket and passes me a tiny bag of Flamin' Hot Cheetos under the table, his eyes gleaming. "Staff room contraband."

I tuck it into the baggy pocket of my shorts, a crunch in my side and a warmth in my chest.

"Now *that's* true friendship," says Mickey.

She and Savvy head over to the drink station to fill up their water cups, and Leo turns to me with a conspiratorial smile. "Speaking of," he says, "seems like you and Savvy had a chance to talk things out, sister to sister?"

I brace myself for commentary from Finn, but he's distracted, watching Victoria talk to the other girls from Phoenix Cabin the table over.

"More like . . . sister adjacent," I say, waving it off. I don't want to make a big deal out of it, because it's a little embarrassing that half the camp knows about our spat in the first place. "And yeah. We're chill."

"I'm glad," says Leo.

He takes one of my hands in both of his, spreading my palm out. Only then do I realize my hand is still kind of wrinkly from all the dishes Finn and I did this morning. I start to pull it back, self-conscious, but then Leo skims the tips of his fingers over my palm, the skin so sensitive that it feels like every nerve is burning for him.

Some vital part of my brain abandons me, and I'm spreading my fingers out and weaving them between his. He doesn't stop me, the teasing smile faltering on his face, giving way to something that must already be on mine.

Our eyes meet, long enough for me to see something I'm not sure I want to—resignation. He squeezes my hand and lets go, and we try to laugh it off. I scramble for what to say next, anything to absorb the awkwardness of what I just did, but it turns out, I don't need to bother.

"Abby, hi," says Victoria, sitting so unexpectedly that I jump in my chair like someone set a firework under it. She doesn't miss a beat, leaning in and propping her elbows on the table in the chummy way adults do right before they ruin your life. Case in point: "One of the counselors went through parent emails and just informed me that we were able to correct the SAT prep rosters. We've enrolled you and the other girls in Phoenix Cabin back in the appropriate session. So sorry for the confusion."

The disappointment is so immediate that it feels like someone dropped an anchor on my stomach. I don't even have it in me to be surprised.

"Oh," I manage.

She pats the table. "Don't worry. Yesterday's session was mostly introductory, so there won't be much to catch up on. You girls can report to the academic building directly after breakfast."

Victoria leaves as abruptly as she came, and I suck in the resigned, heavy breath of the academically damned. I know I deserve this, after lying to my parents about summer school and dodging the prep classes in the first place. But I cut a glance at Jemmy and Cam and Izzy, who look every bit as bummed as I do, and feel a separate wave of guilt, as if this is somehow my fault.

And it occurs to me. This *is* my fault.

"Yowza," says Leo. "Busted."

He's smiling sheepishly, trying to come up with something to cheer me up. Usually he can. But usually I am not preoccupied scanning a cafeteria for a bobbing ponytail with laser eyes set to murder.

"Look, the sessions are what, five hours a day? You'll still have plenty of time to meet up with Savvy and—"

"The only thing I'm doing with *Savvy* is going back in time and smacking myself in the face before I agreed to come with her in the first place."

Leo blinks. "Uh, I'm not following."

I'm seething, looking for a place to channel my rage, but I can't find her anywhere.

"And besides, that's not how time travel works," says Leo, evidently deciding to distract me from said rage with another deep dive into explaining the linearity of time and the possibilities of creating multiverses. I wonder if I can hop into any in which I am marginally less of an idiot. "If you could time travel, future you would have already gone back and—"

"Warned me that Savvy was a backstabber and ratted me and the other girls out to get revenge?"

"You don't know that."

"I do," I insist. "Remember last night?"

Leo's face softens. "Yeah?"

I plow on, ignoring the little tweak in my heart. "Savvy was on the phone, saying she was 'going through parent emails to the camp staff.'"

Plus, Victoria "just" found out. Which can only mean Savvy *just* told her.

"I'm sure she wasn't trying to—"

"Shit. That sucks," says Finn, who ghosted when Victoria showed up, but was apparently close enough to hear the proceedings. He takes a slurp from his juice. "So what are we doing to get back at her?"

Leo pauses in the middle of plucking a banana slice off my plate. I watch his hand linger there, wavering in this moment, Leo on my right and Finn on my left like an angel and a devil on my shoulder.

"I'm fresh out of ideas after last night's stroke of genius, but we could brainstorm. I know a place where nobody will bother us," Finn goes on. "You know that trail by the tennis courts?"

I nod slowly, and Leo goes still beside me.

"Go down it a ways. There's a big old rock there where people meet up sometimes. Great view at the top, too," Finn says with a wink, nodding down at Kitty, who's propped in her case on the table. "Told you I could get you the best shots. Have I steered you wrong yet?"

"Uh . . ."

"So, eight o'clock?"

Before I can say yes or no, Finn ducks under the table and literally rolls across the floor like he's in the middle of an army drill. I blink down at him, wondering what the hell Leo and Mickey put in the waffles, until it becomes clear that he's still avoiding Victoria and her piercing gaze. Only then does it occur to me that he was probably supposed to be at kitchen duty last night, too, but never showed.

I jolt when Leo touches my elbow and is suddenly so much closer to me than he was before.

"You're not actually meeting him, are you?"

Leo's jaw has gone tight and his eyebrows are furrowed.

"We're not going to do anything, like, evil," I say, waving a hand in front of his face. "It's me, Leo." I throw a piece of banana in my mouth.

Leo doesn't shake it off the way I'm expecting. "That's 'Make Out Rock.'"

I almost choke, so fully expecting him to pick the "go easy on your secret sister" moral high ground that I don't know how to respond, the banana taste in my mouth going sour.

"It's a *hookup* spot," Leo iterates.

My heels dig into the legs of my chair. "And what's the problem with that?"

Leo's eyes widen.

"You're into *Finn?*"

No. But I'm decidedly *not* into Leo deciding he has an opinion about my budding friendship with Finn, either. Especially after he made it perfectly clear on the ferry how *over* our almost-kiss he is.

"What do you care?"

It's a way of asking without asking, the coward's way out.

And I get exactly what a coward deserves when that tight jaw of his all but unhinges, and he doesn't make a sound. A quiet, awful confirmation of the thing we've been dancing around for way too long—he doesn't like me the way I like him. And if he did once, he doesn't anymore.

It shouldn't be difficult to wrap my head around. In fact, it should be a relief. It means Connie didn't lie. That my friendship with her, at least, is something I can rely on, something I can trust. But for some unhelpful reason, my face is hotter than a sauna and my eyes are starting to sting. I get up to leave, but Leo touches my elbow.

My heart lifts too fast, like it's on a carnival ride.

"And honestly, I wish you'd give this thing with Savvy a rest. Let it go."

It's the worst thing he could possibly say to me in this moment, even if he's right. Forget carnival rides. This is a high-speed crash. "So you *are* on Savvy's side."

"I'm on your side," he emphasizes. "*And* hers."

I blow my hair out of my face. "Great. I'm already outnumbered by an entire *camp* full of people on her side, and now you, too?"

Leo presses on as if I didn't say anything. "At least let me walk you out there later. People get lost on the path after dark. It's not safe."

I don't let myself blink, mortified that if I do, there's a very real chance a tear is going to slip out. I've never been more mad at my eyeballs than I am right now. As if it isn't enough of a blow to my ego that Leo doesn't like me, he's going to play the big brother card, too?

"I don't need you to Benvolio me," I tell him through my teeth.

"To *what* you?" he asks. He frowns, no doubt remembering my essay. "Are you seriously sucking me into your Benvolio-hatred manifesto right now?"

I take in a breath, trying to focus on my irritation, anything to keep myself from crying or using more Shakespeare character names as verbs. "I don't need a babysitter. I'll be fine."

I grab my tray and start walking it to the sinks, glad I'll at least have the Flamin' Hot Cheetos to make up for the breakfast I'm about to waste to get away from him.

"Maybe you *do* need a babysitter, if you're really going to climb that stupid rock in the pitch dark," says Leo, hot on my heels. The two of us look so equally irritated that other campers are giving us a wide berth in the mess hall. "You walk around like you're invincible, but you have to think of the risks—"

"I'm plenty aware of the *risks*," I say, just as Leo gets ahead of me and stops so abruptly that I have to stop, too.

We scowl at each other. I sigh, opening my mouth to attempt something conciliatory, but Leo beats me to it.

"Tell that to this," he says, grazing a scar I'd forgotten was on my elbow with his knuckles. The lingering touch stuns the anger right out of me. "Or this," he says, gesturing down to my knees, still scraped up from falling off my skateboard. Then Leo looks me right in the face, where the scar digs into my eyebrow. "Or—"

"Would you give it a rest?"

This is new territory for us. I don't snap at Leo. But it's too much. I've always known he keeps track of these little things, of the times I've fallen off skateboards or fences or one unfortunate rooftop straight into a dumpster, but it's different, hearing it all at once. Like I am suddenly aware of my body in a way I never bother to be. Aware that he knows it so fully and doesn't want any part of it.

"I'm sorry," says Leo. He takes a step in, and I have to consciously plant my feet to the sticky mess hall floor to stop myself from moving in, too.

I bite down the hurt, tossing the contents of my tray into the trash, and ask, "What's your problem with Finn, anyway? Isn't he your friend?"

"Of course he is." Leo takes my tray for me, his voice considerably lower. "But Finn . . . he's had a rough year. And there's a bit of an edge to him now. A reckless one. And you're already pretty reckless on your own."

He leans in closer, his eyes trained on mine, and I hate myself for feeling it—that electricity from last night, the thick gravity of the storm between us. I'm almost mad at him for bringing the current back. But he has no way of knowing that current means something entirely different to me than it does to him.

"And for what it's worth, I'm always on your side," he says. "But part of being on your side is telling you the truth. Which is that you should put a stop to this thing with Savvy before it goes full *Lord of the Flies*."

I try and fail to hold in my monumental sigh. He's right. And as mad as I am at Savvy, I am also stuck on the mystery of the magpies, on the brief connection we had this morning. Something fragile enough that if we bend it any more than we have to, it might break.

"We'll . . . do some kind of dumb prank, then," I relent. "Cut off the Wi-Fi in the counselor lounge so she can't update her Instagram or something."

Leo loosens up considerably. "That's not a bad idea. It might actually get her to hang out with us."

I wrinkle my nose.

"Just avoid messing with her job here," says Leo. "It's important to her."

I chew the inside of my cheek, biting down the urge to say that being able to take photos in my free time here was important to me, and that sure didn't stop her from coming for it. "'Course not," I mumble.

Leo's face settles back into a smile, albeit an uneasy one. I hesitate, and then so does he, and finally he says, "Be careful tonight."

I can't tell if he means to be careful climbing the rock or careful of Finn, but maybe that's for the best. "I won't do anything you wouldn't do," I say, trying to ease the tension.

Instead Leo's mouth forms a tight line, his eyes on the other side of the mess hall like he is considering something. I can see the exact moment he decides on it, his jaw clicking before he turns back to me.

"I was being unfair before. Finn's a good guy."

"So . . . you *are* into the idea of me and Finn?"

It's supposed to come out cheeky, but it's choppy and too loud in my ears.

Leo shakes his head and tilts it like he always does at me, except this time there's something weary in it. Something that catches in my chest, the push and pull, the knowing and not knowing where we stand.

"I want you to be happy," he says.

Of all the things he's ever said to me, this might be the worst. Because I know what would make me happy, and it's not something he can give. Instead of answering him I step in closer and reach up, rubbing his hair with my closed fist until it goes all floppy, expecting him to laugh the way he did when we were kids. But his eyes just stay heavy on mine, weighted in a way I can still feel after we've both turned and gone our separate ways.

I file out of the mess hall with the rest of the breakfast stragglers, trying to shake off my unease, and immediately stumble into all three girls from Phoenix Cabin waiting for me outside. I stop in my tracks.

"Finn told us what happened. That Savvy busted us all, and now we have to spend the whole summer locked up in class," says Jemmy, her nostrils flared.

"Yeah," I say miserably.

I'm about to apologize, but Izzy cuts in and says, "He said you're coming up with a plan to get back at her."

I brace myself. This is it, then. Savvy stole my summer and took all my new friends with her. If there really are sides to this battle, there's no doubt whose they'd be on.

But Cam's mouth puckers into a determined line, and the others fall in behind her. She takes a step forward, looking like the leader of some very angry Powerpuff Girls, and says, "We want in."

fifteen

Make Out Rock, as it turns out, may officially be the least sexy place in the entire Pacific Northwest—unless the five of us all competing over who can make the most believable bear noises while chugging an entire liter of smuggled Sprite qualifies as "sexy."

"Finn, you're banned unless you stop the uncontrollable burping," says Izzy, a phrase that may be the cherry on our unsexy sundae. "Also, last check on the final draft of this before we go over Operation Wack."

We shuffle around in the darkness, our faces lit by the glow of Izzy's phone. On the screen is a dummy Instagram account we built that looks almost identical to Savvy's, with all her recent uploaded photos and the bio exactly the same. Except where it should say "How To Stay Savvy" it reads "How To Stay Wacky," and we also uploaded some old adorable pictures of her at camp so it would look like her account was hacked by a nostalgic ghost.

The idea was mine, but the execution was all Finn. While we were stuck in SAT prep, he snuck onto the Wi-Fi to upload his old camp pictures—Savvy and Mickey hamming it up in matching braces and handmade One Direction T-shirts, Savvy sleeping on top of Leo and Finn with drool dribbling out of her mouth, and all of them with two Pringles shoved into their mouths, flinging out their elbows like ducks down by the shore.

Photos I realized I'd seen before, when Leo had shown them to me and Connie after getting back home from camp. But even if I'd memorized their faces, I'd have no way to make the connection between the Savvy she was then and the Savvy she is now, all polished at the edges, every inch of her contained and poised.

The account is private, so nobody will see it except us and Savvy. She'll probably see the lock icon on the profile and figure out it's a prank before she even sees the goofy pictures. But scrolling through them all, I'm glad I took Leo's advice and went for a good clean prank instead of actual revenge. I've seen flashes of this more lighthearted Savvy, but it's something else to see the evidence of it.

The more I look at younger Savvy, the closer I get to understanding the older one. It reminds me that I made her laugh this morning. And for a moment, we were okay.

"These are precious," says Cam, laughing at one where Finn and Savvy are posing with their tennis rackets like lightsabers. She tweaks Finn on the nose. "Look at baby you."

Izzy nods in agreement. "She should post these in real life. To her stories, at least."

"Less admiring how precious twelve-year-old me is, more going over the plan," says Finn, but not with enough conviction for anyone to miss that he's blushing. "Jemmy?"

Jemmy, who is apparently the Dungeon Master of a very large all-girl Dungeons & Dragons group, decided to put herself in charge of this heist. Ultimately she decided the only way to get the junior counselors out of bed without grabbing their phones was to pretend someone had seen a bear—hence our bear noise rehearsal—prompting them to head through their cabin's back exit, which opens into a hallway that goes to the camp office.

At that point, Cam—who, as it turns out, is always clad in neon leggings and shirts because she's a competitive runner—will sprint in and grab Savvy's phone. She'll hand it off to Izzy, who will use some possibly shady but undeniably convenient hacking skills to get into Savvy's phone, log her out of her Instagram, and log on to the How To Stay Wacky one. Cam will then sprint it back in, the five of us will make a mad dash back to the camper cabins, and Savvy will be none the wiser until tomorrow morning's ritual Instagram scroll.

The plan is far from foolproof (I blame the SAT prep for somehow, against all odds, making us all a bit stupider), but none of us really cares. Class was every bit as bone-crushingly tedious as we expected, but all this ridiculous plotting has bonded us enough that I fessed up and told them the whole Savvy and Abby soap opera subplot drama that is our lives.

It took a few minutes for everyone to get up to speed—"I thought this shit only happened in Disney Channel movies," said Jemmy, approximately five times—but it was a relief once we all were. They're not mad at Savvy anymore, but their hero worship went down a few healthy pegs. They see her as a human being instead of an untouchable Instagram god. Which puts us all on the same page, even if that page involves us hiding in different parts of the woods like a junior SWAT team with walkie-talkies we borrowed from the middle school boys' cabin across camp.

"Okay, Abby," says Jemmy, cueing me from the tree she's hiding behind. "Go for the Oscar. Three . . . two . . . one."

I wince, sucking in a lungful of air, and recite the words that Jemmy made me memorize and subsequently rehearse by yelling them into a pillow. "Bear! I saw a bear. There's a bear in the camp!"

My voice carries over the camp from the woods. Rufus immediately starts howling and the lights flicker on in the junior counselor cabin. Even from this distance, I can hear Savvy: "Wait, guys, there aren't any bears here!"

Jemmy nudges me in the ribs, hard, and I obligingly yell, "Oh no! A bear! Ahhhhh!"

She raises an eyebrow at me like she is director Patty Jenkins of *Wonder Woman* in the flesh and I just destroyed her cinematic masterpiece, but it does the trick. Through their window we have a full view of the junior counselors booking it out of the cabin, Savvy nudging Rufus out along with them.

The door shuts, and Jemmy flicks on the walkie-talkie. "Okay, girls. It's showtime."

sixteen

"Let me get this straight," says Connie on the other end of the phone. "You've only been there a week, and you drove your sister to a minor league felony?"

I press the camp phone closer to my ear, my eye on the door as if Savvy might pop out from behind it. "In my defense, how on *earth* could I have predicted an Instagram prank was going to lead to grand theft auto?"

"Back up here. What possessed her to steal a camp van?"

I cringe. "She, uh, did *not* realize it was a fake account. And when she couldn't delete the pictures fast enough, apparently she kind of . . . took off? And drove up the hill to where there was better Wi-Fi in town, so she could fix it?"

"You're joking," says Connie, delighted by this drama.

In fact, I am not. Savvy did just that, and so early in the morning that none of us were awake to see it happen. I was, however, quite awake and trying to get shots of the sunrise when she drove the jacked Camp Reynolds minivan back down the hill, after which I witnessed a chewing-out from Victoria so legendary that I almost dropped Kitty in secondhand horror.

"I wish I were. She got a ton of demerits. Like, the ones they usually give campers," I say. "We've been on cleaning duty together for nearly two weeks and she won't even look at me."

"So I guess that means no progress on figuring out what the hell happened with your parents?"

I hold the phone away from my mouth so she won't get the full volume of my sigh. "Nada." I sense another pep talk brewing, so I'm quick to add, "But you were right, you know. About staying. The rest of it . . . it's actually been kind of fun."

Sure, getting stuck in an academic cage all morning is rough, but the other girls have made it oddly bearable. Once they let us out in the afternoon, demerit duty aside, we're relatively free. We go kayaking. We play dumb camp games and set marshmallows on fire. We swap bug spray and ghost stories and T-shirts. We take enough goofy pictures of ourselves that Kitty is sometimes less of a camera and more of a mirror.

Come to think of it, I've taken so many pictures that Kitty's memory card is probably wheezing with effort to save them— sweeping views of the Puget Sound, of thick, infinite clouds, of unusual birds, of bunnies and butterflies and deer. Pictures that make me proud to go through my camera roll, that finally ease this ache I've had as long as I can remember to get out and see the world beyond Shoreline, beyond the three-mile radius of my house. It feels like something's opened up to me—not only landscapes and sweeping views, but the future. It's not clear, but it's wider than I ever remember it feeling, full of possibility, of places I can go someday.

"Are you guys just gonna do a big old photo dump on your Instas at the end of the summer?" I asked the rest of the Phoenix Cabin girls before dinner one night, when we were swapping a chip bag Leo smuggled for us back and forth. I'd been AirDropping them photos—the ones we took of ourselves, not anything I've been taking on my own—but I hadn't seen any of them volleying for the shared computer in the rec room or wandering around to get bars on their phones.

"Oh, no, this is for our finstas," Jemmy explained, holding

out her phone. "I'm nowhere near the level to be launching a brand yet."

I looked at the screen and saw that like the "How to Stay Wacky" account we made, there were only a handful of followers, and it was locked. Connie had a finsta too, but I was never on Instagram to see it. Jemmy's was in the same vein. Kind of like a scrapbook, without any real theme.

"Oh. I guess mine's a finsta too then, since the posts are only for fun."

"Kind of," said Cam. "Mostly it's good to have your own space, I guess? Get to know your vibe? So when we launch our legit accounts we know what our vision is."

"What are your visions?" I asked.

Cam beamed, adjusting the blond hair she'd pulled into a much lower, non-Savvy ponytail in recent days. "There's a whole body-positive running community on Instagram. I'm gonna start with that, and have my thing be highlighting running brands with inclusive sizing that are actually cute, and match them up with weekly curated playlists." She cast one leg out like a ballerina, showing off the purple leggings with cloud prints she was wearing. "This one's full Ariana, obviously."

Izzy plucked some of the spandex on her calf and snapped it back, making her yelp out a laugh. "Well, I'm gonna be a doctor, so I'm gonna use mine to chronicle everything like a photo diary—premed, med school, residency," she told me. "Like *Grey's Anatomy*, but make it Gen Z. And with like, way less murder."

Before I could react, Jemmy grinned widely, making a bow-and-arrow movement. "Our Dungeons & Dragons group makes all our own cosplay, so I'm gonna chronicle the campaign we're kicking off in the fall. We've all decided it doesn't end until every last one of us is dead."

I stared at each of them in turn, impressed. "Wow, I love all of these," I said. I was so into their ideas that for the first time I wanted to be on Instagram as an actual recreational hobby, and not just something I glanced at once a year to make sure Leo hadn't posted pictures of the clown from *It* on my account on April Fools' Day.

But there was one part that didn't make sense. "If you all have your own Instagram ideas . . . why are you so into Savvy?"

"Well, first off, cuz she's a badass," said Jemmy. "But also because of the workshop she's leading next week."

"Workshop?" I asked. I knew there were specialty classes that rotated every week, but I'd been too busy harassing Mickey and Leo in the kitchens and running around the campground with Kitty and Finn to pay much attention.

"Social Media and the Personal Brand," said Izzy. "Savvy built her Instagram up from basically nothing in two years. If anyone knows how to do it, it's her."

"Don't worry," said Jemmy, "we signed you up, but we can pull your name off it if you'd rather not."

There was this warmth, then—one I'd been too nervous to acknowledge, in case it went away. Like I really did belong here. Like I was capable of finding my place outside the bubble I'd been living in, with the same best friends and the same town and the same endless to-do list on Abby's Agenda.

"See?" says Connie, tugging me out of my thoughts. "You just have to bust out of your shell a bit. Maybe do something totally radical, even, like show your photos to people who *aren't* me and Leo."

"Let's not get too carried away."

"How is Leo, by the way?"

I glance out the window of the main office, wondering if I'll spot him on his way to the kitchen so I can wave him over to say hi, but no luck. Truth is, I was worried Leo might be mad after what happened with Savvy, but even he agreed her reaction was out of proportion. In true Benvolio form, though, he has stayed fair to both parties, hanging out with us each individually without bringing it up.

"He's good," I say. "He and Mickey have been doing these little cook-offs after dinner every night and letting me and Finn be celebrity judges."

"So you're basically living out Leo's *Chopped* fantasies?"

"Or nightmares. Last night he accidentally dumped an entire container of cinnamon into the pork sisig Mickey was trying to teach him to make. She said that's what he gets for going off script on her family recipes."

"I wish I could be there," says Connie. "I'm missing out on everything. It's like Thanksgiving break all over again."

I manage not to wince thinking of the BEI, which either means I've made progress, or have done enough humiliating things to eclipse it since. "Don't worry. You're not missing much," I tell her. "I haven't tried to fling myself at Leo again. I got the message on that loud and clear."

I'm expecting her to laugh, but there's silence on the other end of the line—enough that for a second I think the call was dropped.

"That was a joke," I add quickly.

"Yeah," says Connie, with a weak laugh. "Besides, what about Finn? He sounds nice."

I shrug. "I mean, yeah. But I guess after the whole thing with Leo . . . I dunno. Even if I did like Finn, doesn't seem worth the risk of humiliating myself again."

I don't know why I'm being so frank. I guess because it was rare for me to get Connie alone when we were back at school, and now it's only the two of us, so I can say whatever I want.

Or maybe I need to do it to prove something to myself. Like if I admit I had feelings for Leo, it means I've moved on enough that it can't embarrass me anymore. Like it'll lose its power over me, if I take some of it back.

But there's muffled movement on the other end, like Connie is holding the phone away from her face. When she's back, she says in this careful voice, "Abs . . . do you like Leo?"

"What? No," I say, going so red that I stare down at the floor as if she's in the room with me. "It doesn't matter. Leo doesn't like me. You asked him yourself."

There's a beat. "I think I messed up."

I press the phone closer to my ear, trying to read her tone, not wanting to believe the thought currently racing through my brain. "Messed up how?"

"Messed up like—I—I wasn't entirely honest with you. About . . . what I said about Leo not liking you. The truth is we never talked about it."

My mouth is open for a few seconds before it remembers to form words. "Then why did you say you did?"

"Because I'm an idiot."

She's trying to be funny, but I'm afraid if I give in and laugh I might never stop. "Do *you* like Leo?" I ask instead.

"No. No, it's not like that," she says, the words tripping over each other. "I did it because—honestly, Abby, I thought it was a blip. You looked so freaked out, and I wanted to smooth everything over, so I said what I could to get you guys to move on from it."

"But I didn't move on," I say through my teeth. "I was . . . oh my god, I've been so embarrassed, every single day I've looked at him since."

"I didn't realize you—"

"Why are you only telling me this *now?*"

Connie takes a breath like she's steeling herself. Like she's wrestled with telling me this for a while.

"Leo said something before he left about missing out on a lost chance. And I tried to ask him about it, but he kind of shrugged it off. I thought maybe it had to do with the DNA test stuff, but I think—Abby, I think maybe he was talking about you."

The conversation has shifted so fast that it feels like whiplash. I'm breathing too hard, as if I'm trying to outrun it, like I've been running all this time. It casts new colors on every interaction I've had with Leo in the past few months, on every feeling I've worked so hard to press back inside myself, on every embarrassment I've felt in the moments I failed.

"I'm sorry, Abby. I really am."

This is the part where we're supposed to talk it out, and I forgive her. The part where I'm supposed to say something to save this awful moment, this swooping feeling in my chest.

But it feels like this whole summer has seeped rot into the foundations of all the things I thought I could depend on. My parents lied to me. Connie lied to me. And those lies may have been quiet, with the best of intentions, but they're all imploding the order of my stupid universe.

"I've gotta get back to camp," I say, barely getting it out without the words choking in my throat.

"Abby." She says my name like a plea. I pretend I don't hear it. My heart's beating so loud that it's hard to focus on anything else.

Click.

After I hang up, I stand there, listening to the dial tone, trying to wrap my head around what just happened. We've had plenty of disagreements in our years of friendship, but nothing like this. There's never been anything I wasn't quick to forgive and forget. I wasn't built any other way, and I really do love Connie like the sister I never had.

I set the phone back in its cradle, standing perfectly still, trying to ground myself—trying to make it seem less like we started that phone call far away from each other and ended it further than we've ever been.

seventeen

I'm not crying when I show up for toilet-scrubbing duty with Savvy in the bona fide sewer that is the boys' bathroom, but I'm not *not* crying either. Savvy is elbows deep in one of the stalls when I get there, and for once I'm grateful she's not talking to me. It gives me a chance to hide my sorry face in a stall of my own. And my pee-soaked pity parade is going just fine, at least until Savvy gets up and knocks over the mop water in her stall, spilling it out onto my shoes.

"Shit," she says, so surprised at herself that she forgets we aren't speaking. "Shit, I'm sorry—"

And that's when I realize I *am* crying, because Savvy stops dead with the mop in her hands and the alarm on her face softens into a look a little too close to concern.

"It's fine," I say, reaching up to wipe my eyes. Savvy swiftly grabs my wrist, reminding me that my hands are covered in the primordial ooze of pubescent boys, and I think better of it. Before I know it she's helping me to my feet and out of the mop puddle, and we're face-to-face in the cramped stall.

Savvy blows out a breath, like she's trying to decide if she's going to do something about me or not. By then I have minor control over my face. It's not too late for her to pretend she didn't notice anything, and for us to get back to the Camp Reynolds version of the Cold War.

"Did . . . something happen?"

I shake my head.

"Because if it's camp stuff, I'm kind of obligated to know."

It stings, even though it shouldn't. For a second I thought she cared about me as a person, and not what me being a person meant for her job.

"It's just weird drama. From back home."

"Oh." Savvy mulls this over, and her eyebrows lift. "Did your parents find out we—"

"No," I say, suppressing a laugh. To be honest, I've mostly forgotten there's anything for our parents to find out. "What, did yours?"

Savvy shakes her head. Then she lingers, like maybe she's going to say something else, and I'm so eager for the opening that I end up blurting the words so fast they end up stumbling on one another like mismatched dominoes.

"I'm—I'm really sorry about the whole pranking thing. I didn't think . . ."

The way she's been shutting me out, the last thing I'm expecting is what she says next.

"It was dumb," she says, the tension leaking out of her shoulders. "But what I did was dumber. I don't know what came over me."

Except we both do, even if neither of us wants to say it. Maybe this Instagram thing started out fun for Savvy, but whatever it is now is so hardwired into her psyche that it made her drive a stick-shift eight-seater van up a hill before the sun was even out, and made her forget that there are at least ten camp rules and some actual laws against it.

"But you should know, I wasn't trying to like, punish you, with the SAT thing," says Savvy, her voice low. "I thought it would be better if Victoria knew sooner than later. If she found out in a few more days she would have had to call all your parents, and—"

"They might have made me leave."

She lowers her gaze. "You did say they were pretty serious about all this tutoring stuff."

I shrug, and my weight shifts between my sneakers, making a *squelch* noise that echoes through the empty bathroom. We look down at my feet. They're soaked with mop water. We move out of the stall, over to the sinks. When I look in the mirror, my cheeks are an embarrassing shade of red and my eyes are puffy enough that they're practically screaming for Visine.

"Is that what it was about?" Savvy asks. "The drama back home?"

"Oh . . . uh, no, actually. Just . . ."

I'm not planning on telling her, but she's maybe the only person I *can* tell. She doesn't know Connie. The things I say here will never get back to her.

And maybe I'm imagining it, but it seems like she actually cares.

"It's my friend Connie."

"What, you made her a fake Twitter?"

I laugh, surprising myself and Savvy, who seems pleased that she's capable of making a joke. It loosens me up a bit, and everything spills out.

"No. Learned my lesson with that." I take a breath. "But, uh—so—it's dumb. There was this thing with Leo, a few months ago . . ."

"So he *did* tell you he liked you."

My head snaps up fast enough to make Savvy flinch. "No. The thing was that Connie told me Leo *didn't* like me."

"Oh, he likes you," says Savvy frankly. "He talked about a girl named Abby all last summer. He might not have come right out and said it, but he clearly had some kind of crush. I just didn't make the connection until you were here."

Somehow getting covered in mop water was less of a shock than this.

"Oh."

My voice sounds mangled, and to be fair, I *feel* kind of mangled. There's this swell of—I don't even know what to call it. Something sneaky, something joyful, the giddy idea that Leo liked me maybe even before it occurred to me to like him, too.

But if anything, that only makes Connie's lie worse. Because it doesn't matter, does it? Leo had a crush on me. Leo *had* a crush on me, past tense. And if the little scene in the cafeteria before I went to stupid Make Out Rock is any indication, it's probably too late.

"And you like him."

I don't bother denying it. "It's just . . . Connie lied to me about him. And it kind of complicates everything, because the three of us—well, we're each other's best friends. Always have been." I blow a stray hair out of my face. "I don't want to mess that up, especially not if Leo doesn't feel that way anymore."

I don't know why I'm expecting a lecture. Maybe it's the whole junior counselor power trip, or that she narrates her Instagram stories with the authority of someone twenty years older than she is. But instead she leans against the same disgusting sink and lets out a sigh.

"Well, I don't know if that's true," she says. "But either way, that really sucks."

It feels good to hear someone say this objective truth, even if it's not particularly helpful. It makes me feel like I didn't blow up the problem in my head.

"If you want any advice . . ."

When I look over at her there's nothing smug in her expression. In fact, she almost looks nervous, like I might get offended by the offer. I nod, giving a small smile.

"I have some mildly useful experience in potentially disrupting a friend group dynamic with feelings," she says wryly.

I search her face. "I thought you met Jo through your parents."

"Yeah, but before Jo . . . there was an almost-thing with Mickey." Savvy rolls her eyes, like she's exasperated at her younger self, and explains, "I dunno, we were thirteen, and I had this big crush. I didn't say anything because I didn't want to mess up our little group. Me and Mickey and Finn and Leo, I mean."

She looks reflective for a moment, far from the mucked-up tiles.

"So what happened?" I prompt her.

She blinks, coming back to herself. "What happened is I didn't say anything, and Mickey got a girlfriend."

"Oh."

I'm trying to figure out how, exactly, to roll this into meaningful advice, when Savvy leans in. "And I know I'm with Jo now, and it's all water under the toilet stalls," she says, gesturing to our mess, "but I regretted not saying anything for, like, years. Because who knows what would have happened if I had? I guess what I'm trying to say is, this thing with Leo—you might be mad at yourself for a while if you don't at least ask him about it. If you don't at least try."

It's strange, how little I can know about Savvy's past and still feel her ache like it's my own.

"Anyway, let me know how it goes," she says. "Given the state of the camp bathrooms it looks like we'll have plenty of time to chat."

"Yeah. Yikes."

She hoists herself off the ledge of the sinks, grabbing the mop and holding it there. "And if you want to use some of that time to figure out what happened with our parents . . ."

I've spent the last week compartmentalizing it so effectively that I could almost convince myself it doesn't matter. But it will matter. In a few weeks when we reach the end of camp, the unanswered questions won't be something I can stuff into a box in my brain, but instead two living, breathing human beings who I talk to every day.

But it's more than that. I want to know about our parents, but I'd like to get to know Savvy, too. I can feel myself digging a little closer to the Savvy who Leo and the others must know, the one with the braces and the big smiles and wacky suntan lines.

"Yeah," I say. "I'd like that."

We don't call a truce this time, because something's been settled deeper than that. Like we don't have to put an official end to the fight, because we trust it to simmer out on its own. The whole thing is almost . . . Well. It's almost sisterly.

eighteen

It's unusually chilly the next morning, when I'm lining up by the shore in my swimsuit with the two dozen other campers who were harebrained enough to sign up for the camp's weekly Polar Bear Swim. My teeth are chattering, but maybe it's not the cold—maybe it's just the expected brand of mortal terror that comes with deciding today is the day you're going to tell your best friend you have feelings for him, and alter the flow of the resulting space-time-friendship continuum for the rest of your lives.

I cut a glance at Leo, his eyes bright even with his hair still rumpled from sleep, and feel a cinch in my heart—something gleeful and terrifying, something that chased my dreams all night and woke me with a jolt this morning.

It's going to be today. It has to be. I just don't know when.

Before I can think about it too much, the whistle goes off, and I take off like a rocket with the first wave.

The cold is a heart-stopping zap. My legs pump under the frigid water and my arms flap like they've forgotten how to be arms, but for a freeing, very long second, it's like it is happening to someone else. I breathe in and there's fog in my lungs and ice in my blood, and it pushes out everything in its path— every embarrassment, every confusion, every doubt—frozen and sloughed right off.

I start running back out of the water before I'm even fully immersed, and straight up to where Leo is prepping the hot chocolate. He stops in the middle of whatever he's saying to Mickey, his eyes wide with alarm.

"Are you okay?"

"Yeah," I pant. "Um—I just wanted—can I talk to you?"

"Uh, yeah, of course," says Leo, scanning me up and down like he's not quite sure I'm intact. We take a few steps away from Mickey, and he lowers his voice. "Actually, I had something I wanted to talk to you about, too. What's up?"

"I . . ." For once it's not that I've lost my nerve, but my teeth are chattering like one of those wind-up skull toys on Halloween. I need a beat. "You go first."

"You sure?"

"Yeah, yeah," I say, hopping between my feet and shivering with violence.

Leo glances around us, and something flips in my rib cage. A stupid little hiccup of hope that maybe, just maybe, we are about to tell each other the same thing.

"The thing is, Abby . . . last week I got off the waitlist at another culinary school."

The words are so unexpected that there's no room for the disappointment that follows. I blink dumbly at him. "I thought you'd only applied to the one."

"Just the one in Seattle," says Leo quietly. "This one's in New York. And yesterday, I . . . I sent the deposit. I leave in September."

The ground feels uneven under my feet, like someone suddenly tilted it.

"Oh." I try to smile, but it's wobbly and wrong. "Congratulations, Leo, I . . . wow."

He leans in, talking in the too-fast way he does during his legendary information dumps, except now he's wringing his hands and saying it like an apology. "I didn't think I'd go, but this past week, cooking with Mickey—it's been like a dream. Like this whole world opened up. And this school has all these international exchange opportunities, and an instructor whose Filipino dishes are like, world-famous, plus all of the classes come with an academic session for cultural context," he says. "I think I'm supposed to be there. The opportunities are— Abby, I couldn't pass it up."

"Of course not," I blurt. It sounds graceless and throaty, but at least it's genuine. I really am happy for him. I'm *proud* of him. We've all lived in Shoreline our whole lives, so this decision couldn't have been an easy one. And Leo was so torn between choosing culinary school or an academic track. Now he'll get to do both.

But underneath that happiness, that pride, is a hurt so deep that I can't find the start of it, let alone an end. It's like sitting down in the place where your chair has always been and falling into nothing.

"You'll be so far away," I say, without realizing I've spoken. I catch myself before I say the thing that presses into me like a bruise: *And you didn't think I was important enough to tell.*

The "lost chance" Connie was talking about—it was about this. It was never about me.

"Yeah. I know." He puts a hand on my shoulder, and it should steady me, but I'm reeling. "But it's not going to change anything, right? We'll always be best friends."

He looks so earnestly worried that whatever I should or shouldn't say loses steam before I can say it. *New York.* I've never even left the West Coast. It might as well be another planet. And here I am, working up the nerve to tell Leo I'm in love with him, when Leo's been working up the nerve to tell me he's leaving my life for good.

"Of course," I say, but I don't believe it. Everything's already changed, enough that I'm not even sure if we can use the words *best friend* anymore. Best friends don't lie. Best friends don't keep secrets this monumental. *I thought we told each other everything*, Leo told me, only a rock's throw from this exact spot. But I lied to Leo, and Connie and Leo have both lied to me.

"You said you had something, too?"

I nod, and the last of my hope goes with it.

"Just, uh, Savvy and I . . . we're good."

Leo's face eases into the kind of smile that breaks storms. "That's awesome."

"Yeah," I manage.

Just then the first wave of polar bear swimmers makes it back to shore, and Mickey calls to Leo to help with the hot chocolate distribution. Leo reaches out and grabs me by the hand before he goes, pulling me in too fast for me to stop it and holding me close even though I'm soaking wet. I crush my eyes shut into his chest, and I let myself have this. Just for a moment. Whatever it could have been.

"We'll catch up tonight," he says, pulling away.

I turn back to the shore as he goes, feeling so separate from the next wave of runners getting ready to jump in that I might as well be a ghost. Someone touches my arm.

"Hey," Savvy says quietly.

A beat passes, and I'm praying she doesn't say anything, because I don't know how much longer I can hold it together. Then Savvy—fully clothed, her hair all done up for the day, her eye makeup applied with doll-like precision—grabs my hand and *pulls*, and we're both running, matching each other's strides, smacking the water with the same splash.

I look for Savvy, but find Finn first, his cackling cutting through the mist. Then there's a hand on the top of my head, pushing me fully into the water. My cheeks immediately go numb and my legs start kicking out from under me, and when I break the surface, I'm gasping right into Finn's face.

It's a nice face. And my heart is beating in every nook and cranny of me, angry and confused and too overwhelmed to remember which way it's supposed to beat. And maybe I should do something about it. Maybe I should break the hold Leo has over me, solve one problem with another, do the thing that is obviously occurring to me and Finn at the same time and kiss him.

Finn licks some of the water off his lips, the smirk sliding off his face. I don't have to look back to know Leo is watching, and for this fleeting, selfish moment, I'm glad. Finn leans in, and maybe I am, too—and I get an eye full of water instead.

Finn lets out an indignant crow and splashes back in the direction it came from. Savvy lets out a little shriek, backing away. I catch Savvy's grin, wider than I've ever seen it. Full of the little kid freedom of letting yourself get lost in a moment. It's the Savvy from the old camp pictures, the one everyone else knows, who I'm still filling in the edges of—someone I can actually see myself in.

"You're supposed to get back *out* after you jump in, you bunch of masochists," Mickey calls from the shore.

Someone blows the whistle and we all scramble back out, shivering. Mickey immediately holds out a towel for Savvy, rolling her eyes at us both. I look around for Finn, but he's nowhere to be found.

"Looks like a cold Day in July," says Leo, offering me some hot chocolate.

I let out a sharp breath of a laugh, still wheezing from the run in and out of the water, and take the Styrofoam cup from him. Leo wraps an arm around my sopping wet shoulders again, this time with an unfamiliar tightness—briefly I think it's because he knows I'm upset, but just unsubtly enough, he tilts us, so Finn can get a full view.

I stiffen, and so does Finn, meeting my eye—no, meeting

Leo's. Finn blinks away from him so fast that I almost miss it before he turns on his heels toward another group of campers.

I pull away from Leo.

"You're gonna get soaked," I tell him, even though he already is. Leo reaches out his arm. "I don't mind."

I duck out before he can touch me. I feel raw. Different. Like the cold has crystallized everything, made the things I didn't want to see so clear that there's no way to avoid them: it's not just that Leo doesn't want me. He doesn't want anyone else to have me either.

I make myself watch the confusion streak across his face, the hurt, but it doesn't do anything to chip at my resolve. It's like Leo said when we were watching the lightning. *There are some things you gotta own up to yourself.*

"Leo," I start, but he grabs my arm and pulls, pressing me into him right before Mickey and Savvy barrel right into us.

"I regret to inform you that we're going to have to bury you in this," says Mickey, trying to wrestle the wet sweater off Savvy's body, "because it is permanently stuck to your skin."

The heat of Leo against my freezing cold skin is so inviting that it lulls me, displacing me in time. I'm taken back to two winters ago, when we were sledding on a rare snow day and I went too fast and ended up landing face-first in a pile of someone's driveway slush. Leo kept rubbing my arms to keep me warm while we were laughing and hightailing it back to my house. Back when things were simple. Back when I had no reason to think they wouldn't always be.

Savvy lets out a squeal, bent over with her whole face swallowed up with fabric. "My hair is stuck on the tag!"

"Then hold *still*, you goofball," says Mickey. "I swear to god, Houdini couldn't get out of this. What brand sent you this death trap?"

"Jo gave it to me for my birthday!"

I shiver, and Leo pulls me in tighter. I tell myself I'm only letting him because we're both distracted by Savvy and Mickey's little show, but the lie is too shallow to take root. The truth is, this might be the last time I let him this close. I want to savor it, stamp it to my heart, and hold the part of him I can have, even when I can't have him.

"Jesus, what did you do to piss her off?"

Savvy ducks her head down so Mickey can untangle the tag from her wet ponytail, but the two of them are cracking up so hard at how ridiculous Savvy looks with her head upside down and her arms extended out like she's about to burst into the world's most aggressive jazz hands that they aren't making much progress.

"Probably fucked up the Gcal date schedule," says Savvy, snorting.

Mickey is breathless, cupping Savvy's head between her hands, trying and failing not to laugh. "*Tell* me you're kidding."

I pull away from Leo with absurd slowness, like maybe he won't notice if it happens little by little. But I guess we've been pulling away from each other a lot longer than that. This time he finally lets me go.

He tries to meet my eye, but I don't let him. I'm afraid of what he'll see. Afraid of what he won't.

Savvy shakes her head just beyond us, somehow tangling the sweater even more. "You know what she said?" she tells Mickey. "Why she's not coming this weekend? Because apparently *I* messed up by scheduling it in *pink* instead of *green*, and— Oh."

Whatever is happening, every single person in a ten-foot radius of us catches on before I do, because I have to follow their stricken looks to the source—a girl so tall, pale, and ethereal that I might never stop staring if her eyes didn't look like they could cook me into charred Abby meat within a second of making contact.

Still, it doesn't connect. Not the silence, or the way the girl looks laughably out of place in a pair of loafers and a plaid pantsuit, or even how Mickey has put so much distance between herself and Savvy in the time it took for me to blink that she might have teleported next to me.

"Jo?" Savvy manages.

Jo's eyes narrow, stark and blue and seething. "Surprise," she says. The sarcasm doesn't do anything to mask the hurt.

"I'm— Shit." Savvy straightens up, pulling off the sweater. "Jo, wait."

"Save it," Jo mutters, stalking off toward the parking lot in front of the main camp building. Savvy follows her, barefoot and shivering, not saying a word.

Mickey presses a pair of black sneakers into my hands. "She needs these," she tells me.

I glance over, wondering why she's given them to me, but she's staring so determinedly at the shoes and not at any of us that I know better than to ask. I take them and she sets off in the opposite direction, leaving me on the shore with a pit of dread so low and distinct in my stomach, it seems impossible that Savvy's problems haven't always been tangled up in mine.

nineteen

Getting Savvy's shoes to her ends up being a bust. By the time I reach the parking lot, she and Jo are nowhere to be found, and so is whatever mode of transportation brought Jo here. I end up stashing the shoes at the junior counselors' cabin and hiding from Leo with the Phoenix Cabin girls, who all heard about Jo—or at least, the part about Jo surprising Savvy, and not the part where it turned into an episode of *The Real Housewives of Camp Reynolds*.

"It's so romantic. All my girlfriend's done is send a postcard from Minnesota," Izzy grumbles over dinner.

Jemmy sighs. "Still a leg up from texting John Mulaney GIFs, which is my boyfriend's love language."

Cam snorts. "Well, *my* boyfriend, Oscar Isaac but specifically as Poe Dameron, would be showering me with endless affection if he weren't so busy saving the cosmos."

We all let out an appreciative laugh, and everyone turns to me, expecting me to chime in with some gripe of my own. My throat goes tight before I can, and I take an unnecessarily large slurp of juice to avoid it.

The next morning I'm out even earlier than usual. I couldn't sleep anyway, and I want to make sure Savvy's all right, but she isn't in any of our usual spots. It's like the island swallowed her up.

I do find Rufus, though, who nudges me up one of his favorite paths. I oblige, throwing a stick back and forth as we go. I'm taking a picture of Rufus with his tongue flopping out the side of his mouth when Kitty informs me in no uncertain terms that her memory card is full. It's only eight, so I figure I won't have to wait too long to get to the shared computer and dump the contents into a Dropbox.

Rufus follows me, still nudging me with the stick, but when I throw it toward the main office he disappears around the corner and doesn't come back.

"Yo, Rufus," I call out. "Whatever your little klepto paws are getting into, leave it— Shit."

For the record, that is not the word I envisioned coming out of my mouth when I clapped eyes on Savvy's mom for the first time. Also for the record, what the *hell*.

A week ago I wouldn't have recognized her without her face tilted toward me, but now I've seen so many photos of her on Savvy's phone that her likeness is basically a tab that is eternally open in my brain. By some small mercy, she and Savvy's dad are too distracted petting the heck out of Rufus to notice me. At least, they are for a second.

"Oh, good. Are you a counselor?"

I shove my baseball cap so low on my head that I look like a celebrity trying to sneak out of a Pilates class. "Uh," I manage.

Her dad squints at me as I back away from them, nearly tripping on a rock. "We've met before, right? You're one of Savvy's friends?"

"I'm not—I'm just—sorry!" I blurt, and before they can say anything else, start sprinting for Savvy's cabin like our lives depend on it.

I make it halfway there when it happens: I am running at myself. I am running toward a mirror in the middle of the campgrounds, and am about to smash into the glass.

I skid to a stop, wheezing, and realize when my reflection

wheezes in a much more graceful manner that it's not me at all, but Savvy without makeup, her hair unstyled and in its full frizzy-curled, untamed Day woman glory.

We grab each other by the shoulders.

"Your *parents*," we both say.

I scowl at her and she scowls right back, and we both say, "No, *your* parents."

Simultaneous groans, and again, with matching indignation: "I'm trying to tell you your *parents are here!*"

My mouth drops open in horror, for once I'm the first to figure it out: I have seen her parents. And somehow, ridiculously, impossibly, she has seen mine.

Savvy catches up a few seconds later, going so still her skin is practically waxen. "Where?" she asks, saying the word under her breath like a curse.

I am the exact opposite of still, whipping around like Rufus in a room full of squirrels. "They're going to murder me."

"They're going to murder *us*," Savvy corrects me.

"How the hell did they figure it out?" I ask, way too loudly for someone who should be trying to go incognito. "Did you put something on Instagram?"

Savvy lets out a snort that borders on hysterical, gesturing out so widely that I can't tell if she's trying to encapsulate the camp or the entire known universe. "You think I'd put this shit show on *Instagram?*"

I'd be mad at her for insinuating that my existence constitutes a "shit show," but honestly, I'm getting a kick out of this. Bed-headed, no-fucks-given, slippers-clad Savvy is ten times more dramatic than Instagram Savvy, and she's a heck of a lot more fun to watch.

Except Savvy also looks one light breeze away from losing her marbles, so someone has to take control.

"Okay. Don't worry. It's gonna be okay. We'll head them off

and explain . . . as reasonably as possible . . . that we have gone behind their backs, dug through the last twenty years' worth of their darkest secrets, and run away to an island to hide."

Savvy's eyes are bugged out like one of those rubber squeeze dolls. She wipes at her nose with her oversize shirtsleeve, sounding sniffly underneath the sound of unprecedented panic.

"Are you okay?"

"Yeah, it's just a stupid cold," she says, waving her hand at me dismissively. "Where did you see my parents?"

"By the rec room."

"I saw yours in the parking lot," says Savvy, "which must mean—"

"They're headed to the main office," I finish, glancing in its direction. A gust of wind hits us, and I can't tell if we both shiver out of excitement or dread. Our parents may be pissed, but on the other side of that conversation are the answers to all the impossible questions we've had since we met.

I turn back to Savvy. "Ready?"

She shakes her head at me. "Abby, we don't have a *plan*. We have no idea what we're going to say."

I grab her hand and squeeze it, the way she did mine yesterday, like I can pulse some of my newfound and probably extremely ill-advised bravery into her.

"We'll start with 'sorry' and go from there."

Savvy offers me a wary, watery smile, but she squeezes my hand back before letting go, and we head to the main office, for once matching each other's pace so neither of us is ahead or checking to see if the other is still there.

I'm bracing myself for a hundred different scenarios on the short walk, and about ninety-nine of them start with my parents being astronomical levels of pissed. But maybe they won't be. Maybe they'll see Savvy's parents, and something will just kind of work itself out. They'll all take each other in, and the shared memories of their bad nineties haircuts and cheap weddings and whatever else it was that must have connected them before Savvy and I were born will all come spilling to the surface. By this time tomorrow we'll all be laughing about this.

But even accounting for this nonsense scenario, I still don't manage to account for the one that actually happens: our parents are nowhere to be found. Instead we open the office door to find Mickey, standing next to Rufus and staring out the window looking like she witnessed a crime.

We turn to follow her gaze and in the distance see two cars making their way up the winding hill that leads down to the camp—one a Prius, and behind it, what is unmistakably my parents' minivan in all its clunky, sticker-clad glory. Within seconds they're both out of sight.

"What the hell just happened?" Savvy asks.

Mickey only semicommits to looking at her. In the end, she mostly addresses me. "Um—your parents—kind of took one look at each other and . . . left?"

I manage to find my voice before Savvy. Only because if I don't push past the lump that is suddenly swelling in my throat and burning the front of my face, I'll do something stupid and cry instead.

"Did they say why?"

"No," says Mickey faintly. "Nobody said anything. But, uh . . . whatever went down between your parents? I think it's officially safe to say it was bad."

twenty

What we eventually realize, after wringing Mickey's brain out like a sponge, is this: neither of our parents were coming to confront us about Operation Stealth Sister. Savvy's parents were there because Mickey mentioned Savvy's cold to her mom, who then mentioned it to Savvy's mom.

"And that merited both your parents dropping their lives and crossing a large body of water in less than twenty-four hours because . . . ?" I ask.

Savvy scowls, charging ahead and leading us deeper into the woods. "Why were your parents here?"

Ah. That. I wince, opening the protein bar Savvy handed to me before yanking me onto a hiking path and telling me to follow her.

"There's a medium-to-large-ish chance I failed a class and I'm supposed to be in summer school right now."

"*Summer* school?"

And there it is again. The raised eyebrows, the disbelieving tone. Even with literal twigs in her hair and her nose redder than Rudolph's she manages to ooze the kind of authority that would make my school principal hand Savvy the keys to her office without thinking twice.

"Yeah, yeah, we can't all be Betty Coopers," I say.

"Sorry, I didn't mean to sound . . . judgy. I was surprised, is all."

Well, that's a notch up from her being *unsurprised*, so I'll take it. I'm about to circle back to Savvy's parents crossing the Puget Sound over her sniffles, but Savvy finally comes to a stop.

"Whoa."

The path has given way to a clearing with a wide view and a sharp, unexpected drop—not quite as high as some of the perches I've seen since we got here, but breathtaking. We're far enough away that we can see the camp below, the cabins and the cafeteria and the tennis courts stretched out beyond us, campers starting to mill about lazily for the less-structured Sunday agenda. I don't realize how quiet it is up here until Savvy lets out a sneeze and I flinch.

Savvy touches my shoulder. "It gets really muddy," she warns.

I glance down at the drop from the edge below. It isn't perilous, but it's steep, and it doesn't really look like there's much of a way to get back up if you tumble down.

I take a step back, resenting that I heard all those thoughts in Leo's voice.

"What is this place?"

"Well, it *was* where we did archery, that one summer after the first Hunger Games movie came out and a bunch of kids were into it. But then nobody wanted to hike all the way up here, and the path got overgrown, and . . . most people forgot about it."

Her eyes linger on the base of a tree but wrench away so quickly that I know better than to look at whatever it was.

"But not you."

Savvy shrugs and sits down on a tree stump. I plop down on the stump next to her, still wondering if I really saw my parents' car or if I'm going to wake up in the cabin to find out this was all some bonkers bug spray–induced fever dream.

"So our parents hate each other."

"We don't know that," says Savvy.

"The last time I saw a Prius going that fast, the REI flagship downtown was having a garage sale." I sink my teeth into the protein bar. "Besides, all of our collective parents were here, which means mine probably saddled three boys under the age of ten with my unsuspecting uncle and took the six A.M. ferry. And then just . . . *left?*"

The hurt doesn't really know where to settle in me, or if it even should. They have no way of knowing that I know they're here. And it's not like they left because they were mad at me. Hell, they're *here* because they're mad at me. But the whole thing has me uneasy. The decision to come all the way here must have been a big one. That can only mean the force that drove them out is bigger—bigger, even, than getting to see me.

"Ugh," says Savvy, burying her head in her knees. "I wish our parents would just . . . chill."

"I mean, I blatantly lied to mine and hacked into their emails to avoid my legal obligation to attend summer school, so they're probably at the right amount of un-chill," I admit. "Yours, on the other hand . . . what's got them so worked up about the sniffles? Are you sure they're not here because of Jo?"

"No," Savvy says miserably, her face muffled by her leggings. "Jo's long gone."

"Oh."

I'm not sure if I'm supposed to ask. Being with Savvy is like—there's this closeness, an understanding somewhere in the core of us, in our matching eyes and rhythms and magpie charms. And there's this friendship that we've started to build between us. But it's missing the in-between. The part in the middle of being a friend and being related, where you know things about each other's lives and know where you fit and what kind of person you are when you're with them.

"My parents—they've been like this ever since I can remember. When I was a kid I'd sneeze and end up in the pediatrician's waiting room. One time they kept me home from school because my tongue was green, and it took the whole damn day for us to remember I'd had a Jolly Rancher the night before."

"Were you like, super sick as a kid or something?"

"Not even. But they always seemed to think—"

She stops herself, staring at the half-eaten protein bar in her hands, and licks her upper lip.

"Seemed to think what?"

She stares for a few more moments without answering. I've had to get used to this. Savvy's pauses, the way she is always trying to word things so carefully. It's better not to try to prompt her. She'll usually say whatever it is eventually, but sometimes I can't help myself.

"They seemed to think—well—they've always been paranoid about me having some kind of undiagnosed heart condition. Which, as far as I know, I don't," she adds quickly. "Just one weird blip on a monitor as a baby that even the doctor said not to worry about, but my mom was convinced it was something else, and that if I ever got too sick it would make it pop up and become a real problem."

"That's . . . an oddly specific fear."

Savvy nods, watching me, and only then do I realize her hesitation. Maybe it isn't odd. Maybe it's just specific.

"Nobody in my family had any weird heart things that I know about. Do your parents think we do?"

"I kind of assumed? I was mostly busy being annoyed." Savvy blows out a breath. "But it all kind of rubbed off in the end, I guess."

"Uh, you're like, the opposite of a hypochondriac. I'm pretty sure even if you were at death's door you would challenge the grim reaper to a green juice shot contest and be on your merry way. You're like, the healthiest person I know."

"Yeah, because I had to be. As long as I was doing a whole

song and dance about taking care of myself, my parents would get off my case." She lets out a laugh, extending out her knees and stretching her back, like the words loosened something in her joints and she doesn't know how to hold them. "I don't think I've ever told anyone that."

I nudge her knee with mine, and it settles her a bit. "I think that's the kind of thing your friends probably already know."

Savvy's smile gets smaller, less intentional. Like she's revisiting something. "Yeah." She adds, "To be clear, I like what I do. The Instagram, I mean. Or . . ."

"You like spending time with Mickey."

Savvy straightens up so quickly that I know I'm right, but almost wish I hadn't been. Or at least figured out that I should have kept my mouth shut.

"Are you going to leave?" Savvy asks, her voice quieter than it's been all morning.

I pick at a weed in the ground, stabbing its stem with my fingernails, watching the juices dye my skin green. There's no scenario where my parents don't yank me out of here. But the disappointment isn't as much of a blow as I thought it would be. The time I've had here—the mornings watching the sun rise with Savvy and Rufus, the afternoons on the water with the girls and sneaking around to get good views with Finn, the nights eating food with my fingers with Leo and Mickey—it was always too good to last. Like when you're in a good dream, but you know you're dreaming. I was here on borrowed time.

"I don't want to."

Some of Savvy relaxes, like she can only let herself go a few degrees at a time. "Well, you've already missed summer school, right? The damage is done."

"There's a second session," I say miserably. "And it doesn't start until after camp ends in two weeks, but I'm sure they'll pull me out anyway. I'm kind of surprised it didn't happen sooner."

YOU HAVE A MATCH   173

"Are your parents big into you getting into a good college or something?"

I shrug. We actually haven't talked about it all that much. I always kind of assumed I'd go to the community college nearby until I figured out what I wanted to do, and nobody seemed to have a problem with that.

"Then why are they so fixated on your grades and signing you up for all this stuff?"

"I'm not, like, dumb."

"I know," says Savvy. Not too fast, or too placatingly. "Victoria mentioned your first practice scores were probably too high to justify SAT prep."

Even elbows deep in trying to dissect our parents' drama, I'm oddly tickled to hear this.

"I . . . I don't know. My grades were always fine. But this year . . . not as much, I guess."

What I don't say is that they dipped after Poppy died. That it happened right before the start of junior year. That the grades themselves weren't so bad, maybe, but how I didn't seem to care scared the pants off my parents.

And it's not that I didn't care, exactly. It's just that by the time the school year started, I was exhausted. Everything was changing—not only the big, scary changes, but the little, more practical ones. The shakeups in our routines, the things my parents had to account for without Poppy around to help. I didn't realize how much of the care and keeping of Abby Day had been relegated to him. Didn't realize until my parents shifted to make up for it, and suddenly way too much of their focus was aimed at me.

"They just started putting me in tutoring for *everything*, even the stuff where I was doing okay."

"But you hate it."

"With a burning, fiery passion."

"And you haven't told them."

It's not a question. My reputation for letting problems fester has apparently preceded me.

"It wasn't so bad, at first," I explain. The protein bar starts to taste mealy, like it's too thick to chew. I wrap up the remains and set it on my knee, staring as it stays perfectly balanced, waiting for it to fall. "Poppy—my grandpa—he always used to knock them out of the whole helicopter parenting thing, if they were going off the rails. Sometimes he'd even fake kidnap me, and we'd go up to the trail or to Green Lake with our cameras."

"That sounds fun."

My eyes are still perfectly trained on the bar, and I'm almost glad when it falls, so my eyes have something to focus on instead of tearing up the way they want to.

"Yeah." My voice wavers. "Anyway, joke's on them. The more tutoring they put me through, the worse my grades get."

"Are you doing it on purpose?"

Am I? Sometimes I feel like the last year slipped out from under me, and I can't even measure it in time so much as things that happened in it. Losing Poppy. The BEI. Finding out about Savvy. The rest is this murky haze, like I've been underwater, trying to go with the current, and only just broken the surface and realized how far downstream I am.

"I don't think so. But . . . once I started falling behind . . ."

"It's hard to catch up."

"Maybe if they let me. If I just had some *time* to . . ." I let out a sigh. "I mean, this whole Reynolds-method SAT prep thing? I don't hate it. I'm getting okay at it, even. Because we have time to do our own shit afterward. My brain can like, hit flush. Reset. Whatever."

Savvy nods appreciatively.

"And I will talk to them. Maybe later. When the timing's not so . . ."

"Yeah," Savvy agrees. "And it's hard, I guess. To get mad about stuff they do because they love us."

It suctions something in my chest that, in all the chaos, I've been able to ignore: I *miss* them. I almost want things to go back to normal, just so I can hug them, and talk to them about the boring parts of my day that nobody else cares about, and feel that warm feeling of being theirs, without everything else getting in the way.

But the key is the *almost*. Because I'm understanding now that it's not just that I can't undo this—I don't want to. I don't want to go back to a world where I don't know Savvy. Not because she's my sister, but because, against all odds, I think she might be my friend.

"Yeah." I crush the protein bar wrapper in my hand, steeling myself. "They love us. So they've gotta tell us the truth."

Savvy nods, and we both get up. I start to head back down the path first, but Savvy's voice stops me.

"I hope you get to stay."

I'm not a hugger, really, so I'm not even sure why I'm leaning in until I'm doing it—hugging this girl who is me and not-me, this girl I don't relate to at all but somehow understand. She stiffens, but then hugs me back and squeezes, and it feels solid, then. The understanding between us. No matter what happens, this isn't the end of us. There is going to be a whole lot more bickering and sunrise photo sessions and trying to make sense of ourselves to come.

We turn to leave, and I duck down to tie my shoe. Only then do I see the little carving in the old tree, whittled with a pocket-knife, faded with time: *Mick + Sav*, written in a big, carved star.

twenty-one

What commences after that I can only describe as a stakeout. We plant ourselves by the parking lot and wait. By four o'clock that afternoon, we're all doing rounds: me after breakfast, Savvy before lunch, Mickey right after, and Finn hopping in and out whenever he pleases, like we're a livestream of some puppies and he's coming back to see if they're awake yet.

"Okay, how about this. If things start to go to shit, I'll leap out before they can leave and be like, 'It's ME, your secret *son!*' And once we either cut the tension or unintentionally reveal *another* deep dark family secret, everyone will have a good—"

"Finn, Finn, clam up," I say, my voice rocketing up by about an octave. "Go get Savvy."

Finn whines, spotting the minivan coming down the hill. "But it's finally about to get—"

"*Go.*"

The road is lengthy and winding, so the minivan disappears in and out as it weaves. But we've only got about a minute before they hit the parking lot. Savvy and I discussed what we were going to say, but the closer they get, the more my mind goes blank.

Footsteps are crunching the gravel behind me, but when I whip around it's not Savvy, but Leo. It is a true testament to my current state of panic that I barely feel the wrench in my stomach reminding me my talk with Leo is still very much overdue.

"Hey," he says, glancing where I was just staring.

Shit. He doesn't know what's happening. In the chaos of this morning I not only forgot about all the drama with Leo, I forgot about—well—Leo.

"Hi," I manage. "Um—so I'm—"

"Do you want to—could we talk over dinner tonight? I mean after like, regular dining hall dinner?"

"Oh." Savvy is jogging up from behind Leo, back to her usual put-together self, the sleek ponytail back in place and a strategic layer of foundation hiding her stuffed-up nose. "Uh . . ."

"I'll make lasagna balls."

I nod, only half aware of what I'm agreeing to. "Sure—yes, yeah, okay," I say as Savvy reaches us.

"Cool," says Leo. I finally look at his face, at the anxious, tense line that might be an attempt at a smile. I attempt my own, and we make for a gruesome pair, no doubt both bracing ourselves to say things that the other won't want to hear. "See you later."

"See you."

He turns away as I hear the crunch of wheels on gravel and the distinctive lug of the old minivan pulling in. Savvy and I squint at my parents through the windshield, and I immediately regret it. My dad's mouth is stunned open and my mom's eyes are wider than I've ever seen them, darting between me and Savvy like she's waiting for us to merge back into one kid instead of two.

I don't know what else to do except wave, which is what my stupid arm does, like this is a social call instead of them coming to drag me across the Puget Sound by my ear. There's a beat after they park the car, and my mom says something to my dad, and my dad nods. He gets out of the car alone.

"Shit," I mutter. I've never seen my mom hide from *anything* before.

Savvy unconsciously comes a little closer to me, or maybe I drift closer to her. Either way, we're shoulder to shoulder when my dad approaches, very determinedly not looking at or acknowledging Savvy, staring at me with bloodshot, tired eyes.

"Jig's up," he says, like we can keep this whole thing light-hearted.

"Uh—yeah. You could say that," I try weakly.

"We got a call from the school. Wondering why you hadn't signed up for a summer session yet," says my dad, continuing not to look at Savvy with such commitment that she might as well be a well-groomed, Instagrammable ghost. "Your mom and I are coming to take you home."

"Look, I know I lied, but—well, first off, I'm learning a lot here. Latin roots and circumferences and all kinds of SAT gems. But also—"

"Sorry, Abby," says my dad, taking a step back. "You can take some time to pack up and say goodbye to your friends, but—"

"I'm not saying goodbye to Savvy."

His mouth shuts, and there is this flash of something in his eyes I've never seen before—like I've betrayed him. Pushed him into a corner, one he has avoided since long before I was there to push him into it. But it's coupled with something else that twists the knife, making me doubt myself: surprise. He can't believe I'm doing this to him.

For a moment, I can't, either.

My dad finally looks at Savvy with practiced indifference, like he only meant to glance, but then his eyes snag on her and the recognition in them is unmistakable. The kind that has nothing to do with a face, and everything to do with your heart.

"I'm—I'm sure you and your friend can—"

"She's not just my friend," I blurt. I turn to Savvy, but she looks like she's forgotten how to speak, the guilt wrenching my stomach every bit as visible on her face. "You know she's my . . . you *know*."

"I don't . . ."

I pull out my keychain, the magpie charm catching the light. Wordlessly, Savvy pulls the chain off her neck, holding it next to mine with slow, hesitant hands.

The car door slams. There are tears streaming down my mom's face, so thick that I can't tell what kind of tears they are.

"Girls," she says, addressing both of us. "This isn't the best time to . . . I want to explain. I do. But Abby, can you just—get in the car, and—"

"Savvy!"

We turn, my mom crying, my dad looking like he hasn't breathed in a full minute, our magpie charms limp in our hands, to find that the Prius has—in true Prius form—snuck up on us, and Savvy's parents are out of their car.

Not only that, Savvy's mom is *pissed*.

In her floral wraparound dress and wedge sandals, she does not look like a woman who is about to power walk over to us so fast that I nearly crack my neck following her progress, but in an instant she's grabbing Savvy's arm and glaring daggers at my mom.

"How *dare* you," she says to my mom, squeezing Savvy's arm so intensely that the skin is going red. "You are well aware of the rules."

"I wasn't—"

"We will settle this the same way we did last time. Don't think we won't," she says, pulling Savvy back, as if someone is going to snatch her.

"Pietra," says Savvy's dad, who has only just caught up to Savvy's mom. "Let's hold on a—"

"We're leaving. *Now*."

I keep waiting for my parents to defend themselves. My mom

takes a few steps back, but otherwise is frozen, staring at Pietra like an animal realizing it's about to get decked by a truck.

"Mom, you can't just put me in the car," says Savvy, finally finding her voice. "I *work* here."

"Like hell I can't," says Savvy's mom, a far cry from the beaming, prim woman from the Tully family Christmas card.

My dad cuts in before Savvy's mom just short of firefighter lifts her over her shoulders. "I think we all need to talk to our daughters," he says, without looking at Savvy's parents. "Abby, do you need to grab anything, or can you come with us now?"

"I . . . I have to . . ."

"I'll let Victoria know where you are," says Savvy. Then, before her mom can protest, "And where I'm going. Give me a few minutes, and I'll come with you, okay?"

Savvy's mom nods, not quite calm but definitely embarrassed. She turns to my dad and says, "Yes. I think that's best. But to be clear, I never want to see either of you near my daughter, ever again."

I'm expecting someone, anyone, to protest. But even though my mom's face is still a wreck, her voice is clear: "Understood."

twenty-two

My parents drive me to the small hotel on the island without saying a word, periodically looking at me in the rearview mirror. I try to hold their gazes—*I'm sorry, I'm sorry, I'm sorry*—but every time I do, they look away.

Nobody's spoken by the time we park the car. I follow them meekly, feeling more like a kid than ever, not only because I'm in eighty-six kinds of trouble, but because I'm entirely dependent on them. I left with nothing but my camera and my keychain. I don't even have my phone.

My mom starts microwaving hot water the minute we get into the hotel. I've never had more than a few sips, and as far as I know, neither has she, but the tea ritual has become a defining thing of sorts. If it's a problem, we figure it out. If it's a Problem, Mom makes tea.

After that we all sit, them on the couch, and me on the wheelie chair by the desk. I fidget, and they are ramrod still, only moving to look at each other in some silent conversation.

"We didn't want you to find out like this," I finally say. "We only wanted to—I don't know. Figure out what happened, I guess."

"You couldn't have just asked?" says my dad.

I bunch up the loose fabric of my shorts between my fingers. I should tell them the truth: I knew even then that we were digging up something too big for the world above it. That I didn't want to give them the chance to lie.

And how it *hurt*, knowing they kept this from me. That if sixteen years passed, they were probably planning on keeping it from me my whole life.

"I'm asking now," I say instead. The words take a lot of courage to put into the air, and I don't even realize until I breathe out and my bones feel spent by it. "What happened?"

My mom clutches her tea but doesn't drink it, holding it to her face and closing her eyes briefly.

"You know your father and I got married young."

I nod. I have a feeling it's going to be a lot of nodding from here on out.

"Well—what you don't know is why."

"Because of Savvy?"

My mom shakes her head. "Because . . . your father . . . well—we didn't know if he had a lot of time left."

I let out a laugh, a genuine one followed up by a quiet, uncertain one. Neither of my parents laugh, their faces solemn and drawn. I don't think I've ever seen them this serious. They look like zombie versions of themselves.

"When I was twenty, I got a really bad case of pneumonia," my dad tells me. "It, uh—well, the long and short of it is, I had an undiagnosed heart defect. The pneumonia triggered it. And it really did a number on me. I was in and out of the hospital for a few years."

My mom reaches out suddenly and grabs his hand. I watch them both squeeze—my dad first, and then my mom. I wonder how many times I've watched them do that. I wonder why this is the first time it's made me understand just how much they say to each other when they're not saying anything at all.

"They even had him on the donor list for a while," says my mom. "Things got pretty bad, and we—we were in love, and we just . . . we got married. We didn't think there was much of a future, so we wanted to do as much as we could with what time we thought he had left."

My throat is thick. I can't imagine a world where my mom exists without my dad, or my dad without her. It's strange to think there was even a time when they hadn't met.

"Even having a baby?"

"The baby—Savannah," my mom corrects herself. She says it the way you say a word you've read in a book a hundred times but never said out loud. "That was an accident."

"We were in over our heads," says my dad. "We were married, but we weren't ready for . . . at least not under the circumstances."

"He was so sick," says my mom, "and we were so young, and we were—we were already trying to plan what life would look like without him. I didn't—the idea of—of being in a world without him . . . I thought I was too young to handle it on my own. I know I was."

You don't have to explain, I want to say—but it's not that. I need her to explain, and I think she needs to explain. But she doesn't have to justify it. She's my mom. Even before I knew the circumstances, I understood she'd made an impossible choice.

"So we decided to give her up for adoption," says my dad. "And then . . ."

"You got better."

He nods. My mom's grip around his hand tightens, the two of them pressed so close to each other that they look like a force. I'm starting to understand it now. That unnerving level of calm in the face of every Abby-made or little-brother-related catastrophe that's come our way. They've already faced much worse than what we could throw at them, and come out the other side.

"Right before Savannah was born, they put him on an experimental treatment plan, and it was like it never happened. It still is. He hasn't had any issues since."

My dad sees the question poised in my eyes but misinterprets it. "And as far as we know, neither will you or your brothers. We got all of you tested."

"But Savvy?"

"Does she have . . . ?" My mom's hand goes to her heart, her face paler than it was before.

"No," I say quickly, wishing I'd realized wording it like that would scare them. "I meant—when you gave her up. You know her parents."

"We were friends," says my dad carefully.

It's clear neither of them are going to elaborate. "So . . . what the hell happened?"

My mom folds in on herself. She's always been small—more Savvy-size than I am—but right now she looks like she could sink into the couch cushions and disappear. "It's complicated."

"And the part where you kept a secret sister from me for sixteen years isn't?"

"Hey," my dad warns me.

"It's okay, Tom," says my mom.

I wave in their direction, a gesture of surrender that comes off a little awkward because I've never really had to make one before. Even I'm surprised at myself for challenging them. It isn't easy, but it's not as hard as I thought it would be either. Like I've been saving up all these little moments over the last year where I could have, would have, should have said something, and something so big that I can't ignore it has finally pushed me over the edge.

"I already know the rest of it," I say. "Why can't you tell me?"

"Because . . ." My mom shakes her head.

"And—and what about me? I mean, how do I fit into this?" I ask, before I lose my nerve. I'm shaking. "I mean—you gave her up and had me a year and a half later. Were you, like—super accident-prone, or—"

"Honey, no," says my mom.

"It's okay," I say, and I mean it. "I mean, I always kind of figured I was, and I know it doesn't mean you guys love me any—"

"Honey, you weren't an accident, you were—"

My mom cuts herself off, because in her haste to reassure me, she's given something away.

I feel weak, like I've climbed up something too tall and don't know if I have it in me to get back down. "The whole thing . . . it doesn't make sense."

"I know," says my mom, shaking her head. "I'm sorry. I know."

I can feel my window to ask shutting. They're going to find some way to close this, to seal it tight. I try another tactic. "If you can't tell me now—will you ever?"

They glance at each other, and this time it isn't a mystery. Neither knows what to tell me.

"Because—because I'm going to have to know someday. Savvy's a part of my life," I tell them, and only then do I feel like I might be losing what ridiculously small amount of control I have over the situation. Only then do I realize that this isn't just about what they lost—I have something to lose, too. "We're friends. What we did was shitty, and I'm sorry about that, but I'm not sorry about the part where we found each other, because—"

I have to stop, because my mom's crying again. She puts her face in her hands, shaking her head like she didn't mean for me to stop. But she breathes in and it comes back out in this big, gasping sob, a noise I've never heard her make before, and it clamps my mouth shut so fast that the rest of the words die halfway up my throat.

"I'm sorry," she says. "I'm . . ."

My dad pulls his hand from hers so he can put an arm around her shoulders, steadying her. I don't move, stunned by this unexpected power I have over them, by how quickly it broke

them. I don't want it. I just want to understand. I don't want all
the pain that comes with it.

But the understanding and pain are woven together, tighter
than a knot, and together make something so immovable that it
doesn't matter what I mean and what I don't. It's all going to end
with me yanking on something that can't be undone.

"We're going to turn in for the night," says my dad, helping
my mom to her feet. "There's a deli, just outside, and cash in
your mom's purse—"

"Wait," I say, leaping to my feet. "I know that . . . this is a lot.
But if you could let me stay—"

"Abby," my dad starts.

"—because I'm actually making progress. I really am! I got a
720 on a math practice exam two days ago. A 720! Me!"

They're not even hearing me. I feel like I'm in an alternate
dimension. I don't know what else I can say, how else to make
it stick.

"And I'm making friends, and . . . and I've taken so many
photographs. Beautiful ones."

My dad glances at me. I have his attention, but not enough
to hold it. The next words are some of the most nerve-wracking
I've ever said in my life, but I'm desperate.

"Let me show you."

My dad stops at this, and we stare at each other, trying to
figure out which of us is more surprised. I've never shown them
more than one rare photo at a time before. They've only ever had
good things to say, but they're my parents and obligated to say
nice things. If anything, it only makes me more self-conscious.

This, on the other hand, might fling my sense of self straight
into the sun.

"Send them to us. We want to see them," he says, and though
his voice is grim, and his face ashen, I can tell how much he

means it. That he knows how much it means to me. "We do. But Abby?"

Shit. Shit, shit, *shit.*

"I . . . I don't want you to get your hopes up. It's not anything to do with you, or the summer school thing. It's bigger than that, okay?"

The word tastes like metal on my tongue, but there's nothing else to say.

"Okay."

twenty-three

Somehow, against all odds, I am setting foot back in Camp Reynolds before lunch the next day. It's such a relief I could prostrate myself in front of the academic building and kiss the mud. It is also such a disappointment that instead I stand in the parking lot, watching my parents drive away, my guilt mounting more and more with every turn of the minivan's wheels.

"She lives!"

I'm entirely too exhausted for Finn and his boundless energy, and judging by the visible bags under his eyes, he is, too.

"I thought you were straight-up murdered. I was going to start spreading rumors. Make you the next Gaby, find you a decent tree to haunt—"

"Is Savvy here?"

"She got in last night. Had to report back for duty and all. You're the talk of the camp, you know," Finn tells me. "Phoenix Cabin thought you'd gotten lost in the woods; they were about to start a search party. I swear Leo looked like he was going to cry—"

"I texted him from my mom's phone—didn't he get it?"

"Well, yeah. But we thought you'd be back by dinner. He was convinced you'd been kidnapped or eaten by a rabid animal or something."

Crap. We were supposed to have dinner and talk. Twenty-four hours ago it would have been so burned into my brain I wouldn't have been able to think of anything else. Now I've gone and made yet another bad situation worse.

"So what happened?" Finn asks. "Are you—"

"Abby!"

Savvy looks stunned to see me, breaking away from the other junior counselors so abruptly that they all look like a fellow migrating bird just threw off their formation. From a distance she looks like her usual camera-ready self, but once she gets up close she looks every bit as exhausted as I feel, her eyes rimmed red and her perfect posture off a few degrees.

"You're *here?*"

"I'm as shocked as you are."

"What happened?" Finn asks again, his eyes darting between us. "Did we solve the mystery? Were you secretly split from the same egg the whole time, a genetic experiment gone wrong, the cover-up botched—"

Rufus interrupts by clobbering me with his usual muddy overexuberance, right as Savvy says, "Meet me after lunch?"

"Yeah," Finn and I say at the same time.

Savvy raises her eyebrows at him.

"Ugh, fine," says Finn. "I'll go find a secret sister of my own."

The instant Savvy and I are somewhat alone, we spill everything we know, comparing notes. My parents' and her parents' stories line up perfectly. They told Savvy about not being able to have kids, and a friend of theirs being in a position where they needed to put their baby up for adoption. Neither story goes any further than that.

"I tried to find out, but my mom got really upset," says Savvy, shifting uncomfortably.

"You're telling me."

"I wonder . . ." Savvy shakes her head. "What made your parents change their minds about letting you stay?"

"I'm not sure."

But maybe I am. It could be the SAT thing, but it could also be that they just woke up this morning and decided it was easier not to deal with me than to spend another two weeks fielding questions. Easier not to walk around the house with a living, breathing reminder that what happened eighteen years ago is out in the open, pushing at the edges of the world they've built since. I'm not just their problem kid anymore. I'm a time bomb.

The one thing I know for sure is that it's not my photography. Nobody even tried to access the Dropbox of my photos last night. It should be a relief, but if it is, it sinks way lower than any kind I've felt before.

"I wish we knew what made them hate each other so much," says Savvy.

"I just wish we could fix it."

"Savvy, have you seen Amelia?"

We both jump, but Victoria seems unfazed.

"Uh . . . she was in the mess hall," says Savvy. "Why? Is there anything I can help with?"

Victoria sighs. "There's some problem with the dock. No ferries in or out since this morning. So now the teacher for AP Lit Prep isn't here, and I need Amelia to sub in until they get things up and running. Let her know to come find me if you see her."

"Absolutely."

The moment she leaves, our eyes snap to each other's: our parents are all still here.

Savvy's eyes light up with sudden mischief so familiar to me that I might as well be back home, playing referee between my brothers as they pummel one another with plastic lightsabers and Silly String.

"I've got an idea."

twenty-four

I have done some pretty stupid things in my life, but this plan of Savvy's—Savvy, the *responsible* one—might be the stupidest thing I've done yet.

In fact, *plan* is a generous word. She wants us to go out and find our parents, and by our parents, I mean each other's parents. As in I am walking through the woods, one pair of binoculars away from getting labeled as a certified stalker, because Savvy is sure I'll find Dale and Pietra on this specific trail. Meanwhile, Savvy is using her one break during the day to hitch a ride with one of the morning teachers up to the little stretch of town.

"We'll ease them in this way," she reasoned. "We'll 'accidentally' bump into them, chat them up, make it seem like our own parents said something about missing them, and nudge them in the right direction."

"So lie to them."

"It's not lying. They clearly *do* miss each other. You saw those pictures."

"Yeah. But Savvy . . ."

"But what?" Savvy asked.

I sighed. "Say we find them. Then what?"

"We draw them back to camp. Maybe they'll be loosened up and it won't be as weird."

I raised my eyebrows, wondering when Savvy became the

lawless one and I became the rule follower. I didn't know what her night looked like, but I personally had a vested interest in never seeing those looks on my parents' faces again.

I expected her to say something challenging—*Got any better ideas?*—but instead she tapped my camera, this quiet little pulse, like it was more a part of me than tapping my actual arm.

Her voice went quiet. "If we want to see each other ever again without them getting majorly pissed about it, this might be our only shot."

Most of the fear deflated out of me. She was right. And it was even grimmer than that, considering we have another year and some change before I turn eighteen.

"And if your parents hate me?"

Savvy relaxed, recognizing she'd won me over. "Trust me," she said, taking her hat off her head and putting it on mine. "They won't."

The only comfort I have is that my odds of running into them in the woods, specific trail or no, are somewhat slim. It's not that I'm not committed to the plan—I *do* want them to get along, so we can get whatever happened out in the open and move on from it—but I am also acutely aware that I'm not exactly winning Kid of the Year out here, compared to her. Savvy is a trophy child. I'm more of a participation award.

I take Kitty with me, feeling like I shouldn't be carrying Poppy's camera around when I'm deliberately plotting against my mom. At some point the trail forks into one that's clearly the main path and one that's thin and steep and a little muddy. It takes a minute to maneuver myself up the muddy one without sliding down, but it's worth it when I do. There are three deer, a fully grown one and two skittish, frozen little ones, all peering at me like we accidentally stepped through a veil into each other's worlds.

"Hi," I whisper, moving as slowly as I can for my camera.

There's a clearing beyond them, the sun's rays peeking out from behind a cloud, crisscrossing their thin faces and the trees. I can already see the end result, and I'm salivating like the photo is something I can taste. "Stay right there, little buddies . . . ooooone second, and I'll—"

"Dale, are you *sure* we can't ask one of your friends with a boat to—"

The deer take off like rockets, and I'm sliding buttfirst down the hill to avoid them before the woman down below can even finish her sentence. I manage not to yelp, but there's no chance of not giving myself away—I have transitioned so fully from girl to mud monster that I'm pretty sure I can feel some in my armpits.

"*Savvy?*"

I don't know Savvy's mom's—*Pietra's*—voice well enough to recognize it, but I do know the universe well enough to assume I have been completely screwed over. So it's no surprise when I look up and Savvy's parents are hovering over me with worried eyes, their faces shiny with sunscreen and shadowed by matching brimmed hats.

"Nope. Just the knockoff version," I manage, pulling Savvy's hat off.

Pietra shakes her head, embarrassed, before getting her wits about her. "Are you all right?"

"I'm fine. I have a sturdy butt."

Thanks for nothing, brain-to-mouth filter.

"Let me help you up," says Dale.

Before I can protest, he takes my hand and hoists me up so easily that my feet fully lift up from the ground before they find purchase in the mud again. I blink, righting myself, and they're both gaping at me like they've seen a ghost.

Pietra looks away, her gaze a fixed line on her shoes, but Dale's eyes widen on me. "You really do look like her."

My face burns. "We've been getting that a lot."

"No, not Savvy. Like Maggie," he says.

I'm not used to hearing people say my mom's first name, but Pietra reacts before I can.

"You're bleeding," she says, half scolding, half concerned. She touches my cheek, and I'm too stunned to react. She's every bit as stunned at herself as I am. Like it's something she'd do to Savvy, maybe, but only accidentally did to me.

My face is stinging, but I already know from experience that whatever it is, it's not that bad. "I'm really fine."

"Are you—"

"Your camera, on the other hand," says Dale.

Kitty is lens-down in the glop, and not looking so hot. Dale picks her up for me, trying to wipe some of the mud off. He sucks some air between his teeth, making a grim prognosis. Pietra doesn't look away from me for the whole exchange.

"I'm sure she's fine," I say, taking Kitty and saying a silent prayer up to the DSLR camera gods.

"We should get her to camp, have someone take a look at that," says Pietra to Dale, as if I'm six and not sixteen. I square her up more easily, now that she's not shouting her head off. She's one of those mothering types, the kind who does it to everyone, not just her kid. "I'm sure I have some coconut oil in the car that we can put on it."

She takes off, and Dale tilts his chin to indicate that I should follow. It seems that, much like Savvy, Pietra is a woman unused to hearing the word *no*.

I follow them in silence, hearing our feet squish in the mud in different rhythms. I'm supposed to think of something to say—Savvy would—but everything I think of is too blunt.

Instead, I am occupied by a much larger, weirder thought: if someone had like, shaken up the eggs or something—if I'd bullied my way down a fallopian tube first—I would have been born before Savvy and belonged to these people. And maybe I would have been the one with a closet full of pastel spandex and Instagrams full of comments with heart-eyes emojis and a head full of rules.

"So you're into photography?" Dale asks.

He's clearly the kind of person who fills silences. He reminds me of Finn. Someone who puts the grease on awkward moments, with a little forced cheer, and makes them go down a little easier.

"Um—just—mostly landscapes. Sometimes animals, like birds and deer and stuff." I unconsciously touch the magpie charm on my lanyard, wrapped around my wrist.

"You sure your camera survived?"

"It's definitely seen worse." I turn Kitty back on to check, and sure enough she flickers back to life, her lens whirring into place. A few lives left to go, I guess.

"Is that—that's from the hill up there?"

Dale is tall enough that I doubt anything gets past him, let alone the hot second the Puget Sound popped up on Kitty's screen. I freeze, horrified for being so careless.

But this isn't about me or my stupid photos. There's way too much at stake for me to worry about Dale seeing one of them, even if my palms are sweating enough to create their own small pond.

"Nah, that's, uh—from another spot," I say, clearing my throat. "A trail on the other side of camp."

Dale peers down at the screen with such sincere interest that I don't even notice he's reached out to take Kitty from me until she is in his grip. To my mortification, he starts to scroll, going through the different vantage points I took photos of the sunrise from yesterday morning.

"These are lovely."

It feels weird to say thank you, like I'd be agreeing with him.

And although my brain has abandoned me more than once in the last few days, it is not so far gone that I don't remember that Savvy's parents are Serious Art People. I can't tell if he's complimenting me because he means it, or because he feels like he has to, a charitable gesture toward a kid whose work doesn't have any teeth.

"These three here," he says, lowering the screen down to my eyeline. "You can blow them up, put them on canvas side by side. Where are you displaying your work?"

I laugh, but it comes out as a wheeze. "Uh, nowhere."

"Not even Bean Well?"

It's Pietra, surprising me and Dale both. She immediately turns back around, staring ahead at the trail, but not before I see a flicker of something she wants buried streak across her face.

I don't want to say anything. I've lived sixteen years pointedly *not* saying anything in situations like this. But if I don't, I'll be kicking myself when I report back to Savvy and tell her I came up empty.

"You've been to Bean Well?"

Pietra takes on a breezy tone that even I, a person who has known her for less than a day, can hear right past. "That's the name of it, right?"

"Pietra," says Dale, chuckling, "you practically lived there."

She turns to Dale sharply. "It was a long time ago."

It takes me a moment to wrap my head around the idea. Savvy's parents come from money. And while anyone was welcome at Bean Well, it was a far cry from Medina mansions and charity galas, which seem entirely more Pietra's vibe.

Still, it's more information than I had five seconds ago, and I can't waste it. I channel my inner Savvy and ask, "Is that how you met my mom?"

Pietra winces, but softens when she looks over at me.

"It was a long time ago," she repeats, in the gentle, firm way of someone closing a book they have no intention of reading ever again.

It's a cheap shot, but it's all I've got. "Well, it won't be Bean Well for long. We're selling it."

"No. Why?"

I didn't think ahead this far. They're both watching me so intensely that it feels like I just lit a spotlight on something that I haven't even figured out the shape of, a hole in me I'm still trying to figure out how to fill.

"Well . . ."

I don't have to tell them, in the end.

"Oh. Abby, I'm . . ." Pietra has stopped walking, and so has Dale. I'm the one who stops a beat late, caught in the unexpected net of their grief. "I'm so sorry."

Dale puts a hand on my shoulder. "Walt was a good man."

My throat goes achy, my fingers clutching Kitty like a life preserver. I wish for Poppy's camera instead. I wish for it even though that means it would be the one muddied up, and that Dale wouldn't have seen my photos, and we would have finished the walk back without a word.

But instead of knocking me off course, the ache grounds me. Gives me something to level the distance between me and these absolute strangers. They knew Poppy. They understand how special he was.

I forge ahead.

"You could come by," I offer. "Before it sells, I mean."

Dale lets my shoulder go, and Pietra takes an uneasy half step.

"I don't think your parents would like that."

I shake my head. "They miss you."

Pietra lets out a shuddering breath that might have started as a laugh, looking up at the sky. I watch her carefully, this woman who is clearly frazzled within an inch of her life, and I'm hoping she'll tip over and accidentally reveal something else and also hoping she won't. The closer I get to knowing, the scarier the knowing seems.

"They said that?" says Dale.

I turn to him. "Yeah." A lie. "Well—I know they do. Last night . . ."

"Abby, honey, we appreciate what you're trying to do. You and Savvy," says Pietra. She has the same borderline desperate look my mom had, and just like that, I feel myself losing my nerve. "But you have to understand that what happened was—it can't be undone."

I can't believe that. I actively have to not believe it. Savvy and I may be related, but my parents and her parents—they're family. Or they were, once. One look at that wedding photo, one glance at the faded magpie charms, is all it takes to know that. And to me, that's the thing that can't be undone.

"I'm sorry. I don't know what happened, I just . . ."

Pietra starts walking again, slowly, with more resignation than anger. "Don't be sorry. I know Savvy put you up to this."

I open my mouth to protest, but I catch the knowing glint in her eye. It makes me smile, and then she's smiling back—I've been caught out, and we both know Savvy too well to pretend otherwise.

Still, she hasn't fully caught me. She thinks Savvy put me up to finding out the truth. What Savvy put me up to was finding a way to get our parents in the same space together.

"At least consider going to the Bean Well closing party at the end of the summer," I say quietly. "If you really did spend time there, Poppy would have wanted you to come."

Pietra opens her mouth—to gently shut me down, I'm guessing—but Dale says, "We'll consider it. But only if you put some of your photos on display for the party. They really are quite stunning."

"You've got your grandpa's eye for light," Pietra agrees.

I try not to let the embarrassment swallow me whole. But it's a different kind of embarrassment, maybe. There's a thrill beneath it, humming under the surface. Like maybe they mean it. Like maybe I am as good at this as Poppy was always saying.

"You knew him well?"

This time I'm not asking to pry. I genuinely want to know.

"I worked for him."

I try to swallow my surprise, but I'm not sure how effectively. She's not looking at me though, her eyes and thoughts somewhere else.

"But you're . . ." I duck my head, knowing there's no way to end that sentence without sounding rude.

"I found myself like most girls in their twenties do, having a rough patch."

Whatever it is couldn't have stuck too badly, because she seems almost nostalgic about it. Just nostalgic enough that I decide to push my luck.

"And that's how you met my mom."

She turns her head to the opening of the trail, which has appeared in front of us sooner than I expected.

"You remind me of her."

I hold my breath so I don't laugh. I'm nothing like my mom. She's organized and whip smart and—well, a lot more like Savvy than like me.

"Blunt," Pietra clarifies. "In a good way, I mean. You seem like someone who says what they think."

Well, she's wrong about that, if the last sixteen years of my life are any indication. But maybe that's starting to change.

"I *think* you and my parents should talk out whatever happened."

Dale lets out another sigh from behind me. "I *think* we should table this discussion for a time when we've all had a chance to cool off."

Pietra has already shifted gears, going back into mother hen mode, squinting at the cut on my face. "Maybe some turmeric," she tells me. "It's a natural antibiotic, and I definitely have some in the first aid kit in the car. Oh, and coconut oil, to prevent scarring."

"You're going to smell like a farmer's market when she's done with you," Dale informs me.

I nod, following them to their car. Considering there is about a bajillion years' worth of science behind the perfectly good modern medicine just down the path at the camp office, it doesn't make much sense, but one thing does: I know exactly where the roots of Savvy's Instagram came from now.

And, as if conjured by my brain, there is Savvy, flanked by my parents. Pietra is elbows deep in her first aid kit, and Dale is crouched to let Rufus lick his face, so I'm not expecting them to pop up as fast as they do, or the low "What the *fuck?*" that comes out of Pietra's mouth.

Then there's a "*Shit*" and a "Hold on" and "What were you *thinking?*" until Savvy and I can't keep up with who's saying what. Our eyes connect, and through the chaos, there is a pulse of understanding that goes deeper than friendship, deeper than sisterhood: it is the pulse of understanding between two people who are simultaneously and extremely fucked.

twenty-five

I'm not even sure, in the end, what gets said. Mostly it's a lot of yelling. Pietra yelling at my mom, Savvy yelling at Pietra, my dad yelling at me, Dale yelling at Rufus to stop barking his head off, which is mostly why we are having to yell to be heard in the first place. Once Finn and Mickey come sprinting around the corner, we go quiet at once, six people clearly unfamiliar with making a scene.

Mickey yanks Finn by the elbow, and he lets himself get led away, and then we're all panting in the parking lot like we were in an hour-long battle royale instead of a minute of slightly raising our voices.

Pietra's hand is firmly wrapped around Savvy's arm. "We're contacting our lawyer the minute we get off this island."

Savvy and I both blink at her. "Lawyer?" we ask in unison.

I'm surprised how firm my mom's voice is, how much resolve is back since yesterday. "That won't be necessary. The girls won't be—"

"I'll decide what's necessary. Especially when I see you blatantly breaking the terms of our settlement by coming anywhere near *my* daughter, let alone coercing her somewhere without other witnesses present."

The words *lawyer* and *settlement* rattle loud in my ears. It's not that I didn't believe my parents when they said it was bigger than we were. I just didn't think it was bad enough to say things like that.

"Oh please," says Savvy, too fired up to notice. "You *all* know that Abby and I did this."

I try not to shrink. My parents' eyes snap to me, and even though I avoid them, I can feel the heat of them coming at me like a flamethrower.

Dale sucks in a breath, and I think, dumbly, that he is saying something to de-escalate the situation. Instead, he says, "We can't take legal action. Savvy is eighteen. She'd have to put a restraining order on them herself."

Pietra firms her resolve. "Then that's what we'll do."

"In what universe do you think I'd agree to *that*?"

"Nobody has to take any legal action," says my mom. "The girls won't be allowed to see each other anymore. That should settle the matter."

The words jolt me back into my body in an instant. "You can't do that."

My dad's voice is quiet and grim. "We can for the next year."

"This is—are you *shitting* me?" I exclaim. "She practically lives down the block. You can't just lock me up in a tower, like some kind of prisoner—"

"Maybe it's time we have more rules for you anyway," says my mom, in that "quit while you're ahead" voice I usually only ever hear her use when my brothers are at one another's throats.

The rage is white-hot and entirely inconvenient, given I am supposed to be focusing on the very urgent, Abby-made disaster at hand, but I can't help myself. "More *rules*?" I demand. "You have me scheduled within an inch of my life and you want *more* rules?"

My dad's lips are a thin line. "Pack your bags, Abby. We're leaving in the morning, and you're coming with us."

I am not a person who lets herself cry in public, but the idea of them taking this place away is gutting. This place where I can learn and still have enough room to breathe, so I actually *enjoy* it. This place where I have friends on all sides—old ones, new ones, ones who I happen to be related to and didn't know about for sixteen years. This place where I can stumble into a new corner of the universe every day and take photos of things I've never seen, drink up the world and feel like a part of it, instead of like it's passing me by.

I've been waiting for this feeling ever since Poppy died. Now it's gone, too.

Savvy sees that she's going to have to rein me in, and jumps in before I can spiral further. "Or the four of you can get over yourselves, and whatever happened, so we can *all* see each other. Like normal people."

"That's impossible."

"Why? What's so unforgivable that—"

"Savannah," my mom starts, "it's not—"

"No. Tell her," says Pietra.

My mom takes a step back as if Pietra has slapped her. "Pet," she says. A nickname. A white flag. It hovers between them for a second, but Pietra lets it go with the breeze.

"Tell her what you did," says Pietra. Her face is splotched with tears, but her voice is eerily firm. "Tell her how you gave her to us, and then you *changed your mind.* Handed her to us, then scooped her up from the nursery and left the goddamn hospital with her."

My mom isn't crying this time. "I . . . Pietra, you know I—"

"Tell her how you said it was a mistake. Just 'postpartum brain.' Tell her how you told me everything was fine, and let us take her home, and how a week later we were served papers from some lawyer, trying to *take our baby back,* because after everything we'd been through, you'd *changed your fucking mind.*"

"If we could go back," says my dad. "If we'd known—"

Pietra shakes her head, unwilling to hear it. "I knew I couldn't have kids. I waited my whole life for her. And she was *mine*—the moment you asked me to take her. Before she was born. She was *mine*." Pietra is sobbing now. Dale is tearing up too, his hands on her shoulders, like they are used to absorbing this specific pain from each other. "The terror of losing her. That you would win, and get her back. You can't imagine what it was like."

The words may be an excuse, but my mom says them like an apology. "You can't imagine what it was like, giving her up."

Savvy and I stare at each other as if we're on opposite sides of a hole we've blown into the earth. We've wanted the truth for so long, but this feels less like a truth and more like a grenade.

"But you could have other kids," says Pietra.

"Oh my god."

All four adults' heads swivel to me, which is how I realize I've said the words out loud.

"I wasn't an accident." I'm just repeating what my mom said last night; it's the final twist of a key that just got shoved into a lock. The last bit of information I need to confirm an ugly truth. I look over at them to ask, but the answer is already in their faces, was already tense in the air between us back in the hotel. "You had me so fast because you were sad about Savvy, and needed a replacement baby."

Everybody goes quiet, the battle temporarily forgotten. I wish I hadn't said anything. It's worse than their anger, than the lies, than everything else that's built up to this: it's pity.

My parents stare at me, ashen, and then at each other. They're trying to do that freaky thing where they come up with a solution without saying a word. Trouble is, they can't think of one fast enough.

I swipe at my eyes with the heel of my hand. "Nice." I mean for it to sound scathing. Instead it sounds pathetic.

My mom shifts toward me, and so does Pietra, like they both want to soothe me but don't know how. And suddenly the whole thing is excruciating. My dumb eyes all watery, them staring at me, even Rufus coming over to cuddle himself against me like my self-pity is so thick that he can smell it in the air.

"Let's . . ."

I don't let my mom finish. "Fuck off," I bite out, stunning us all. The words make me feel solid again, rock-hard and unforgiving. I don't even mean them. They're just better than crying. *Fuck you.*"

I need to get out of here, *now*.

"Abby, wait!"

It's Savvy who calls me back when I take off, and unfortunately there's no way to outrun the queen of cardio and HIIT. Sure enough, she's reached me before I'm even halfway to my cabin, and I go skidding to a halt to avoid crashing into her.

"Savvy—"

"Abby, wait. Just listen. We're making progress, I know it. Come back."

My mouth drops open. I was going for indignant, but I am sabotaged by the fact that I am openmouthed wheezing and Savvy basically glided over here on wings.

"Progress?" I repeat. "I'm sorry, were we watching the same car crash?"

Savvy shakes her head. "It's gotta get worse before it gets better. Get all the poison out. And it's finally getting out, and—"

"And we should have just left them *alone*."

My voice sounds wretched. I don't want to be mad. I've spent my whole life avoiding this feeling, and now it's itching under my skin, swelling in my ribs, I know exactly why—but right now mad is all I have. If don't stay mad it's going to turn into something much worse.

"And then what?" Savvy asks, lowering her voice and pulling

me off the main path. Yet again we have piqued other campers' interest—not as two sisters, but as a camper mouthing off to a junior counselor. "Never see each other again?"

I'm supposed to lower my voice, but somehow that information doesn't get past my brain.

"At least we would have had two more weeks. And maybe a chance to do something without setting the whole thing on fire," I say. And then, privately: *Maybe a chance to keep existing in the world without knowing I was nothing more than a fix-it. Runner-up. Second place.*

That's not fair, and I know it. Not to my parents, who never once made me feel like anything less than the center of their universe, even with all my brothers. And not to Savvy, who didn't ask for any of this.

But it doesn't make the hurt go away, and right now, I need to go away with it. Give it a place to breathe. A place to scream.

"That's just like you, though, isn't it, Abby? Avoiding the issue." She doesn't say it in an accusatory way. It's worse—she's encouraging me. There's the same motivational gleam in her eye she gets in her Instagram stories, before she shares her mantra of the week, one of "Savvy's Savvies." I wish I could swipe out of it, but real life doesn't come with force quit. "You're miserable with all the tutoring, and you won't tell your parents. You want to be a photographer, but you're too scared to give your work a fighting chance. You have a thing for Leo, but—"

"Would you *shut up?*" I blurt. The embarrassment is blinding, white-hot, stabbing into every single pore of my skin. "Do you realize what just happened? Everybody wanted you. *Everybody* did. And instead of getting the kid who followed the rules and got good grades and did all the shit my parents wanted out of a daughter, they got me. Thoughtless, stupid, untalented *me.*"

This time I'm the one who notices the people pausing

around us. Izzy, Cam, and Jemmy chief among them, hovering between us and the cafeteria with the same conflicted looks of people who want to help but don't know how.

I duck my head, my face so hot I can practically feel it burning the ground I'm staring at.

"Abby," says Savvy, her voice low and encouraging. "I don't want to waste a bunch of time telling you how untrue all of that is."

"Then don't. The last thing I need is one of your Instagram pep talks."

She frowns but doesn't back down. Instead she squares her shoulders, her resolve hardening. "It isn't about *Instagram*. If you would just be receptive to a little advice—"

"Because that's done *wonders* for me."

"What's that supposed to mean?"

What it's supposed to mean is that I *did* listen to her. I worked up the nerve to tell Leo my feelings, and before I could get a word out he crushed them into fine dust. I got over my self-consciousness and tried to show my parents my photos, and they didn't care enough to look. Every piece of "advice" Savvy has given me has led me down a path where I'm worse off than before.

"You act like you know everything, like you have the answers to fix everyone, but you're just as messed up as the rest of us, Savvy." Her eyes are wide from a blow I haven't even landed yet, but it doesn't stop me from throwing it. "I saw those old pictures. You used to be fun and hang out with your friends, but that stupid Instagram is your whole personality now. You're just a control freak with nice hair."

She blinks hard, hurt flashing in her eyes, and I've done it— cracked the impenetrable force that is Savannah Tully. All these years of holding it in, of not letting myself get angry, and now I've gone so far over the edge I don't know how to get back.

"That's not fair," Savvy says, so quietly I almost don't hear it.

Of course it isn't. None of this is *fair*. But I can't hold my tears back long enough to answer. I point myself in the direction of the nearest trail, wait until I am out of her line of sight, and start to bawl.

twenty-six

By the time I slink into the kitchen after dinner I am less of a girl and more of an emotionally derailed swamp creature, my face puffy, my hair in so many directions no tie could hope to tame it. I can't decide how to be when I walk in—sheepish, defensive, or apologetic—but Leo's there, with a plate of food next to him that has way too many Flamin' Hot Cheetos on the side to be meant for anyone but me, and all pretense goes out the window.

"You heard our little sideshow?"

Leo nudges the plate across the counter. "Clear as Day."

I'm too upset by everything else in my life that it eclipses any reason I have to be upset with him. Even when I am at my worst he knows exactly what to say to soften my edges, still looks at me like I am something precious to him.

I let out my usual groan, and our bit has played out, some tentative order between us restored. I'm bracing myself for Leo to try to make peace between me and Savvy, but he lowers his voice and says, "Do you want to talk about it?"

I do, but I don't. I do, but not right now, when there's really nothing to say that doesn't lead me right back where I started: mad at everyone, but mostly at myself.

"I'm too hungry."

He lets out a laugh and grabs the plate and walks over to me, but instead of handing it over, he sets it down on the shiny metal counter by the door. Then he puts his hands on my shoulders, this quiet beat of asking permission. I don't even let myself look him in the eye. I lean in the rest of the way, because I'm tired. I'm so tired. My brain feels hollowed out and my heart hurts, and if I really do have to quit Leo, maybe I can put it off until tomorrow, when I leave camp for good.

I burrow my face into his shirt, into sweat and cinnamon, a little bitter, a little sweet.

"I'm sorry I ditched you for dinner," I mumble into him.

There's no way any regular human could decipher what I said, but Leo still manages. "When you didn't come back I was worried something happened to you."

I stiffen, only because it's hard to tack the guilt of that onto the guilt of everything else.

"I know," he says, misinterpreting the stiffness. "Yet again— what did you call it?—Benvolio-ing you."

I pull away, nudging his shoulder with the heel of my hand.

"It's probably my last night here," I tell him.

Leo nods, pulling back to look at me. He tilts his head toward the door. We wander outside, wordlessly settling back on the bench where we watched the lightning streak—except this time the sun is only just starting to set, the sky clear enough that we can see the light gleaming across the water and the beginnings of yellows and oranges where mountains meet the sky.

Leo and I sit with a full foot of distance between us, an invisible barrier. I can't decide whether it's a disappointment or a relief, so I decide not to decide at all. Instead I tuck into the dinner Leo saved for me, only realizing just *how* hungry I am once I take the first bite and start coming at it like a lion.

"What *is* this?"

Leo glances toward the water. "Pork menudo. Another Filipino dish. Mickey taught me how to make it," he says, embarrassed but pleased. "Except traditionally there aren't Flamin' Hot Cheetos crushed into it."

I crack a smile. He knows me too well. "I'm glad you and Mickey laid down your spatulas and decided to make peace."

"Turns out making menudo is a hell of a lot easier than making war," he says. "Also, Mickey was kicking my ass."

"Eh, you held your own."

I shift some of the dinner on my plate, easing into the bench, recognizing this moment for what it is—not a chance to confront Leo, but a chance to have the kind of conversation we had before I let my stupid feelings get in the way. Maybe the last one we'll get in a long while.

Except Leo leans in with one of those stupidly compelling grins of his, one where he's so excited about something that he's a little bit out of his own body, and the thought of keeping my distance is shot to hell.

"But she's gone *way* beyond dishes now," he tells me. "Like— she tells me all the stories behind how she learned them from her aunts, the ones here, and the ones in Manila, too. And tons of stuff about her family. Like how her grandma's convinced that if you leave rice on a plate it means you won't ever get married. Or how her aunts think when someone drops something in the kitchen it means someone's coming to visit."

He's at an infectious level of "information dump," the kind that pulls me in with its own force.

"The way Finn and I took care of kitchen duty, we should be expecting a lot of visitors."

He laughs, pulling out his phone and opening it up to an infinitely long thread.

"Her younger cousins have been putting her in random WhatsApp groups to prank her all summer. They ambushed me last week and put me in one, too. Now they're all spamming us with K-pop links and Disney lip dubs they're making on some app."

"Well that's ridiculously precious."

"Eh, it's all fun and games until they swore up and down they were teaching me how to say 'good morning' in Tagalog and I ended up telling Mickey to 'go eat shit.'"

Even in the depths of my possibly bottomless self-pity, that gets a laugh out of me.

Leo knocks his shoulder into mine, another reminder of how fast we've filled up the air between us. "Yeah, yeah, *kumain ng tae.*"

"I would, but my mouth's already full," I say, tilting my head at the plate I'm eating from so sloppily that several curious birds have flitted their way over. Carefully, I ask, "Do you think it's helped at all? I mean . . . with the not knowing?"

Leo considers the question, staring down at my half-eaten plate.

"In some ways, kind of? I mean, who even knows if my parents came from anywhere near where her family is, but . . . it's nice to learn about anyway."

There's a beat, then, that I know isn't the end of the thought, but the thought taking a new shape. I watch it in his face the same way I always have, wishing I could take it for granted. Wishing I knew if there would be a chance to watch it again.

"It's weird to think . . . in some other life . . . Carla and I would be living there. Like there's some alternate version of us who do. You know?"

I almost laugh. My alternate version is a few hundred yards away, no doubt busting gum chewers in the rec room and fuming over what I said earlier. Leo catches the ghost of it on my face, and his head dips as if he's thinking the same thing.

"The test, though—I'm kind of relieved I didn't find anybody," he admits. "I don't know if I was really thinking about what might happen if I did. What it might dig up."

I nudge some dirt on the ground with the heel of my shoe. "I hope what happened with me and Savvy wasn't what scared you off."

That hope is dashed when Leo answers without hesitation.

"That's just it, though. It's different. This thing with your parents—they must have known you'd find out eventually. This whole mess is more on them than on you." He shakes his head. "But with me—if these people are even still out there—they set the terms. Nobody ever lied to anybody about it. Which means there's a chance if I did find them, I'd be digging up something they're not prepared to handle. Something *I'm* not prepared to handle."

I'm not really sure what to say, or if there's anything *to* say. We both know he's right. But it makes me ache for him anyway, knowing Leo well enough to understand that the decision is less about protecting himself and more about protecting other people.

And if there's anything I've learned in the last week, it's that we all have a lot more to protect than we think.

"I'm letting it go for now." Leo says the words more to the ground than to me. It's clear he's been thinking about this a lot more than he let on, and the decision isn't easy for him. But he looks up at me with fresh resolve and says, "I want to focus more on the future. On this school in New York. It's kind of opened this door where I can learn more about cooking, but also about my background. It's not what I was trying to do, but maybe—maybe I was meant to feel like this so it could lead me here. Maybe . . ."

I nod, compelled by the possibility at the end of that *maybe*, by the weight of it. He's always been so driven, always thrown his whole self into his ideas. And I've always been the first one to jump with him. It's weird to think I won't get to anymore. No matter what happens between us, something is definitively ending—his future is thousands of miles away, and mine's still mired in high school and big decisions and the mess I left in the parking lot earlier today.

"So you think you'll ever go out and meet Mickey's cousins?" I ask. "Teach them how to say 'good morning' in Elvish?"

"I'm going to talk to Carla about taking a trip next summer." He pauses, some thought poised on the tip of his teeth, and adds, "And I think—well, this is a *long* way off, and assuming I don't get laughed out of New York—but Mickey and I started talking about one day opening, like, a fusion restaurant. Menudo meets Cheetos. Lasagna balls meet banana leaves. Mickey's childhood meets Leo's. You know?"

I do know—I can practically see it. Somewhere medium-size and homey and warm, the kind of restaurant where everyone who goes there once immediately finds an excuse to go again.

I wonder if it will be in Seattle. I swallow down the lump in my throat, too scared to ask.

"Well, shit," I say. "If I'm going to invest in this I've gotta find a way to get rich, *fast*."

Leo lets out a rushed laugh, like he's been waiting to float this past me for a while and is glad he finally got the chance.

"We'll settle for you taking staged food pics for the website."

"As long as I get to eat everything I shoot, you two have got yourself a deal."

We both settle into this quiet that becomes less of a coincidence and more of an understanding. The grins on our faces falter at the same time, our eyes struggling to hold each other's.

"So . . . tomorrow."

"Tomorrow," I echo, turning back to the water.

"You're really leaving?"

I lift up my palms in a half shrug. "Doesn't look like I have a choice."

"You're not gonna push back?"

I try not to stiffen. Leo may know that I'm not good at fighting my own battles, but he doesn't understand this battle isn't mine. It's just one I've been in the cross fire of since before I was born. "No."

Leo lowers his voice, the question gentler than the one that came before it. "You're not mad?"

I don't really want to talk about it, but it's Leo. I can tell myself to put him out of my mind, to keep my distance, but nothing can erase more than a decade's worth of spilling my guts out to him.

"I was. I am. But mostly I guess I'm just—"

I'm going to say *scared*, but it feels too dumb. These are my parents.

And I'm not scared of them, really. I'm scared of me. I'm scared things are going to change, now that the truth is out in the open. I'm scared that we will be tiptoeing around one another forever, trying not to wake the sleeping beast in every room.

I'm scared I won't get to see Savvy again.

The fears build up, one on top of the other, one badly constructed, extremely flammable mound. I hadn't put reason or words to them before, but that's the thing. Leo is my touchstone. My compass. The steadying force that puts all the shaky things into view.

So I skip past all that and say the thing that scares me most—the one that has followed me since long before I found out about this.

"I'm—I'm scared I'll always feel like I'm not good enough."

Leo jumps on this like he's the lifeguard of my brain, plucking out a drowning thought. "Your parents don't think that. I know they—"

"It's not only them. It's . . . everything. With this thing with Savvy, with school, with . . ."

I'm getting too close to *us*—to the BEI, and what happened after. To how Leo and I are so far apart that I didn't even get to be a part of the biggest decision he's ever made. To this perpetual feeling that only gets heavier with every year, that I'm not cut out for what the world has in store.

"Abby . . . things are always going to move for different people at different times. You've gotta be patient. Set your own pace." His voice goes so quiet that it sounds like one of the little waves that laps on the shore, like he's pressing some quiet current into my ears. "It's like I told you at the beginning of the summer. You're an original."

I huff out a laugh. I can hear the smile in his voice, even though I'm not looking at him.

"Good things are coming, Abby. I know that because I know you. You're talented and you're stubborn and you're braver than you give yourself credit for."

I want to believe the words so badly—not just because I've been trying to grow into words like that my whole life. But because the words are coming from him.

"I wish you saw yourself the way I see you."

I press my eyes closed for a moment, but when I open them I'm every bit as shaken. "Leo . . ." It's not confronting him, really, but it's as close as I can get after a day like this. "You didn't even tell me you were thinking of leaving."

His mouth opens slightly, fast enough that he can't hide the surprise on his face.

"Abby, it wasn't like that, really," he insists. "I just—I didn't even think I could get in. I didn't tell Connie either."

I wince.

"Yeah, but we're . . ." *Different,* I want to say. But I guess we're not.

I glance over at him, grappling for a change of subject. But his eyes are so earnest that mine get stuck on them, tipping me

over into some part of him that's always been mine. Some ache
under the surface we've always shared, except now it's as plain
as ever, the light of the dimming sun exposing it in every plane
of his face.

"I'm gonna take your picture."

Leo watches me for a beat. "No, you're not."

"I am."

"You don't photograph people. Like, ever."

"Yeah, well—I'm getting some practice." This is not exactly a
lie, given the Phoenix Cabin shenanigans I've been document-
ing. He's right, though. I don't photograph people.

But *this*—the sky casting its warmth on him, like his face
was made to catch light. The gold in his eyes, the straight plane
of his nose, the sharp curve of his jaw—these parts of him I've
tried so hard not to notice, now on such full display that trying
to look away would be like trying to deny every moment I pined
for him, when it feels like the last thing I want to do is forget.

I pull out Poppy's camera, glad I snuck into the cabin to grab
it during dinner. It takes an extra second to turn on, one that
seems to last so long that it's not the camera, but the universe:
Are you sure about this? Is this what you want?

I don't understand why it's asking until my eye is in the viewfinder, and Leo is staring at me through the lens.

This isn't a photo, I understand. It's a memory. I've spent my
whole life trying to capture perfect moments, treating each of
them like a victory. This is the first one I am capturing out of
defeat.

"Abby?"

The next twelve hours will be a minifuneral, saying goodbye
to everyone and everything here, but this is a goodbye, too. Leo
will spend the rest of summer here, and I'll spend it in summer
school. Then I'll go back to Shoreline High, with all my classes
and tutoring sessions, and Leo will be gone. The problem is

solved before it could even become a problem; I'll never have to tell Leo the truth about how I feel about him. We're out of time.

I should be relieved. Nobody's feelings will be hurt. Nobody's pride will be compromised. And nobody's heart will break except mine.

I focus Leo in the frame and click.

There's this uneasy silence that follows, me poised with the camera level with my chest, Leo's stare fixed on me like the camera was never there at all. I think about uploading the photo, and it scares me, thinking of what I might see. What I won't.

Leo breaks his gaze first. I'm not the coward anymore.

"I wish . . ." Leo leans forward, frustrated. "Oh my god. Abby!"

"What—"

"Your camera, get your camera, it's—"

"Holy *shit*."

There they are, off in the distance. A pod of orcas. They're unmistakable, slick and gleaming as their backs slide in and out of the water, their distinctive fins cresting over the ripples.

"Take the picture," says Leo. "It's the perfect shot."

Poppy's camera is too old. It doesn't have a prayer of capturing them at this distance. I could sprint to the cabin maybe, grab Kitty, and get back in time to catch something magnificent. The kind of photo I've dreamed of taking for years.

But no photo will capture this—the soar of my heart in my throat, the swell of my whole body, this weightlessness that makes me feel like we're in free fall, untethered to the earth. Without consciously deciding to, we take off at a run to the edge of the water, giddy and disbelieving, chasing this feeling louder than words.

We watch them in silent awe, our excitement pulsing off each other like something we can touch. Then it happens—one of them leaps out of the water, this joyful, enormous, impossible thing, so far offshore but somehow close enough that it feels like he is leaping just so the two of us can see.

We turn, our eyes cracking into each other's like the lightning on the first day at camp. It is energy and chaos, but rooted in something so deep that for once, it doesn't scare me. I feel strangely invincible, like the moments happening right now don't count for anything, but somehow count for everything at once.

Somewhere buried in the back of my mind, I know I shouldn't let this happen. It's the exact opposite of how I was going to handle this. But maybe it's like Savvy said, about things getting worse before they get better. Well, this is the worst thing I can think of: giving Leo another chance to reject me. And if he doesn't, giving myself a chance to know what this might feel like, even if it can never be mine.

I'm not seeing anything beyond Leo by the time my eyelids slide shut, something stronger than any one sense guiding us forward, pulling us into each other. It's inevitable. Thunder after lightning. Order after chaos. Hope after—

"Have you seen Finn?"

The kiss is interrupted before it can begin, but neither of us jump. We're frozen. His eyes are so wide on mine that I can only assume he never meant for it to happen. I'm the one who has to take control and take the quiet step back before Mickey comes into view. Leo is blushing furiously enough to warrant a trip to the nurse, but oddly, I am calm.

The feeling was enough, I think. Just to know it. To have it in my bones, make it a part of my history. There was a beautiful *before*, without an *after* to wreck it on the other side.

"Not since this afternoon," I answer for us. "Why?"

Mickey didn't even notice us nearly playing tongue hockey in full view of half the camp. Her brow is furrowed, and she's rubbing her arms so anxiously that I'm afraid she might peel Princess Jasmine clean off.

"I can't find him anywhere. I tried to cover for him, but Victoria's gonna notice soon, and—"

Leo clears his throat, wiping his palms on his shorts. "Have you checked in with Savvy?"

Mickey shakes her head. "I can't find her either, but I know Jo called, so . . ."

Leo finally steps away from me. I can sense him searching my face, but when I look over, I don't know what to make of it. It's almost like he seems disappointed, but I can't tell if it's in himself, or in me.

"Abby has to go pack, but I'll help you look," he says to Mickey. "I've got a few ideas."

They talk it over and are off in separate directions within the minute, leaving me out on the beach with my camera still dangling around my neck. I look out over the water, unsurprised to find the orcas are gone.

twenty-seven

Considering I am far less familiar with stories about Gaby the camp ghost than the dozens of Camp Reynolds returners, I should probably be the last person to follow her straight to Finn. But there I am, a mere five minutes later, standing at the base of an allegedly haunted tree with the shadow of a Finn-shaped human making long shapes on the ground.

I crunch down on a spare branch when I come to a stop, and Finn's face pops down between the branches. He takes one look at me, closes his eyes, and says, "Shit."

"Good to see you, too."

He turns his head away, toward the skyline, which is getting darker by the second. "I'm not stuck."

"That sounds like something a stuck person would say."

"Is Savvy with you?"

I don't even have the wherewithal to be offended. Even if I did, we've got much bigger problems judging from the sound of his voice, which is very much that of someone trying not to panic and doing a very bad job of it.

"Just me."

Before he can bleat out some other excuse or Finn-ism, I tug the strap of my bag so Poppy's camera is on my back, flex my wrists, and start climbing the tree. It isn't exactly an easy feat without much light, but that's the problem. There's no time to turn around and get Savvy, or turn around and get anyone, really. I've got about five minutes to coach him down before the sun ghosts us and the whole camp goes dark.

"You don't have to . . ."

I'm fast, faster than Finn's expecting. His eyes go wide at me closing in on him, big and red-rimmed and giving him away before he can turn his head.

"What are you doing up here?"

He's clinging to the tree and another branch for dear life, but at least he seems to relax once I'm up there. There's nothing between us but bark and the faded MAKE A WISH sign. Whatever plans he had of not looking at me are immediately foiled when a twig of a branch cracks under my hand and he full-body flinches.

"Don't you have your *own* problems to deal with?" he asks, voice strained.

I'm high enough now that I'm eye level with him. "Nice deflecting."

He's looking at me without looking at me, half peering and half laser-focused on the arms he has wrapped around the tree.

"Finn."

He rests his head on the tree trunk. "I . . . was climbing. And I guess I don't usually climb it by myself. And I'm . . . a little bit . . ."

"Stuck," I provide.

He blows out an embarrassed breath.

"Well, I'm here now. I'll help you down."

It feels like someone else is saying it. I'm not used to feeling like someone with authority, someone with a plan. That was always Connie in our group, or my parents at home, or the army of teachers and tutors at school. I kind of assumed I'd be bad at it.

And maybe I still am, but there's no time to overthink that now.

"Yeah," says Finn, except it sounds less like a *yeah* and more like he choked on his own spit.

I try another tactic. "Why'd you come up here in the first place?"

"For *wishing*," he says, a flash of his usual self. "Duh."

I try to think back to the wishes we made, but it feels like it's been years since he first brought me here. Leo told me once that all your skin cells replace themselves every two or three weeks, but this time it's like I felt it, every single one of them dying and being reborn, making some new version of me with edges and pieces I don't fully know how to use yet.

My wishes were so specific then. I may not have been able to fix my problems, but at least I could give them names. Now I wouldn't even know where to begin.

Which is how I remember exactly what Finn said, because it's exactly what I feel all these weeks later.

"For things to be less fucked up?"

He lets out a wheeze that might have started out a laugh, tilting his head away from me. Problem is his limbs are too occupied glomming onto the tree to swipe at his eyes or stop the quick tear that slides down his cheek.

"You know I wasn't even supposed to go to camp this summer? We were going to go on a big trip across the U.S. together, me and my mom and dad. We'd been planning it for years."

My chest is tight, wondering what's on the other end of this, knowing from the look on his face that it's about to go from bad to worse.

"But then—my mom just—*left*."

He says it with the bewilderment of someone it just happened to, like he's not stuck in this tree, but stuck in the leaving.

I wait him out, thinking he'll go on, but he's miles from these tree branches, somewhere I can't reach.

"Like she left your dad, or . . ."

Finn shakes his head, a piece of him coming back. "I mean— she just—came into my room one morning and told me she was going to Chicago to see my uncle, and did I want to come, and I said yeah. She said she'd wait for me downstairs. And I said, 'Wait, right now?' and she said yes, and I said 'I have school,' and—" Finn's ramble stops like a train that yanked its brakes, realizing it was about to go off the tracks. "I mean, I was barely even awake. I didn't think . . ."

It's almost fully dark. Whatever chance we had of using the sun's light to get us down is a lost cause, so I stop trying to rush him. I sit and let the time go with us.

"She lives there now, in Chicago. She just decided she didn't want to be with my dad anymore, so she left us both."

I latch on to what he said before, knowing it won't help but at a loss for what else to say. "But she wanted you to come with her."

Finn lets out a terse breath, finally moving his forehead off the tree to look at me. "No, she didn't. Not if she asked me like that, she didn't. You only ask someone something like that if you want the answer to be no."

I glance into the murky darkness below, trying to understand what might have been going through her head. She didn't want him to come with her because she knew his world was here. She didn't want him to feel like he had to say yes and leave everything behind, but still wanted him to know that she loved him. Because sometimes trying to protect people from your own fucked-up decisions is so impossible that there's no right and wrong way to do it—everything will explode in the end. You can only try to anticipate which direction the explosion will come from.

The thought sidles a little too close to the anger I'm not ready to let go of yet, pricks like a needle trying to deflate it. The trouble is, I understand exactly why my parents did what they did. It just doesn't change the way I feel about any of it right now.

"It wasn't a choice. It was a trap. And anyway . . ." His voice goes low. He doesn't seem afraid anymore, at least. Only tired. Ashamed. "I messed some things up after that. I told her I hated her and I never wanted to see her again."

My own *fuck you* is still rattling like a pinball through the camp.

"You didn't mean it," I say.

"I think I did, when I said it."

We're quiet for a moment.

"It's shitty," he tells me. "The way she left, I mean. I did some stuff I shouldn't have done. Messed up my grades. My dad made me come back for the whole 'Reynolds method' thing basically to punish me, but I think he just doesn't want to deal with me anymore. And my mom . . ."

"You thought she'd come home. When shit started going wrong."

His face tightens, like he's trying to hold himself still, but his jaw starts to shake. "Your parents were here in the blink of an eye," he says, sounding younger than he ever has. "They're *still* here. And mine are too mad at each other to remember I exist."

He is staring at the MAKE A WISH sign with enough intensity to set it on fire. I don't think he even means to. It's just directly in his line of sight, and there's too much darkness to look past it and see anything else.

"I thought when I got here that it would help, being with my friends. But they're all busy with actual camp jobs, and I'm . . . I got left behind."

It resonates in a way that I wish it didn't. It kind of crept up on me, that exact feeling—months of Connie being too busy to hang out, and then heading off for Europe. The shock of Leo leaving for good. Maybe it's why I've been gravitating toward Finn this whole summer. We're both trying to catch up to people who seem like they're already gone.

I know he's thinking the same thing when he says, "I'm glad you're here, though."

"Well, I'm probably not the one to be giving advice on families right now," I admit. "But I think you have to call your mom."

For once he isn't fidgeting or trying to stay a step ahead for a laugh. "What am I supposed to do, apologize?"

"Maybe nobody has to say sorry," I say quietly. "Maybe you just have to talk."

The words settle there in the branches. We're closer than we've ever been, but entire universes apart—Finn in his bedroom, me in the parking lot, both trying to relive things that happened too fast to fully live when they happened.

Finn interrupts the silence with a groan. "You know, I was gonna spend the summer trying to impress you. And here I am snotting it up stuck in a tree."

"I mean, I'm still impressed," I say, trying to lift the mood. "This height's no joke. You're basically the alpha of every squirrel on the island now."

"Except how the hell am I supposed to get back down?"

"Slowly. And at the mercy of Gaby the camp ghost."

"May she be as merciful as she is super dead."

I reach out and touch his hand, a light graze so I don't startle him. "Did you make your wish yet?"

"Nah, I was too busy trying not to become a forest pancake."

"We'll make one together. Then we'll go down."

Finn nods, shifting to tighten his grip on the tree, and closes his eyes. I shut mine too, my wish so immediate that it feels like it's been taking shape all day. It's short this time, but bigger than the word alone can hold. I wish for some kind of peace. For the lost years to count for something. For everyone to come out the other side of this stronger than they started.

Finn and I finish our wishes at the same moment, breathing them out into the black. His eyes gleam back at me, cutting through the darkness, so wide on mine that I see myself in them as much as I do him.

I lean forward and kiss him on the cheek, but it's less of a kiss and more of an understanding. There isn't a thrill, or a swoop, or some desire for it to be anything more. There is only my lips on his skin, and the quiet comfort of being seen, understood.

"Okay," I tell him, my voice firm like Savvy's when she's directing campers. "Here's what we'll do. I'll use the flashlight on my phone to light the way down. I'll go first, so you can watch what I do and copy it."

Finn swallows hard. "Yeah. Cool."

"We'll go slow."

And that we do. The same tree that took me less than a minute to climb up takes an excruciating ten to get back down. I talk Finn through every step, pausing during the occasional panic. I start to understand things about Finn that everyone else here must have already known: he is not a risk-taker, not a rebel. He's a confused kid doing his best at acting like one.

"Almost there," I tell him.

Just then my phone buzzes to life in my hands, a picture of Savvy lighting up the screen. I flinch in surprise, and there's a crunch—the slightest, stupidest misstep—and I take the last five feet of the tree tumbling, reaching out for a branch that isn't there, hitting the ground with a *thud*.

"Shit. Abby—are you okay?"

"Fine," I grumble. I don't know whether it's a lie yet. I'm still too stunned to take account of myself, but I don't want to scare him. Poppy's camera is miraculously unharmed, and that's all that really matters to me anyway. "Hold on, I'll grab the light so you can . . ."

I suck in a breath, because when I grapple for my phone in the dark, I feel it. The twinge in my left wrist that shoots all the way up my elbow, my shoulder, straight into the *oh no* part of my brain.

I ignore it, using my other hand to find the phone and shining the flashlight up toward Finn, even as the pain starts to beat in time with my heart and settle throughout my entire arm. He works his way down and scrambles over to help me up. I wave him off, using my right hand to hoist up my very bruised self.

"You're sure you're okay?"

I make a show of stretching myself out. Everything else, at least, seems to be in regular order.

"Trust me. My butt has endured *much* worse."

I can't see Finn in the dark, but I can feel his uneasy smile. He reaches out in the dark and grabs my good hand, squeezing it.

"Thanks," he says.

I squeeze back, and it feels less like we made a wish, and more of a promise. Now we just have to figure out how to keep it.

twenty-eight

"Holy *crap*, Abby."

Not the most pleasant way to wake up, and it doesn't get better from there. The throb in my wrist has escalated to a five-alarm-fire kind of pain that only seems to get worse the more awake I am. I blearily open my eyes to Cam, who is staring at my arm like it's a horror movie.

"Did you get into a fight with a *bear*?"

I follow her eyes to my wrist, which has swelled to approximately the size and shape of a mutilated balloon animal. I try to jerk it under the covers, but end up hissing in pain before I can move it more than an inch.

Izzy's head pops over to my bedside. "You need to go see the nurse."

"S'happening?" Jemmy, who is not a morning person until someone puts food in her, mumbles from the top bunk.

"My wrist looks like an angry potato," I inform her.

"Potato," she murmurs, fully asleep before the end of the word.

"Seriously," says Izzy, "nurse. Now. We'll walk you."

I sit up, my head aching and my body stiff from a crying hangover. I need water, Advil, and maybe someone to saw off my arm.

But with the pain comes an even more brutal clarity: I need to find Savvy and apologize. I never got a chance to call her back last night, and if I'm going to get dragged out of here without any idea of when I'll see her again, it has to happen with the air cleared.

"I'm fine," I say. Off Izzy's look, I add, "Okay, I'm terrible, but I'll be fine to get myself over to the office. Go grab breakfast. Save me a seat."

It's the opposite of *goodbye*, which is what I should be saying to them. But it hasn't sunk in yet, even though I figure I have about half an hour before my parents roll up. They called Victoria last night to let me know when to expect them. It's not nearly enough time, but it's the only time I've got.

I pull on a sweater to hide my gross wrist, even though it's already hot enough that stepping out of the cabin feels like breathing in lukewarm soup. I don't want Finn to see and feel bad, and I don't want my parents to make a big scene about it before we go.

I'm outside the kitchens when I'm accosted by none other than Finn, who looks about as tired as I feel. He slows to a jog when he reaches me, looking pale in the light of day, but with some of that Finn spark back in his eyes.

"I wanted to make sure you're okay," he says, skidding to a stop. "And thank you, for last night."

I wave my good hand at him.

His smile is smaller than usual. "I mean, I'd probably still be up there if it weren't for you. They'd probably have had to call the fire brigade or something. And my 'cool guy' rep would have really gone down the drain."

"That's mostly why I helped. Heaven forbid a cooler guy upstage you here."

Finn lets out an appreciative laugh, rocking back on his heels and pushing his mop of hair back with his hand. "Well—I'll find you somewhere on the internet. See you when camp's out?"

"Sure."

Some of the usual mischief sneaks back into his face. "Maybe then I'll take you on a real date. Not a terrifying one that's forty feet above sea level."

Before I can react, he wraps me in a hug so tight that my feet leave the ground. I give him a one-armed hug back on autopilot, aware of the sudden and searing heat of Leo's eyes on us both. Finn pulls away and tweaks me on the cheek. "Bye for now, Bubbles."

"Bye."

There's a beat when Finn is scampering off and I'm standing there watching him leave that I consider not turning around. Just walking around the other side of the building and going to breakfast, leaving Leo and his eyes there to make holes in the dirt.

"Well, I guess I know why you didn't text after you found him," says Leo. He's trying for casual, but failing so spectacularly that I can hear the edge in his voice even with my back turned. "You and Finn are really a thing, then?"

I guess we're cutting right to the chase. I turn around, braced for his irritation, but not everything else—the hurt shining in his eyes, heavy in his shoulders.

I take a breath. He isn't allowed to feel hurt. Not after the past few months, and certainly not after the last two days.

"So what if we are?" I say. Whatever was brewing in me yesterday is right back, looking for trouble. This time, I don't mind.

Leo blinks at me, like he had some script for how this conversation was going to go and I tossed it in the mud.

"Okay." He says it slowly, his eyes on me but his face already tilting toward the ground. "Well. I hope you two are . . . happy."

The words ring stilted and false, and he hovers there, like he can't decide if he wants to keep pressing into this or turn and leave. I surprise both of us by making the decision for him.

"Okay, that's it." He snaps to attention, rising to meet my words. "So what if I'm with Finn? Why do you even care?"

"Why do I *care?*"

I press my heels farther into the dirt, squaring myself for this. Here it is—the moment that was going to happen on the other side of the BEI, and last night's repeat of it. This was the inevitability. This was the bend that wouldn't break. The truth neither of us would face.

"Well, first of all," he says, taking my cue, "he's a bad influence. You don't think I heard about him dragging you up that stupid *wishing* tree last night? Or last week when you two tried to climb the roof of the cabin? Or the other day when you snuck off the damn property to take pictures from the neighboring camp's docks, or—"

"He's not putting me in danger, he's doing those things because he's helping me—"

"Because he's trying to get you *alone*—"

"—and actually cares about my photography."

I say the words dismissively, trying to cut past this argument to the heart of it, which is extremely not about Finn and very much about us.

"You think I don't care about your photography?" Leo asks, with an indignant laugh. "I don't . . . even know what to say to that. I mean—if you think I'm not supportive of you, there's an entire Instagram page full of your photos that shows just how wrong you are."

I grit my teeth. We both know what I'm talking about.

"You sure seem to like holding me back."

"When have I ever—"

"Not with the photography," I cut in. The chaos of my anger has tighte elf e a shape I can hold on to, giving every word that comes out of me its own weight. "It's the push-and-pull this whole damn summer. You don't like me enough to want me, but you don't want me to be happy with anybody else."

Leo stares at me, so stunned that I might have curled the accusation into a fist and hurled it into him. But it's like a dam has burst and everything is rushing up behind it, fighting its way to the surface.

"I mean, I get it, Leo. You don't think of me the way I think, or *thought*, of you." My resolve is already leaking out of me, so I have to bite the words out, saying them more to Leo's chest than his face. "And who knows what would have happened if Connie hadn't—" I shake my head. "But it's fine. I made myself get over it, because that's what friends do. Because you're *important* to me. But you don't even care enough about me to *consider* telling me you're leaving before you up and go."

My voice breaks on the last word. Something in his face splinters, and I know I've finally gotten through to him. I don't live in the comfortable in-between now, of pretending Leo knows and doesn't know the way I feel. It's all laid out bare, and me right along with it.

"You think I didn't tell you because you're not important to me?"

I can only stare at him. I don't know how else to answer without giving too much more of myself away.

"Don't you get it?" Leo's eyes well up, and I'm the one who's stunned into silence. "I almost didn't leave at all. Because I—of course I like you, Abby. I've wanted to tell you, but I—I knew I couldn't do it if I was ever gonna leave."

The breath I was going to let out catches in my throat, my anger dissolving so fast that my bones have almost forgotten how to hold me up without it.

"What?"

He doesn't say anything, but he doesn't have to. I see my own confusion and hurt reflected back at me. I see the gears turning in his brain the way they're turning in mine, the enormity of what he just said, of what it means and what it doesn't.

"Leo, I . . ." I want to be happy. I've waited for months, hoped against hope, to hear him say this to me. But I never thought he'd follow it up with something so bleak. "You think I'd stand in the way of you going? After everything we've been through, is that really what you think of me?"

Leo closes his eyes, breathing something out that's heavier than air.

"No, Abby, that's just it. I was afraid I'd stand in my own way. Because I knew if you felt the same way, I'd never be able to go."

We're both holding our breath, knowing the next few moments are going to define a lifetime's worth of what we are to each other. We took reckless steps to get here, but we'll have to take careful ones to get back.

I shake my head. "I'd have made you go. You know that, right?" I'm not even thinking when I take a step back toward him and lift my hand up. "That's what—"

"Oh my god. *Abby.*"

His eyes are locked on my wrist. The pain has seared through my arm, an inconvenient and ill-timed reminder that I am broken in the figurative sense and in a very literal one. I try to shove my sleeve over it, but Leo's too fast, his touch feather-light but firm enough that I know better than to jerk it back.

"What the *hell* . . . Finn," he says, answering his own question. There's less anger in it, more worry. He's gone into full Benvolio mode, and there's no getting him back. "This looks really bad. We've got to—"

Leo looks up at the sound of footsteps. I already know who it is from the look on his face, but that doesn't make me any more prepared to hear the quake in my mom's voice when she says, "We're going home. *Now.*"

twenty-nine

The dumbest thing I can do is try to hide my wrist, both because it's clear that my mom has already seen it, and also because it hurts like a bitch. But that is exactly what I do, and the pained squeak that comes out of my mouth only makes it worse.

"What happened?" ask my mom and Leo in unison.

I look over at my mom and see that she has my duffel bag in her hands. Somehow, in the last ten minutes, she has taken the liberty of inviting herself into my cabin, shoving all my stuff into it, and carting it out. She means business.

"I fell."

She opens her mouth, clearly not accepting that as an adequate answer, but she's entered fight-or-flight mode and she is decidedly in *flight*.

"We'll stop and get it looked at on the way," she says. "Let's go, your dad's waiting in the car."

"Wait—I can't—I have to say—"

"Please don't make this difficult."

There is this resignation in her voice I'm not used to hearing. Something about it blisters in my ears, reminding me of the truth I've been trying to come to terms with not only in the last few months, but all my life—I'm a problem.

Well, serves them right. They had me to solve one. Figures I'd create a dozen more.

My voice is hard, matching hers. "Let me say goodbye to Savvy. You at *least* owe me that."

She falters for a split second, and I seize on it, backing away from her. "I'll be right back," I tell her. I turn to acknowledge Leo, but he's gone. I quickly scour the area for him, but he must have gone back into the kitchen.

"Crap."

I take off, but before I find Savvy I nearly run headfirst into Mickey, who's coming back from a run with Rufus. She pulls her headphones out of her ears, squinting at the hobble I've adopted in an attempt not to mess up my wrist.

"Have you seen Savvy?"

She glances at my arm, drops her mouth in horror, and looks back at my face. "Uh—"

"Seriously, my parents are here, I've gotta find her."

The horror slides off Mickey's face into a deeper, disquieting kind of fear. "She's not with you?"

"No. Why?"

"Because she didn't come back to the cabin after she talked to Jo last night," says Mickey, the words coming out too fast. She was breathing hard before, but now she's on the verge of hyperventilating. "I just figured with everything going on that she was with you. She's not with you anymore?"

The chill that goes through me is more immediate than the one from Polar Bear Swim, more ancient than anything I can shake off. "She hasn't been with me at all."

There's a beat, and then Mickey starts whisper-screaming, "Shit. *Shit.* Shit, shit, shit—"

"When did you last see her?"

"She was outside the cabin, taking the call, and I was—I didn't want to hear it, I . . ." Her face has gone ashen. "She was trying to get better service and walked out toward the main office, and that's it. That's the last time I saw her."

Only then do I remember the flash of her phone number lighting up my screen, right before I fell from the tree. I pull out my phone and call her back, Mickey's eyes glued to me for the few long seconds it takes.

"Voicemail," I mutter.

Mickey looks like she's about to bawl. "Rufus wanted to go with her, but I was feeling sorry for myself, and I made him stay and cuddle with me. Oh my god. Oh my *god*—"

"It's okay," I hear myself saying. The girl with angry parents in the car, and a wrist ballooning more by the second, and a brain that's basically in free fall, is telling someone it'll be okay. "We'll find her. Is there some kind of camp protocol? Anyone we're supposed to call?"

Mickey sucks in a breath, drawing herself up and blinking until her eyes are clear. "Yeah. I'll go tell Victoria."

"I'll . . ."

Mickey is full-on sprinting away already, leaving me in the dust. I stand there, glancing back to see if my mom has followed me. But it's only Rufus, staring at me fully alert, sans slobber or stolen camp paraphernalia in his mouth, like he's waiting for a command.

My parents are gonna kill me.

"Let's go."

thirty

I'm not a runner, but today I sure as hell am. Rufus starts sprinting ahead of me, recognizing the trail I'm headed for before I reach it, and my adrenaline somewhat cancels out the pain of my wrist. Whether it's going to cancel out the pain of being grounded for the rest of my life is another matter entirely.

What's strange is that I'm not panicking. Maybe it's naive, but I know that Savvy is okay. First of all, if she were really in danger, she would have called an authority figure long before she called me last night. And second of all, I doubt there's much this island could throw at Savvy that she doesn't have some solution for hidden in one of her leggings' pockets.

Rufus and I make slow but steady progress, kicking up mud from last night's rain. The trail is way more slippery than I remember. I nearly topple over twice and actually do a third time, just barely catching myself with my unmangled hand.

Still, even with the mud working against us, we make it up to the abandoned archery spot Savvy showed me within minutes. We pass the tree where Savvy's and Mickey's names are carved into the trunk and skid to a stop—at least, Rufus does. My feet stop, but my body doesn't, the mud creating some kind of nature-made Slip 'n Slide. And before I know it, I'm slip 'n' sliding right to the edge of the spectacular view of camp, and kissing it goodbye as I swoop down, down, down on my butt, finally coming to a stop with a muddy *thunk* at the bottom of the minicliff.

Once I'm pretty sure I have stopped sliding into an abyss of mud, I open my eyes to see one mucked-up, frizzy-haired, wild-eyed Savannah Tully, who is—praise be to Gaby the camp ghost—very much intact.

"First off, are you okay?" she asks.

I am too embarrassed to answer, knocking my head back into the mud and feeling it congeal in my hair. She correctly interprets this as a yes.

"Second off, please for the love of all that is holy tell me you brought help."

Rufus lets out a woof, before promptly disappearing from our sight.

"Other than Rufus, whose last two brain cells are committed to eating strangers' iPhones."

I close my eyes. "No."

There's a silence, and then: "I am so fucking hungry. Abby. I'm at the level of hungry where I might actually eat you."

"I'm not Instagrammable enough to eat," I mumble, still too humiliated to move. "There's some gum in my pocket?"

"You're dead to me. Hand it over."

I pull myself up with my good arm and reach into my front pocket, pulling out my lanyard and some admittedly warm cinnamon gum that's been chilling there for I'm not sure how long. Savvy rips open two pieces and crams them in her mouth, half crying, "God, I wish this were food."

"Well, people definitely know you're missing now, so I'm sure it's only a matter of time before—"

"People only *just* started looking? Are you *kidding* me? I've been stuck down here for—what the fuck time is it, anyway? My phone's dead."

I reach for my phone, but it's not in my back pocket. Savvy's eyes go so wide and murderous on mine that I almost want to strangle myself so she doesn't have to put in the effort.

"It must have slipped out of my pocket when I fell."

"Dead. To. Me."

"Fair enough," I say, trying to scoop as much mud off my legs as I can manage. "But for what it's worth, I'm really glad you're okay."

The words puncture past her frustration, then past something deeper than that. She sighs, then settles down next to me, leaning in and resting her head on my shoulder. I rest mine on top of hers, and the two of us take a long breath and make some quiet forgiveness.

"I guess if I'm gonna be stuck down here, it's nice to have company."

For a few moments there is this weird, completely inappropriate relief, considering how screwed we are. Our well-being may be in semidanger, but this, at least, isn't. Whatever *this* is, it's solid now. Not enough to have a name, maybe, but enough to withstand a storm.

We both stare up at the little ledge that brought us down.

"You're sure there's no way out of here?"

"Trust me, I've tried. I also just considered standing on your shoulders and abandoning you long enough to cram some food in my face and get help, but that's a no-go, too."

"I'm touched."

Savvy's eyes close. "I would commit a felony for an egg sandwich right now."

"You know, you are not the first person whose rescue mission I have phenomenally messed up in the last twelve hours."

"Oh yeah?" Savvy asks, raising her eyebrows. "What did I miss?"

I hold up my wrist. Savvy hisses.

"Not to story top or anything," I say, resting it back down at my side.

"Uh, yeah, come talk to me when you've spent the whole night in a ditch and *nobody notices you're gone.*"

I knock my shoulder with hers. "To be fair . . . a lot of drama has gone down since then. This place is basically the set of a reality show."

Savvy snorts. It's the most graceless sound I've ever heard her make. I love everything about it. "You're telling me."

"Mickey said that Jo called."

Savvy turns to me abruptly. This close I can see there isn't only crusted mud in her hair, but actual leaves and twigs. She looks like that time our school put on a production of *A Midsummer Night's Dream* and the theater kids got a little too method about their costumes.

"Mickey heard that?"

"Heard what?"

"Me breaking up with Jo."

My eyebrows lift. "You broke up with Jo?"

"How much did Mickey hear?" Savvy demands, way more paranoid than someone whose problems include being trapped in a muddy ditch without a way to contact the outside world should be.

I shrug. "I mean, I'm guessing not much. She said you took the call and she was in some kind of mood and made Rufus cuddle with her or something, so . . ."

"Jesus." Savvy hikes her knees up and rests her forehead on them, streaking herself with mud. It's unfortunate that I've never noticed our resemblance more than in this instant. "I'm making a mess out of *everything.*"

"Okay, this time I definitely get to story top you, considering I told my own parents to fuck off." I kick at the mud with the heels of my shoes, making little mud piles in front of me. "So . . . what happened with Jo?"

Savvy groans. "I broke up with her and the universe immediately punished me by plummeting me into a muddy ditch and giving me a sister who doesn't answer the one call I'm able to make before my phone turns into a glorified brick."

My ears don't perk at the word *sister* the way they normally would. For the first time, it doesn't feel weird. Maybe it's hearing it like this, mid-rant with a tinge of annoyance, that finally makes it fit—she throws out the word *sister* the way I throw out the word *brother*, with the carelessness of someone who's allowed to be careless because they know that sister or brother isn't going anywhere.

"Why would the universe be punishing you? I mean . . . I don't know Jo or anything. But it kinda seemed like it wasn't a match made in teenage heaven."

"I mean, yeah," she admits. "It wasn't working."

I approach the topic with caution. "Too busy to keep up with each other?"

"No—well, yeah." The defensiveness leaks out of her, and she adds, "But if I'm being honest . . . that's probably why we lasted so long in the first place."

"Ah, yes. It was . . . what was that incredibly romantic word you used? *Convenient.*"

"Also, she was . . . she didn't want me hanging out with Mickey so much." Savvy's expression is wry. "She was sure Mickey had an agenda, which is dumb, obviously. Mickey was dating that girl for years. If she'd had an *agenda*, I'd have known by now."

If Savvy's bad attempt at hedging around it hadn't already confirmed that she is still harboring at least *some* feelings for Mickey, referring to her ex of several years as "that girl" sure does.

"Anyway, that was always going to be nonnegotiable. Mickey's my best friend."

I think of the way Mickey went redder than a fire hydrant the day we first met and I mistook her for Jo, how she always seems to have her eyes peeled for Savvy and anticipates whatever gloriously Type A thing Savvy is going to say before the thought has taken root in her brain.

I think of Mickey handing me Savvy's shoes after Jo showed up, looking every bit as defeated in that moment as I felt over Leo.

"I dunno," I say. "Watching the two of you, sometimes I get the sense that—"

"Oh my god, you sound just like Jo."

I try another tactic. "Okay, fine, then here's a thing Jo definitely didn't say—you might be mad at yourself, if you didn't at least ask her about it."

Savvy's lips quirk upward. "Gee," she deadpans. "What great advice."

I nudge my muddy sneaker into hers. "Yeah, the girl who gave it to me isn't half bad."

Savvy nudges my foot back, and leans farther into the muddy hillside, staring outward and mulling something over.

"How about we make a deal," she says. I brace myself, thinking it will have something to do with Leo, and I won't know what to say. "I'll feel things out with Mickey, if you agree to have a serious conversation with your parents about your photography."

Just like that the sting is back, a fresh reminder of the untouched Dropbox.

"Well, joke's on you. I already tried."

"Try harder."

I shrug. Even if I wanted to, now doesn't feel like the right time. There's too much going on to pull this out of the periphery and into a spotlight taken up by the rest of the chaos I've brought on.

"If it helps, my parents are judgy as hell, and they love your work."

"Really?" I ask, not entirely convinced they weren't trying to play nice with their kid's biological sister.

Savvy rolls her eyes. "Of course they do."

"Uh—ouch?"

"No, sorry, I—I didn't mean it like that," Savvy adds quickly. "I just mean they've always kind of like—I don't know. Seemed kind of baffled by my whole Instagram thing."

"I guess if I grew up without Instagram, I'd be baffled, too," I say, trying to be diplomatic.

"Yeah, well, they grew up without ordering the Amazon Alexa around, and they seem to be adjusting to *that* just fine," Savvy says flatly. "You'd think they'd be more supportive, since they basically groomed me for it. What else was I going to do after a lifetime of being raised by the biggest hypochondriacs in the greater Seattle area?"

"If only we could all so easily monetize our parents' paranoia."

Savvy loosens a bit, letting out a laugh. "Anyway, it makes sense they'd jump all over your photos. That's exactly the kind of thing they're into. Everything about you—the whole creative, seizing-the-day thing."

I sidestep the "Day" pun for my own sanity, and add, "Or as my parents would call it, that whole reckless, bad-prioritizing thing."

"Your parents seem so chill. I mean, I couldn't get a single nugget of information out of them, so that was a bust. But other than that they seem chill."

"Of course they're chill to you. You're the dream kid." I caught myself before I said *their dream kid*, but I might as well have. It's heavy in the humid air, taking up space even though it didn't take up sound.

But Savvy doesn't seem to notice, turning more fully to look me in the face.

"Abby, you've got to stop thinking you're like, a 'bad kid' or something. So your grades aren't the best. So what? Grades stop counting pretty much the minute you get your diploma. Especially when your talents are outside of school." It's the last thing I'm expecting to hear from the most aggressive rule-following Capricorn to ever walk the earth, but less surprising than what she says next, which is, "Truth is, I'd kill to be more like you."

"Excuse me?"

She leans back. "You know what's dumb? I'm trapped in the middle of the woods, and yeah, I've thought about food and water and getting eaten by a wild bobcat—but mostly I've obsessed about how nobody's updating the Instagram. No scheduled posts, no stories, no DMing with followers. I've basically gone dark for the first time in two years."

There's reservation in her face after she finishes, like she's expecting me to make fun of her.

"How's it feel?" I ask instead.

"Super shitty." Savvy swipes sweat off her brow, accidentally streaking more mud on her forehead. "It's wild to think I used to do this for fun."

I peer at her cautiously. "Was it ever really fun, though?"

"It was," she insists. "Actually, it was kind of a relief. I just wanted . . . control, I guess. Over the stuff my parents wanted me to do, all the rules they had. You saw what happened when I got a days' worth of sniffles," she says, gesturing widely the way someone would at a catastrophic mess. "It's always been like that, and nothing I said ever really stopped them. There was always this big scary unknown that I could never talk them down from, because they never told me much about my bios. I didn't know enough to understand where the fear came from in the first place." She tilts her head, considering. "But running the Instagram—showing them I was taking their advice seriously—for a while it worked."

It hits a little too close to home, hearing her say that. Savvy, for all her bravado, is as guilty of taking the easy way out as I am.

"And even when it stopped working, it was fun, when it was just me and Mickey. But now it sort of feels like—this whole other beast. I started it to feel like I had control, but it controls me."

I nudge her with the shoulder of my good arm, and she sighs.

"Sometimes I think about all the stuff I missed out on, because I was distracted, or because I didn't want to break some rule I made for myself, and . . . I think—I know I'm missing out on stuff. And that makes me anxious. But not sticking to my plans makes me feel worse."

She looks over at me the way little kids do, when they're looking to someone else to confirm something is or isn't true. But we both know she's right. I think of my nights hanging out in the kitchen without her, the calls she took while we were pointing at constellations, the sunrises she spent scowling into the screen on her camera.

"And you . . . you're just yourself. You're brave. You do what you want. No apologies."

Brave. It's a word I'm still getting used to, after a lifetime of ducking from my problems. But maybe I'm growing into it, in my own way. A little less running and a little more talking. A little less wandering and a little more found.

"Plenty of apologies. I drive my parents nuts."

"Listen, I got jack shit out of them, but I *do* know they're proud of you. Before I found them they were mooning over your photos of the camp."

I haven't been able to access the Dropbox link for more than a day. "You're sure they were *my* photos?"

"Sure I'm sure. I think if you talk to them, you can find some common ground." She lowers her voice. "You love this, Abby. There's no point in making yourself miserable about it, and as long as you're hiding, you always will."

The lump in my throat aches all the way down into my chest. I don't know if it's been hiding so much as protecting. This one thing that was mine and Poppy's has turned into something that's only mine. But that's something I don't want to fully reckon with right now in the mud, so I just nod.

"Well—same goes for you," I say. "With the rules thing, I mean."

Savvy slouches, her legs sinking into the mud even more. "That's the problem. I don't know if I can give them up."

I'm at a loss for what to say, but remember what Leo said to me last night, about setting your own pace. "I don't think it happens overnight," I tell her. "But you can start. And maybe I can help."

I pause, wondering if she's going to laugh at me.

"We can start with this," I say, tracing two lines into the mud. "It's called a pros and Connies list."

Savvy's eyebrow lifts.

"The next time you want to do something—instead of thinking about what would happen if you did it, think about what would happen if you didn't do it. The stuff you'd miss out on. The people who'd miss you, too. Those are the Connies."

It is at that precise and inconvenient moment, sitting in the mud a whole island away from our usual stomping grounds, that I miss Connie with a near impossible force. There's so much I want to tell her. So much I want to understand. I feel like I am straddling some line between who I was when I left and who

I've become, and Connie is somewhere in the middle, just out of reach.

"How about this," says Savvy. "No matter what happens when they finally drag us out of here—even if we have to wait for you to turn eighteen so we can see each other—we find some way to be in touch. To hold each other accountable."

"Savvy's Savvies meets Abby's Days?"

Savvy groans. "Leo's puns are rubbing off on you."

The truth is there are very few parts of me that Leo hasn't had a part in. If I am the way I am—the way Savvy thinks of me, at least—then Leo is the one to blame. If I'm brave, it's partially because I always knew Leo was looking out for me. If I do what I want, it's partially because of Leo supporting me. We've been catching each other's slipups and rooting for each other's dreams before they counted for anything. Long before now, when a lifetime of them are so tangled in each other that I have no idea what shape they'd take without him.

I clear my throat, pushing it to the back of my mind. There's nothing I can do now—not about what Connie said, or the months Leo and I wasted tiptoeing around each other, or even the fact that, somewhere within a mile radius of where we are currently trapped in a ditch, our parents are probably losing their collective shit.

I lean farther into Savvy, who is, surprisingly, much calmer than I am. It's as if she's been waiting to get this off her chest for a while, and is slumped in relief, muddy and banged up and brand-new.

"Well," I say lightly, "when you've got names like ours, it's kind of hard not to resist the lure of a pun."

Savvy blinks, the blue in her eyes sharpening.

"Your mom's name. It's Maggie, right?"

"Yeah. Why?"

Savvy yanks my lanyard from where it's hanging out of my front pocket and hands it to me. "Magpie," she says softly.

I stare at it resting in my palm, its gleam sharp against my skin. This thing that knows the history of me, maybe better than I know it myself. This gift that held my biggest secret in it, and just gave us a key.

"Maggie and Pietra."

thirty-one

We fill up the next few hours talking about nothing and everything. Savvy tells me about growing up in Medina with oddball rich parents in a typical rich town—about things like trick-or-treating at Bill Gates's house, or going inner-tubing on Lake Washington on her friends' parents' boats, and stressing out all year about winning a Hula-Hoop contest at the Medina Days festival every summer. She tells me how she and Mickey met through an art class they took in second grade, inseparable ever since. She tells me she's secretly really into Lord of the Rings, and that the same year Leo tortured me and Connie by trying to send coded messages in Elvish, she'd been learning it with him.

I tell her about the mini-adventure trips Poppy would take me on—how we'd drive out to Snoqualmie Falls to photograph the waterfall, or to Mount Saint Helens to squint at it through the fog and watch the seismic activity tracker jut up and down in the museum. I tell her how badly I'd wanted a sibling, and how my parents told me about Brandon by taking me out for cupcakes, and that somewhere in the archive there's a video of me bursting into happy tears and getting cookie dough frosting up my nose. I tell her about all of them—Brandon and Mason and Asher—and their little quirks, like how Brandon is obsessed with different kinds of knots and keeps experimenting on our

sneakers, or how Mason recently discovered his passion for guz-
zling large amounts of milk and burping out pop songs, or how
Asher has an almost eerie knack for remembering where everyone puts their stuff down, so things are never lost for more than
a minute when he's around.

It's the kind of stuff that fills in the edges, like we were whole
people to each other but now the colors of us are a little brighter.
It's the kind of stuff we would have told each other over the next
two weeks, except crammed into two muddy hours occasionally
interrupted by one of us groaning about how hungry we are or
how badly we need to pee.

"I wonder if I'll ever get to meet them," Savvy says at one
point, when I finish telling her how Asher got so enthusiastic
blowing out Brandon's birthday candles that he almost set the
house on fire.

It's nearing noon, the heat settling in low in our little ditch.
From our shadows, our hair has identically poofed up to full
frizz potential. I touch mine absentmindedly, mulling over Savvy's words and wondering the same.

"I hope so."

Three weeks ago the idea made me queasy and possessive.
But we've pushed so far into each other's lives, it seems strange
that she might not be there, or that there will be parts she can't
see—at least not until our parents either make a big decision, or
the boys get old enough to find out about Savvy on their own.
I know it's not my place to tell them. But that doesn't make the
disappointment sting any less.

"Do you think they'd like me?"

"*Another* big sister to torture? They'd have a damn field
day." I smile at the thought, and it's the first time getting sent
home hasn't felt like the end of the world. I really do miss those
twerps. "That is, if they aren't too busy trying to kidnap Rufus.
They've been begging for a dog since—"

And, then, as if his name summoned him, we hear a distinct *woof*! that can only belong to Rufus.

Savvy snaps to attention so fast she looks like a human jack-in-the-box. "Rufus!" she calls up. "You beautiful, stupid, ridiculous—"

"Girls?"

It's my mom. I'm on my feet in an instant, and Savvy and I open our mouths to yell some variation of the same thing—*be careful*—but we're both so flustered that Savvy only manages to squeak and I say something in gibberish and all of it gets drowned out by Rufus's barking anyway.

"Maggie, watch out!"

"Oh my," I hear my mom gasp. Savvy and I wince, half expecting my mom to slide down here with us, but instead she says, "Thank you."

Pietra doesn't respond, because by then other voices are joining the fray. She and my mom are calling down to us, and our dads are calling from somewhere not too far off, and we're calling back, and the whole thing is a clusterfuck of yelling before Savvy manages to trump everyone by shouting, "Does anyone have any *food*?"

"Are you okay?" Pietra asks instead.

"We're fine," Savvy answers.

"Abby?"

"Just hangry."

Which is really all I can think of until someone tosses a Luna Bar down, and I, like the colossal, dehydrated idiot I am, try to catch it with the arm on my busted-up side and end up yelping like a Chihuahua. Savvy catches it out from under me and has it unwrapped and in her mouth so fast that I have no idea what she says next, but it sounds an awful lot like she just promised to give the name Luna to her firstborn.

"How far down are you?" Pietra calls.

"Not that far—maybe ten feet?" I guess. "But don't come too close, you'll slip right down."

There's more talking above us, the muffled noise of a decision getting made, and made fast. Savvy and I glance at each other in surprise—our parents are actually talking to one another.

"Dale is going to get help, girls," my mom tells us. "Sit tight."

"How did this *happen*?" Pietra asks.

"I thought it might be fun to spend the night in a ditch," Savvy calls up, with the most impressive eye roll I've ever seen.

"What's the verdict?" my dad asks. He tries for a joking tone, but we can hear the strain in his voice. We may not have been having a ball down here, but I can't imagine what's been going through their heads.

"Zero out of five stars," I say. "The checkout procedures are . . . really fucked up."

"Language," my mom chides me.

There's a snort from above that sounds uncannily like Savvy's. Pietra adds, "I think they get a pass."

My mom laughs. The sound is breathless and manic and tinged with exhaustion that goes well beyond the last few days' worth of drama, but they're laughing that same laugh together. Even Savvy stops chewing to listen, the two of us staring at each other in disbelief.

"Just this once," my mom concedes.

thirty-two

Once the fire department hauls us out, my parents take me to the small hospital on the island, equipped with an X-ray and a very nervous resident who informs us that my wrist is broken and seems a little *too* pleased with himself when he successfully puts a cast on it. After that, one shower in the hotel room and the equivalent of four ibuprofen running through my veins later, I almost look like a human being.

When I come out of the bathroom, there's a telling hush in the room. My parents glance over, not even bothering to pretend they weren't talking about me. I wish they would—it's the first time we've had quiet all day, and suddenly I have no idea how to fill it. No idea of what I want to say, or where I'd even begin if I did.

My dad rescues us all from ourselves by saying, "Should we get some dinner?"

I thought for sure we'd be catching the next ferry out. "Is Colin not begging for mercy yet?" I ask, trying to imagine my uncle surviving another full night with my brothers.

My mom grabs her phone and says, "There's a Thai place down the street that's still open."

"Sounds good to me. Abby?"

They're so calm. So weirdly patient. Usually when there's a problem, or something that needs to be said, they'll do it right then. Rip the Band-Aid off and move on. Between all six of our schedules we don't exactly have the luxury of time to stew.

But I guess as far as *things* go, we've never had to deal with one as big as this.

"Yeah. Sounds good to me."

The place is small and cozy, with dim, yellow lighting and warm colors on the walls, a far cry from the camp and its high ceilings and pine smell and somewhat orderly chaos. Even the seats are big and plush, and only once I put my butt in one do I realize I'm so tired I could fall asleep as fast as it would take to close my eyes.

But the way my parents position themselves, the two of them on one side and me on the other, makes me realize this dinner wasn't a whim. It was a tactical move. They were deciding what to say while I was in the shower, and they've chosen a public place so nobody can raise their voice or walk away. After yesterday I can't really blame them. The usual bets are off.

I try not to squirm, wishing I'd at least used some of my time in the shower to rehearse what I was going to say instead of holding my wrapped-up arm out of the water spray. But before my parents can open their mouths, the front door to the restaurant opens and their eyes snap away from me so fast that there's no doubt in my mind who walked in.

Sure enough, I turn and meet Savvy's eyes so fast it feels like we planned this.

"Three?" the hostess asks, before Savvy or her parents can get their wits about them. "It's probably going to be a half-hour wait."

"Oh," says Pietra, doing a very bad job of pretending not to see us, "that's—you know what? We'll come back another time—"

"There's plenty of room at our table," I say, before I can lose my nerve.

Dale clears his throat. "We wouldn't want to . . . interrupt, if you—"

"Please," says my mom, unexpectedly pulling out the empty chair next to her. "We really wouldn't mind."

We're the ones doing the inviting, but it feels like it's the other way around. Everyone holds their breath, the poor hostess trying to make eye contact with literally anyone to gauge the temperature of what's going on, until Pietra says quietly, "If you're sure."

Before we can awkwardly put too much thought into who's sitting where, I get up and sit on my parents' side of the table, so when Savvy sits down she's facing me and we're both sandwiched by our parents. I try not to smile so we don't look like we're scheming, but Savvy's eyes glint at me, and I nudge her sneakered foot under the table.

The waitress comes to take our order, looking at my parents first. My dad orders a beer, and my mom surprises me by ordering a glass of white wine, something I've only ever seen her drink when all my brothers are in bed. She turns to Pietra and says shyly, "And I assume a glass of red for you?"

Pietra goes stiff, bristling slightly at the familiarity, but slowly she eases into her seat and nods at my mom. "That would be lovely."

Everyone buries their heads in their menus after that, my parents scrutinizing the appetizer list like it's a legal document from one of their cases, Savvy's parents finishing nearly half their first glass of wine before the waitress makes it back to take our food order. Savvy and I are both dead silent, communicating only through the occasional glance, like we're too afraid to remind them we're here and distract from this rare moment of them not being at one another's throats.

"The spring rolls, maybe?" my mom asks.

My dad shakes his head. "Dale's allergic to cilantro."

Pietra reaches over Savvy to nudge Dale. "He *says* he's allergic."

"It tastes like soap."

"That's not an allergy," my mom and Pietra protest at the same time, with the exact same inflection.

Dale holds his hands up in surrender. "Wow, it's been eighteen years since the two of them have ganged up on me, and somehow it's still just as terrifying."

"Well, they're not the only girls ganging up on you anymore," says my dad mildly, acknowledging me and Savvy.

I freeze like a bunny in an open field, but Savvy leans forward, addressing us all in turn with a meaningful look. "Okay. We're all here. We've survived a public spat and a mud pit and cilantro. Can you tell us the rest of the story, maybe?"

Crickets from the parents, until Dale takes it upon himself to say, "There's not much to tell."

Savvy falters, and I pick up the slack. "Sure there is. You told us the end of it. What happened at the beginning? How did you all meet?"

I feel my parents' eyes on me, but before I meet them I know it's less from annoyance and more out of surprise. I'm not usually the one taking charge of conversations. And while I'm still getting used to this new Abby, they haven't seen much of her at all.

I can see the adults starting to relent. My mom drops her shoulders. My dad stops staring at his empty plate. Dale stops cracking his knuckles, and Pietra stops intermittently taking large sips of her wine. It's like they're all finally willing to go the distance, but have no idea where the journey begins.

I pull the keychain out of my pocket and set my magpie charm on the table. Savvy pulls hers off and does the same.

"It's your names, isn't it?" Savvy asks. "Maggie and Pietra."

The look on my mom's face when we first pulled these out is so fresh in my mind that I almost keep my head down, but her posture softens, her lips giving way to a quiet smile. She and Pietra stare at the little charms, disappearing to some other time together, far from the rest of us.

My mom looks up, but it's Pietra's eyes she meets, not mine. Like she's waiting for Pietra's permission before she says anything. Or maybe the beginning is Pietra's story to tell.

Pietra leans forward, grazing the charm with her fingertips. "We bought these at Pike Place Market. Some little artisan seller. They were the last two."

"We were both near broke."

"Worth the money, though," Pietra murmurs. "They've held up through the years, haven't they?"

"That they have."

Pietra lets go of the charm, looking from me to Savvy. "I was twenty-two when I started at Bean Well. I'd moved out of my parents' place—less than politely. Told them I wanted to make it on my own. Ended up crying in the first coffee shop where I could find parking, certain I was going to turn right back around and undo the whole thing." She turns to look at my mom, her eyes misty, but her voice wry. "But some nosy teenager butted in with a free scone and wrangled out my whole life story instead."

My mom ducks her head, and when she looks up I can imagine her as that nosy teen, smirking this exact same smirk. "Well. Dad helped."

"He did." Pietra's smile widens. "And for some reason I could never begin to fathom, he offered the girl scaring all his customers away a *job*."

"I had to train her." There's a pause where my mom bites her lip, and her eyes meet Pietra's, and she says, "She was *so bad*."

Pietra puts her hand up in surrender. "I'm a tea drinker, I'd never made coffee in my life—"

"Forget coffee—you couldn't even figure out how to turn on the *vacuum*," my mom says, trying to muffle her laughter.

Pietra's mouth drops open in mock offense. "You mean that piece of junk your mom dragged out of the *eighties*? Honestly, I was half expecting it to turn into a Transformer."

My mom does what appears to be an impression of Pietra trying to figure out where the "on" button of an invisible vacuum is, and Pietra lets out a sharp laugh, saying, "Mags, you *jerk*."

I watch, riveted. My parents tease each other, but not like this—not this lawless, almost teenage banter, the kind of shit I would get away with saying to Connie or Leo in full awareness that I could never say it to anyone else.

Pietra leans over the table and sips some of my mom's wine in what appears to be retaliation. My mom lets her, easing back with a smug look on her face. "At least you were a quick student."

Pietra rolls her eyes, returning the wineglass. "I was managing the place within the year. I was *your* boss, if you recall."

"Hmm," says my mom, glancing up at the ceiling. "And yet *your* lattes were never so good that you had lines out the door to order them."

"Puh-lease. The boys who were mooning over your lattes were just trying to get in your—"

"Is everyone ready to order?" asks the waitress, saving me from nearly choking on my Sprite.

The waitress takes down everyone's dinner orders and flits off. I'm afraid there's going to be a lull, but Pietra jumps right back in, her cheeks flushed from the wine and her voice giddy in that way adults are when they're talking about something they almost forgot about from a long time ago.

"I worked there for years. Long after I made up with my parents. Your grandfather started letting me work with local artists. We featured some of their pieces in the shop."

"You're the one who started that?" I ask.

My mom nods. "It was more than that. There was Bean Well After Dark, for a little while. Open mic nights and mini art shows. We even had a few poetry slams."

"It was all very late nineties," says Pietra, sharing my mom's smile. "And Maggie had this idea . . ." She nods over at my mom.

"It was around when I was studying for the LSATs, and interning downtown at the women's shelter. I knew I was going to be working with families, and I—well, *we* came up with this idea for a hybrid art gallery café." My mom's voice is lower, self-conscious. It occurs to me this is probably the first time she's talked about this in years. "We'd have classes there. For art and photography. And offer free classes to families in adjustment periods, just so they'd have something fun to focus on, a place they could be together."

"We were going to call it Magpic."

A quiet settles over the table. Savvy's looking over at me, but I can't quite bring myself to look back. Bean Well isn't really a part of her history the way it's part of mine. She didn't grow up scarfing Marianne's scones, or letting Mrs. Leary's dog fall asleep in her lap by the window, or getting free life advice from the string of college-age baristas who came and went and still visited whenever they could. She doesn't have scratches in the doorframe of the supply closet marking her height every year, or a favorite chair, or a sunny spot in the back she used to tease Poppy for taking naps in. She never called it home.

My mom leans across the table and picks up Savvy's charm, dangling it so it spins and catches the light. "I didn't realize you'd kept yours," she says.

"I didn't, actually," says Pietra. She clears her throat. "It was still on my keys to Bean Well when I sent them back to Walt. After everything that happened, I . . . didn't feel right having them anymore."

The table is at once tense enough that it feels like there is something seismic underneath us, something that will either rumble or explode. I watch my mom nod quietly, watch Pietra's eyes dim. There's a second when I think this is all going to come unraveled again. But Pietra reaches across the table and takes my charm, holding it up next to Savvy's.

"About two years after Savvy was born, Walt sent it back to me," she says softly. "He said he respected that we wanted a clean break, but he wanted Savvy to have something in case we told her the truth. He told me to give it to her. To help explain everything when she was old enough."

"My dad told me to give my charm to Abby, too." My mom's voice is shaking. "He said he thought she should have it, since it was a symbol of how we all brought each other together. But he didn't say anything about telling her."

I stare down at the napkin in my lap, fighting the smallest smile. I'm almost certain Poppy knew our parents weren't going to tell us the truth. This was a seed he planted to bring me and Savvy together. The idea is comforting, and for a moment, it feels like he's here, listening in, chuckling at handiwork sixteen years in the making.

"He also sent me a picture," Pietra says quietly. "Of Abby's birth announcement."

My mom's hand grazes her mouth, like she's trying not to choke up again. "I didn't know."

"We were still so angry. But we—we were happy to hear about her. About you," Pietra amends, shooting me a wry look.

My cheeks flush, embarrassed to have four pairs of adult eyes suddenly on me. I'm relieved when Pietra continues.

"If things had been different . . ."

Savvy and I might have grown up together. Might have had a lot of dinners like this, ones where we sat back in our chairs and laughed without looking over our shoulders. Might have shared much more than the unexpected things we do now.

"I know I've said it before," says my mom, addressing Dale and Pietra both. "But I really am sorry."

Pietra's lips thin into her teeth, like she'll never be quite ready to accept the words fully, even if she understands them. She sets the charm back down and rests her hand over it. "Love makes you do things you never thought you would."

Pietra carefully reaches out and puts the magpie charm back in my hand. My fingers curl around it, feeling a new warmth at its edges. "What did you mean before . . . about you guys bringing each other together?" I ask.

"Oh, he probably meant us," says Dale, with an exaggerated lean back in his chair.

My dad is also sporting a knowing look. "I wondered if our names were ever going to come up."

"Really is just like the good ole days, huh? Your wife forgetting you exist, my wife forgetting I exist . . ."

"Excuse you," says Pietra. "What Walt meant is that if it weren't for us, neither of you would be married in the first place."

I blink at the four of them. "Uh. I mean, isn't that . . . how deciding to marry each other works?"

Dale's eyebrows shoot up, excited to be a part of the conversation. "No, she means—your dad was taking an art class with Pietra—"

"To impress some other girl, it turns out," my mom cuts in.

"I hadn't met you yet!" my dad protests.

Pietra's eyes are gleaming. "You and that other girl would have been a disaster, but the moment I saw Tom I knew he was Maggie's. So I brought him over to the coffee shop—"

"She told me there was a student discount."

"There wasn't," says my mom, leaning toward me and Savvy conspiratorially.

"And when I got there, she just—poof!—disappeared. Left me in that café all alone with Maggie, who took one look at my John Grisham paperback and started talking my ear off about how secretly reading her parents' 'murder books' as a kid is what first got her interested in law."

"Lucky you."

My dad's smile softens. "Lucky me."

"And lucky us, because Maggie paid back the favor. I mean, it was a little less romantic and definitely not intentional—"

"Uh, Dale, it was *completely* intentional," my mom cuts in. "I'd been talking to Pietra about you for weeks."

"Wait, what? Then why did you wait until we were in the middle of a training run on the hottest day of the year to drag me into Bean Well for free water?" He leans over to me and Savvy for context, adding, "Maggie and I were in the same running club."

"Because you seemed like the kind of guy who would, I don't know, overthink the whole thing completely and come off way too strong."

"Instead he came off as kind of smelly," says Pietra, looking over Savvy to tease him with a smile.

"Anyway," says my dad. "That's how we met."

There's this lull where nobody says anything, until Savvy asks, "So you two kind of . . . picked each other's husbands?"

"No," says my dad, without missing a beat. "They picked each other."

My mom and Pietra both get so immediately teary-eyed that there is no mistaking it for nostalgia, or that specific brand of weepy you get when you're thinking about your best friend. It's quiet and ancient. It's years of regret and grief, and an entire lifetime buried under it—a lifetime where my mom and Pietra were two entirely different people, on some entirely different plane. A lifetime where they teased each other and dreamed each other's dreams and willed each other's happiness into existence.

And no matter how messy it turned out, it's still there, I realize. That happiness. It's in every part of my world—the old things, like walking hand-in-hand with my parents to get ice cream as a kid. The new things, like making massive Oreo towers with my little brothers. Even the newest, sitting across from me right now, blinking back with eyes like mirrors, the two of us coming to the same understanding.

Their friendship may have ended years ago, but it's lived on in us all this time.

My mom reaches her hand across the table at the same time as Pietra, and they squeeze, and there is something so powerful in the pulse that it feels like some kind of spell is broken. It's a *thank you* every bit as much as it's an *I'm sorry*, the weight of it without the words. We hold our breath in the aftermath, like they were all bound to something for so long that they don't know how to move themselves without it holding them back.

And then my mom looks at me and Savvy and says, "Seems like they did, too."

thirty-three

Only after we're all fed, watered, and deposited in our respective hotel rooms does it occur to me how strange it is, being with my parents on my own like this. I've gotten so used to my brothers' footsteps darting up and down the hall, the clanging of things that probably shouldn't be clanging, the unsteady soundtrack of our steady lives. In the absence of it—in the just me, Mom, and Dad of it—I feel inexplicably littler and older at the same time.

We end up sitting in the same configuration we did the last time I was here, them on the couch, me on the chair. I sensed A Talk long before we drifted into position for it, but this one already feels different. We're looser. Lighter. A lot fewer secrets and, for the adults at least, a lot more wine.

There isn't exactly a silence to break, only a contemplative quiet, but my mom is the one who interrupts it.

"I know the last few days have been rough on all of us. And there's a lot to process and decide on, regarding how we're going to move forward. But before we get to that, we wanted to talk to you about—"

I shake my head. "You don't have to."

"No," says my dad, "we really do. What you were saying, about feeling like the . . ." He winces.

"The replacement kid," I supply, wincing right back. "And I—"

"It couldn't be further from how we felt, how we feel."

"I know—"

"What we went through was—unimaginable. Even now. But when you were born—"

"I know," I say, firmer.

Even if I didn't know it in my bones, I can see it in their faces. I don't need an explanation, because it isn't an explanation, really. It's a lifetime. It's sixteen years of never having to wonder who to call or how long it will take for them to pick up. It's looking at them and knowing I'm every bit as much theirs as they are mine.

"Do you?"

I look at them, and at my lap, considering. It feels important to say the right thing here, like the result of this conversation will mean more to them than it does to me. So I have to let them say it. I have to let them get this off their chests if I'm ever going to get anything off mine.

I lean back, feeling the way I sometimes do when I take that first step off the ground—up a tree, or a rickety old ladder, or someone's car. That sense of pushing off of something solid, leaving something behind, and thinking, *No going back now.*

My mom takes a breath, and when she speaks, it sounds like she's been waiting to say the words a lot longer than I've been waiting to hear them.

"When Savvy happened—we were young, and confused, and . . . I honestly can't remember a lot of that time. It's murky to me still. Sometimes it's easier not to think about it too much." She clasps her hands together, like she is trying to press the words into the feeling, leaning forward so I can feel it, too. "But with you—I remember every moment. You were *ours*. Before you were even real."

She's getting teary-eyed, and I go completely still, wondering if I should say something. But my dad is watching me over her shoulder, and something in his expression tells me to wait.

"We decided on you together," says my mom. "The day you

were born was the happiest day of our lives. Like . . . something had lifted, maybe. Out of all the darkness. The thing we'd been waiting for."

I blink back my own tears. It's not that I have trouble believing her. But it's overwhelming, hearing it all like this. I think in life you can know you're loved without peering too closely at the edges of it. It's almost scary, seeing that there aren't any—it doesn't have a beginning or an end. It just kind of is.

My mom lowers her voice and says, "But if I were in your shoes, thinking what you thought, I'd be upset, too."

They're both watching me—no, waiting. This is the part where I'm supposed to say my bit. Put it all out there. Talk to them the way Savvy told me I should, the way I haven't, really, since Poppy died and everything felt like too much of a mess to untangle from the outside.

But it's one thing to finally have the resolve. It's another thing entirely to find the words.

"I think I was—surprised, is all." I clear my throat. "And mad, maybe."

They nod, in sync the way they always are. I wait for one of them to say something, to give me an out so I don't have to dig any deeper than that, but neither do.

So I dig.

"There was this big, giant secret that I didn't see coming. And I know there were good reasons for why everything shook out the way it did, but it rattled me." I look away so I don't lose my nerve. "And I know you don't think of me as—a replacement. But the other thing that I can't stop thinking about is how Savvy's kind of—well. She would have been a lot easier to handle than me."

My dad almost starts to laugh, but when I look up sharply and meet his eye, he blows out air instead. "Why would you think that?"

It feels pathetic to say it out loud—worse, maybe, that I have to explain it to them. My parents and I have barely even discussed Savvy's existence, so the jump from "I found out I had a sister" to "I might have a complex about how inadequate I sometimes feel compared to my sister" is justifiably more jarring to them than it is for me, having had a full month to marinate in it. But I feel like it's something I have to say now, in one of these rare moments when there's nothing to interrupt us, and real life seems suspended somewhere outside the rainy windows.

"She's a lot more—on track than I am, I guess. And sometimes with everything the way it's gotten . . . the tutoring, and the extra prep courses, and everything being so intense . . . it kind of feels like you don't think I'm on one." I think I'm finished, but the last part slips out unbidden: "Like I'm letting you down."

Neither of them jumps in right away, and I feel my face burn. I don't want to accuse them of anything, or blow this out of proportion. People have worse problems than their parents harping on them about their grades.

But it feels bigger than that. Like it's not rooted in my grades, but something deeper—the way Savvy's parents and their worries about her health were. And when my parents exchange this pointed glance, like they're trying to decide which one is going to answer me, I'm pretty sure that hunch is right.

"First of all," says my dad, "we've never felt like you're letting us down. Everyone needs extra help sometimes."

I fidget, shifting my weight on the seat and working up the nerve to keep meeting their eyes.

"I'm just not sure if I . . . need that help."

I straighten my spine, channeling my inner Savvy. Channeling something that I must have been born with too and am only just figuring how to use. "Honestly, it just made things worse. I've been so busy that I don't even have time to catch up after all the tutoring. And like, here—we had all this time. Free time. And I kept up with everything. I'm actually doing well."

They don't seem wholly convinced of my theory, but receptive. Enough that my dad says, "Victoria mentioned that."

"She did?" I wasn't aware that I was on her radar for anything other than gum smuggling and sneaking out before sunrise.

My dad adds, "She also mentioned you'd made a lot of friends here."

"I have."

It's not an attempt to stay. All things considered—the lying, the broken wrist, the still very confusing aftermath we all have to navigate—I'm lucky to be having a conversation this calm at all. I'm not going to try to take advantage of it by angling to go back.

"And that's been great, too. I don't think I've made a lot of friends outside of Leo and Connie for . . . a while, really," I say. My throat tightens, thinking of them both, but that is its own volcano of issues that I am not touching with a ten-foot pole tonight. "It made me feel—I don't know. Excited for what comes after high school. I don't think I've really even thought about it much, but it was nice, to meet new people. See new things. And I think . . . I want more time to do that. Not just when senior year is over."

They consider this, my dad more actively than my mom, whose gaze is on the table between us. "So you want to just— full stop, on the tutoring?" he asks.

I press my lips together. "I mean, yeah?" I glance at them. "Is that a . . . trick question?"

"I'm not saying we're going to stop caring about your grades." My dad's voice is wry. "We do need you to graduate."

My ears burn. "Yeah, well. That I can do."

"And you know," he adds, taking care to take some of the defensiveness out of it, "you could have talked to us about this before."

And there it is. That deeper root I thought I was pulling on, finally brought up to the surface. It isn't one I would have touched a few weeks ago, but I'm a long way from the Abby I was then.

"It just seemed like it mattered to you guys a lot," I say carefully. "And honestly . . . things were so nuts after Poppy died, I didn't want to make it any worse. I didn't want to be a problem."

"Honey, you've never been a *problem*—"

I don't mean to cut my mom off with the look I give her, but it stops her in her tracks.

"I feel like I have," I say, trying to soften it. "I mean, you guys have to drive me all over for tutoring. And before that I was getting in the way of you working full-time, and before that I was getting in the way of school . . ."

"Abby, those were *our* problems. Not yours. You understand?"

My mom doesn't say anything for a few moments, and I can't tell if it's because she's not sure how to say it or if she should say it at all. But it's almost like we're shaking something loose, something we've all been walking around with for a long time, and it doesn't make sense to leave the weight of any of it on us now.

"We knew it would be hard, having you during law school, but that was our decision," says my mom. "And a huge part of why we were able to do that was knowing that your grandpa wanted to help. I don't know if you ever realized how much that meant to him, having you—he'd been so quiet after we lost my mom, but after you were born everything changed. He couldn't wait to take you places and teach you things. It was like watching him come back to life."

I nod, only because my throat feels too thick to say much else.

My mom smiles sadly. "And I know you and Poppy were always close because of that. And we were there whenever we could be, but it seemed like we . . . missed out on some stuff. It felt like sometimes we weren't giving you your best shot."

"Like maybe we'd been selfish, having you when we did. Instead of waiting until we could have given you more," says my dad.

The idea of this is so ridiculous to me that I'm not even sure how to react. I'm so used to being the one they've had to soothe or reassure—now that the script has flipped it turns out I'm total crap at it.

"I've never wanted *more*," I say. "I mean, sheesh. I got ten years of you all to myself."

My mom smiles. "Well, things got calmer after the first few years of work, and we were around more," she says. "And the feeling went away. The fear that we were letting *you* down."

I bunch my fingers into my shorts, wishing I could find the words to tell them that they didn't. That to me it's always felt the other way around.

"Then, when your brothers were born . . . obviously things got hectic," my mom continues. "And it was like the pattern repeated. You were older, and more independent, and we still had your Poppy to keep an eye on you."

I nod, and they pause. I wonder why, until I feel a tear burn down my cheek, falling onto my bare knee. My mom's already crossed the distance to me before I fully realize what's happening, wrapping me up in her arms and letting me snot into her shoulder.

Usually I'm not sad when people bring up Poppy, because I'm already thinking about him most of the time. He's in the weight of his old camera strapped to my shoulder, in the periphery of every photo I take, squinting at the same views and humming his approval. He's the person I talk to in my head, when I need an imaginary person to help me think things through.

I was lucky to have him to myself as a kid, and luckier still to go on the adventures we took after my brothers were born. But those adventures are over, and I've been too busy to really think about how scary it is that I'll have to choose the next adventures on my own.

"I miss him," I say.

It's something we've all said a hundred times to each other, but this time it's different. It's like I opened up part of myself to make room for so much—a first love. A sister. A past that half belongs to me and half doesn't. And it cracked me open just wide enough that I can feel all the parts of me still aching for Poppy, which are still adjusting to a world where he doesn't exist.

"I know," says my mom, squeezing me one more time before she lets go. "Me too."

"I miss the things we used to do together. I miss . . . I miss having time to shoot. I feel like I can still kind of be with him when I do, and with all this tutoring, there's just . . . no time."

"I think maybe we thought the tutoring would be a cushion," says my dad. "Something we could help you with even when we couldn't be there ourselves."

"What we're trying to say is that sometimes—there's just this sense—" My mom looks at my dad, who nods. "This sense that we still want to give you everything we can. Set you up for success. Like we can be there when we can't always be *there*."

"Guys," I blurt, "you're *always* there. I mean like—in the stuff that counts. Aggressively there."

My mom is mirroring me, bunching her fingers in her cotton skirt. "We try to be."

"You *are*." Even when they shouldn't have the time, they make it—whether it's nights spent awake helping me with essay drafts, or the sleepovers they hosted for me and Connie and Leo when we were little, or the long car ride talks about whatever's been on my mind, ones where sometimes we just circled the block so I could keep on talking. "I'm . . . I just think maybe you could be a little, uh, *less* there with the tutoring and stuff."

"We can try that," says my dad. "Well, right after summer school."

Woof. I'd almost forgotten. "Yeah," I say, the cringe every bit as much in my voice as my face. "After that whole thing."

He peers at me, and I wonder what flavor this lecture is going to take, knowing full well there is one overdue. "Why didn't you tell us about that?"

"I wanted—well, part of it was Savvy. I really did want to get to know her."

Or at least, back then, understand her. It seems unthinkable that only a month ago she was worse than a stranger to me and I could barely find any common ground with her at all. It's hard to apologize for the lie that got me here, when my friendship with Savvy is what happened because of it.

"But the other part was . . . I knew if summer school happened it was going to snowball into more tutoring, and I'd never have time for photography. I guess this was a way to steal the time back before anyone found out." My voice is sheepish when I add, only half meaning it, "But I am sorry for lying."

"I'm not even sure how you did it," says my dad. "All the different things you hacked into—I'm honestly a little impressed—"

"Uh, maybe we don't encourage her," my mom cuts in.

My dad smirks. "I have a feeling it wouldn't stop her either way." He leans in and says the thing I've been waiting to hear most. "Abby, we've always known you're a talented photographer. Your grandpa was showing your photos to us even when you weren't, and they speak for themselves. I guess we just thought it was something the two of you did for fun. You were always so shy about your work—I don't think either of us realized how serious you are about pursuing it."

My face flushes, but I'm not as embarrassed as I thought I'd be. So I'm not surprised by my answer, so much as how firmly I deliver it. "I really am."

"Well—I'm glad," he says. "If there's anything we can help with on our end, we want to. Keep us in the loop, kiddo. Tell us what's going on before you duck out the door every once in a while."

"Yeah. I will."

It sinks in, then, that this lack of communication is every bit as much my fault as it is theirs. Maybe more. They've been busy, but I've been—well. *Lazy* is the wrong word, maybe. But less than proactive, for sure.

"Maybe if there's some shots you guys looked at from the past few months—I mean, if you like them, and think it wouldn't look too weird—maybe we could put some up at Bean Well, like you guys planned? Before it sells and all."

Their faces fall, but even then, with every context clue in the damn galaxy, I have no idea what they're going to say before my dad says it.

"Abby, the thing is—the realtor called. We had a buyer last night. Offered a lot more than what we were asking."

I forgot to anticipate this. I've been so worried about everything else that the possibility slipped my radar, too quiet under the noise of the past few weeks for me to even think about it. It comes at me sideways, makes me feel uneven though I'm fully seated in the chair.

"We're sorry, hon," says my mom.

"No—of course. This is—that's a good thing, right?" I manage. I ball my fingers into fists and flex them back out, letting them go loose. "That means someone cares about the space a lot. They're gonna turn it into something good."

My mom's eyes are watering. She's thinking of Poppy, and not the shop. But to me they were always kind of the same thing.

"I sure hope so."

My dad gets up to join us, and they both wordlessly squeeze me, turning me into an Abby sandwich. The hug goes on so long that it feels like it could make me invincible, as if all the things outside it can't do anything to me while we're here. It makes me feel small, and everything around us even smaller. I wonder if there will ever come a day that I'm old enough not to feel like the center of my universe is this.

"For the record," I say, "I'm really glad I'm your kid."

"For the record, we wouldn't change one thing about you," says my mom.

My dad waits three full seconds before adding, "Except we might have gotten accident insurance on all your screens a little sooner."

We laugh, my dad's warm and low, my mom cackling the same cackle she did with Pietra, me barely managing not to snort. Nothing changes when we break apart, the way nothing really did before we came together—not anything important, anyway. Maybe just the view.

thirty-four

My parents end up going to bed early enough that it's still light out. I hook my phone up to the charger and use it to call Leo, unsurprised when it goes straight to voicemail. I try the camp's front office phone next. My name must come up on caller ID, because Mickey picks up and says, "Oh, good. Can I put you on speakerphone before half the camp riots? Phoenix Cabin is freaking out that you're gone. This whole night has been s'mores with a side of anarchy."

I laugh into my sleeve so I don't wake my parents. "Actually . . . is Leo there? I really need to talk to him."

"Hold up."

I hear the tap of her putting the phone down on the front desk, my heart fluttering in this way that feels more in my throat than in my chest. I don't know exactly what I plan on saying, but for once, I'm not worried about it. The kinds of things I want to say right now can't be planned.

"Hey, Abby. Leo's busy."

It's a hard stop, with no quip to soften it. Not a *Try calling back later*, or even a *Sorry*.

"Is he?"

Mickey blows out a breath. "Do I even want to know?"

I rest my head in my hands, smushing the phone farther into my cheek. "My life is basically a CW drama right now, is all."

"You're telling me." She drums her fingers on the desk, the faint noise echoing on the other side of the line. "Don't worry. I'll knock some sense into him. I know it's none of my business, but I'm emotionally invested in the two of you getting your heads out of your asses and confessing your love for each other already."

I don't bother muffling this laugh because it sounds too much like I'm being strangled.

"Sorry," says Mickey, not sounding it one bit.

"Don't be." I hesitate, but not nearly as long as I should. "Also—while we're, uh, inserting ourselves into each other's business—Savvy and Jo are extremely done."

There's a pause. "Huh."

"Do with that information . . . what you will."

I can almost feel the heat of Mickey's cheeks burning through the phone. "It's tough out here for a Ravenclaw."

"Didn't you say you were a—"

"Humans are in constant evolution, Abby. Ever-changing, constant growth, et cetera," says Mickey, a smile in her voice.

"Let's hope."

After we hang up I sit there against the wall of the hotel room, my phone still juicing up. I'm connected to legitimate Wi-Fi for the first time in weeks, so I find myself poking through it—looking at Connie's Facebook pictures of gelato and pizza and what appears to be her very smug-looking cousin drenched and posing by an Italian fountain. Scrolling through all the photography Tumblr accounts I follow. Doing anything I can to distract myself from the fact that the one person I need to talk to most is the one I have no way to reach.

My finger hovers over the Instagram app. I don't even know if I'm logged in. I press it anyway, waiting for it to load, and—

Oh.

Oh my *god*.

At first I think I'm logged into someone else's account by mistake, because there are so many notifications that the app looks like it's going to crash trying to account for them all. That, and the follower count—it's over twenty-six thousand. Pushing twenty-seven.

I scroll down. My jaw about unhinges from my face.

It's my account, all right. @savingtheabbyday, just how Leo set it up. But it's not only pictures from the time Leo and I met up before camp. It's pictures from the last few weeks—specifically, the ones I dumped from my memory card into the Dropbox we were all sharing to work on our Anthro projects.

I tap the most recent one, posted two days ago. No caption, but underneath a bunch of periods are at least a dozen photography hashtags, none that I've ever heard of. It's an image of the fog rolling in on the Sound, a photo I took one sleepy morning so early that even Savvy wasn't around yet. One sleepy morning when I was, unsurprisingly, thinking of Leo.

It has thousands of likes. Dozens of comments. I sit up straighter, accidentally squeaking my shoes against the hotel's linoleum floor, sure I'm hallucinating this whole thing.

I pan out to the grid and see dozens of them—a photo from on top of the Wishing Tree. Another of the sunset gleaming through the crack in a rickety old bench nobody uses anymore. Another I took when Mickey, Leo, Finn, and I were wandering around after dinner, of the embers of one of the campfires blowing in the wind.

There are none of the goofier, spontaneous ones I took of Rufus, or the other girls in my cabin, or the staged ones we took for their Instagrams. Leo went through with a careful eye, picking the exact ones I would have chosen myself—maybe even chose better than I would have. A photo of the mismatched kayaks all lined up at the shore in their yellows, blues, and reds that I dismissed as soon as I took it has more likes than anything in the last three weeks.

If that's staggering, the amount of DMs flagged in my inbox is enough to knock me off my feet. I tap on them, hit by a wall of everything from why no people in your feed, girly? bet ur a stunner to omg!! how can i BE you to one that I click on too fast to process, so fast that I have to read it three times before I can even begin to let it sink in.

> Hello Abby,
> I hope this DM finds you well—we couldn't find an email for you. We work with a scholarship program through Adventure Lens, and we're sponsoring teen travel photographers to go on short trips and take photos as wildlife ambassadors. It's for graduating seniors. I wasn't sure if you qualified this summer or the upcoming summer, but either way we'd love for you to consider the opportunity. The travel dates are flexible, and all expenses are paid, with the expectation that your photos are used as a part of our campaigns that subsequent year and featured on your personal Instagram. Please let me know if you'd like to hear more details!

I click out of it, breathing hard, pressing the phone between my hand and the floor as if something is going to leap out of it. I had no idea. I had *no idea*. All this time Leo hasn't been keeping my photos safe—he's been building them a home..

My eyes squeeze shut, but it's like the grid of photos is tattooed to the inside of my eyelids. Every single one of them carefully plucked, posted, and hashtagged. A little ritual Leo must have committed himself to, one he kept up even when we weren't keeping up with ourselves. Like these posts aren't just posts, but messages that mean something—*I'm sorry*, or *I'm still here*, or maybe even the hope for something more that swallows all of them, even now.

I can't reach him tonight. He won't pick up the phone, and it's too dark to sneak back to camp. Tomorrow I may get a chance before I leave, but if I don't—he has to know the truth. And I know exactly how I can make him.

My dad's computer is still out on the table. I upload the memory card on Poppy's camera, pulling up all the photos. It only takes a moment to find the one I need. It's the first time I've seen it at full resolution, the first time I've really been able to look at it, but even in that split second I know it's more precious to me than any photo that's come before.

I hit "Share" and close it before I can see reactions come in. I fall asleep with the phone in my good hand, willing him to see it and hoping he sees the same things I do when he does.

thirty-five

I wake up the next morning to my wrist throbbing and three missed calls from Connie. I rub my eyes, aware my parents have long been up and gone in search of breakfast from the way the light is hitting the window. It's probably the latest I've slept in years.

My parents left a glass of water and some ibuprofen on the coffee table. I chug some immediately, and before I can overthink it or chicken out, call Connie back.

She picks up on the first ring and speaks before it's even over.

"I'm sorry. I mean, you know that, but I'm going to start with that and end with that, and possibly say it into perpetuity."

I close my eyes, trying to acclimate my brain to what's happening.

"I just—the whole thing was—so dumb. I really didn't think it was gonna, like, be a whole *thing*, you know? Or maybe that's it. I was worried it *was* gonna be a thing, and either you'd both leave me behind, or you'd have some big messy breakup and the whole thing would get ruined and I'd have to pick a side, and shit, Abby. I love you both so much."

I open my eyes again. "So you . . . you told me Leo didn't like me."

"Yeah. But what you don't know is . . . after, you were so relieved about it . . . I told Leo you didn't like him."

"Hold up. One sec. Sorry. I just woke up, so I don't . . . really know what's happening." I take another swig of water and see that there's a banana, too. I rip it open as if I didn't eat my weight in Thai food last night, hoping it will make the ibuprofen work its magic faster.

Then my eyes snap fully open. "You told him *what?*"

"You're pissed."

My mouth is too full of banana to allow me to be much of anything. Or maybe it's that, when I try to summon the anger I've felt since figuring out what she did, I can't find it. If it's there it feels like the smoke it left behind, something too thin to hold on to.

"Kinda."

Connie's not crying, but her voice is at that specific decibel it gets just before she starts. "I ruined everything, haven't I?"

I sit up on the couch, trying to clear my head and decide what to say. I should tell her how much this hurt me. I should tell her how I spent the last few months tiptoeing around her and Leo both, nursing the kind of ache I couldn't tell anyone about, least of all the two people it affected most.

But I can tell she already knows that. And making her feel worse isn't going to do anybody any good.

"No, you haven't."

I just watched an entire lifetime of friendship get imploded by a misunderstanding. I'm not going to let this rock us. We've got way too much behind us and way too much ahead to lose it over something that I think—I hope—can still be fixed.

"I'm fixing this, I swear. I was on the phone with Leo last night. I was trying to reach you, but someone found him for me and I told him everything," she says in a rush. "Just—so he knew. Why there was weirdness. If there was weirdness."

"A surplus of it," I say. It's a relief, weirdly, to be open about it with her. I'm dying to ask her what Leo said—an even vainer,

YOU HAVE A MATCH   283

louder part of me wants to know what Leo said about *me*—but I know it's not Leo I need to ask about. "I was . . . mad when you told me what you did. And I didn't give you a chance to explain."

Connie lets out a sigh. "Well—I guess part of it was that so many things have been changing, and I just wanted to—hit pause, you know?"

"Yeah," I say after a moment. "I know."

The relief of hearing that seems to speed her up, making her words trip over each other on their way out. "It kind of felt like the two of you were going somewhere I've never been, and—if I'm being honest, might not ever really want to go," she says. "I've never really had feelings like that for anyone before, I guess, and I . . . I didn't want you guys to get wrapped up in it and leave me behind. We've all been so busy as it is."

It's like we'd been driving in the same car for ages, and only just looked down and saw the hole in the floor—like we could convince ourselves everything was still okay, as long as we were chugging along in the same direction we'd always been. I try to remember the last time Connie and I really talked to each other, really *talked*, without homework or extracurriculars or a phone screen in our way, and I'm coming up empty.

"Well, you know what? We'll change that. Spend more time together this year, like we used to," I say. "I'm going to have more free time. So if you find some, we can just . . . hang."

"You're not gonna third wheel me?" Connie's voice is light, even if there's still a slight wobble to it. "Not gonna make me the Harry to your Ron and Hermione, the Peggy to your Steve and Bucky, the PB&J cinnamon rolls to your brothers and any other living creature—"

"I'm gonna go ahead and cut you off right there," I laugh. "Connie, nobody could ever third wheel you. You're like four wheels all on your own."

"This is a fact."

I press the phone closer to my face, as if she can feel the intention and it will make my words count for more than they already do.

"And even if things change—I mean—I guess what I'm trying to say is, things were going to change no matter what. Leo's going off to school. You and I are gonna peel off somewhere in a year, too. But that doesn't have to be a bad thing. After Hermione and Ron got together, Harry and Ron were still best friends."

"Did you just . . . willingly make yourself Ron in this metaphor?"

"That's how much I love you, Con."

"Well, shit." She sniffles into the phone, relieved. "And Abby—I mean—I know I'm not exactly the patron saint of budding relationships right now, but I think . . . well. Even my meddling didn't stop you two from feeling things for each other. I really think it could work out."

"You know he's leaving."

And like that, Connie is back in full Mom Friend splendor, the words so firm that I can hear her hand land on her hip for emphasis. "Abby, you've waited your whole damn life to get out of Shoreline and see the world. I'm pretty sure there isn't anywhere either of you could go that the other one wouldn't follow."

I'm not so sure about that, but I am sure I'll do whatever it takes to find out.

thirty-six

It turns out scoring a farewell tour back to camp is as easy as asking my parents for a lift. That, and Mickey wasn't kidding—there were full-blown rumors circulating that I'd been eaten by a bear, so Victoria encouraged a drop-in before the whole of Phoenix Cabin turned the place upside down trying to find out the truth.

I'm expecting to see Finn hanging out at the front desk in that lazy way he always does in the morning, but he isn't there.

"He's got a flight to Chicago tonight," Jemmy informs me, after she and Izzy and Cam finish squeezing in a hug made awkward only by how vigilantly all three were avoiding my cast.

"Yeah," says Izzy, popping the top off a pen with her molars. She gestures for me to hold out my wrist, and starts signing the bright blue plaster. "But he seemed pretty happy about it."

So am I. I hope it works out between him and his mom. I have a feeling I'll be hearing from him and find out soon enough.

"I can't believe you're leaving. Half the camp is ditching us," says Cam.

My arm gets shifted in turn so each can sign, and then all three stare at me solemnly. I'm afraid they're going to ask what happened. Afraid that I'm going to blurt it out and tell them, because I'm bursting to tell *someone*—Connie had to leave before I could tell her anything important.

"Stay in touch," says Izzy instead. Like she's putting a bookmark in the conversation; like she doesn't have to ask now, because they're going to ask later. "I'll put you in the group text when we're all out of here."

"You better."

My parents are still busy talking to Victoria when I pop out of the front cabin to look for Leo. I don't have to look very hard—he's already walking toward the office with long, purposeful strides, looking windswept and frazzled and like he didn't sleep much last night. Our eyes find each other's and he stops in his tracks so fast that my face burns, realizing he must have also been looking for me.

And somehow, just like that, this seems like the least scary thing I'll ever do. I cross the distance to Leo, letting myself look him fully and completely in the eyes for the first time in months, drinking them in without any self-consciousness or fear.

He stares back, and it's already there. It isn't something we've realized. Just something we've always had, maybe, that got lost, and is finally found.

I hold out my hand.

"Do you want to go for a walk?"

He stares at my fingers, his eyes flitting over to the cast on my other side before settling back on my face. I keep my hand out, waiting.

"Yeah. Let's."

It's almost embarrassing, how fast the warmth floods through me when his hand wraps around mine. The surge is quiet but powerful, the kind of burn that steadies me. Neither of us says anything, not even when I squeeze his fingers and he gives mine a quick squeeze back. But I start walking, and he follows, and the rhythm is so easy that we might have been walking like this our whole lives.

I lead him down a path I've walked with Savvy and Rufus before, an early-morning one that I know well. We walk, hand in hand, until I'm almost certain I can feel his heartbeat against my palm as loudly as I can hear my own.

"I saw the Instagram post," he finally says.

"I think it's my best work."

Leo lets out a sharp laugh, kicking a heel into the grass. "I've seen enough of your work to know *that's* a lie."

I squeeze his hand another time before I let go, settling into a spot on the grass that overlooks the water. Leo hesitates, then sits down next to me, staring out at the shore.

"You read the caption?"

"There was a caption?" Leo asks. He looks worried. "I haven't been captioning any of your posts—"

"Here," I say, handing him my phone. I already had the page pulled up, so we don't have to worry about it loading. I hold the phone out to him and let him read, watching the expression on his face shift.

He reads the quote, half murmuring it under his breath. After weeks of working on that Benvolio essay, I have the character's quote memorized: **Soft! I will go along. And if you leave me so, you do me wrong.**

He spent enough time crafting his own essay for *Romeo and Juliet* in his junior year that he knows it, too.

"Abby . . ."

I take the phone from him, my fingers grazing his and lingering. It's the kind of deliberate gesture that might have terrified me a few days ago, but I feel buoyed in it now—in this faith I have in myself to say what I need to say.

"So, I'm gonna be starting summer school. In like two weeks."

Leo's shoulders slump a bit closer to the grass, expecting me to break the silence with something else.

"I read over the email last night," I tell him. "We're doing an intensive in *Romeo and Juliet*. Same essay all over again."

He's as engaged as ever, even in this moment when it is suddenly clear to me that he thinks I'm about to disappoint him. He leans back, like he's settling into something—not the ground beneath us, but acceptance.

"Just—different thesis."

I hold my gaze on him, waiting him out. Watching the way his eyes are brewing as they watch the water, the curve of his set jaw, the rustle of dark hair against his ear. Watching until he realizes I'm not going anywhere, and he has no choice but to look back.

"I was thinking . . . I had it wrong on the last one. Or at least, my heart was never in it." I lean in closer, lowering my voice. "This one will be about why we all need a Benvolio."

Leo lets out this little breath of surprise, a quiet understanding that spreads into his face, sparks in his eyes, and curls the edges of his lips. "You're going to need supporting evidence for that thesis, you know."

I grin back. "I think I've got enough of it right here."

There is an undeniable crack in his expression then, something that splits deeper than his face. "Abby," he says. "I'm . . . I'm still leaving in September."

"Yeah. To New York, not to Mars." I lower my voice. "You read that quote. I mean it, Leo. There's nowhere you could go that would change my mind."

He presses his lips together, his eyes searching mine. "You say that now, Abby, but it's a year. Thousands of miles. And I want this. I want *you*." He takes my hand in his, tight enough that I know he means it, but loose enough that it would be easy for me to let go. "But you're . . . you're a forever kind of person to me. You always have been. And I don't want to start something this important when it might be ended because of things we can't control."

I can't claim to know what the future holds—whether the two of us will be equipped to go the distance, or what kind of people we'll be in a year or two or more on the other side of it. I can't even say where I'll be, let alone where he might.

But it isn't the knowing that matters. It's the feeling that does—and this is deeper than the miles between us, more enduring than any odds we might face.

"Our lives are going to take us a lot of places," I say softly, tightening my grip on his hand. "Like you said—things happening for different people at different times. But the way I feel about you . . . that's never going to change. So if you really feel the way that I do . . ."

"I do," he says. "Plain as Day."

We both start to smile, but our grins snag on each other, pulling us closer than we expected—then as close as we can get.

Kissing Leo is so easy that I almost miss the moment it happens, the way you don't remember opening the front door when you come home, or how you don't wake up in the middle of the night to the same loud noise you've heard a thousand times. Like this isn't the important moment, not the one that really defines anything; it's just a moment built smack in the middle of all the other ones. A moment that carries you through to the next but isn't any more or less important than the others because the end result will always be the same.

What isn't easy is once it starts happening, because there is no way to make it fit—it isn't just the clench of my gut, the heat pooling out of it, the tingle of skin on skin. It's the overwhelming flood of sensations, and everything they're built on. Knees knocking on top of the jungle gym. Late-night texts under the covers. Stolen bites of still-cooking meals. This current that has hummed under me my whole life, roaring and breaking the surface, crashing into every part of me. I could kiss him and never find the start of it, never find the end. I could kiss him and lose myself in a world we already share, now lit up in colors I never thought I'd see.

When we pull apart we're both grinning, foreheads pressed together, eyes with identical sparks.

"I can't even tell you how long I've wanted to do that," says Leo.

Confidence blazes through me, making me feel like I could snap fire into existence, strike lightning at will, control the tides.

"So show me."

Leo laughs, and so do I, and he catches my laugh with his lips and this time when we kiss, I know I've finally reached the one height he'll never ask me to come down from.

thirty-seven

I can count on one hand the number of times I've seen an actual drunk person, courtesy of never going to any of the student government parties Connie always invites us to, but I imagine that this is what it feels like: stumbling like the earth's axis tilted, sneaking glances at the person next to you and giggling for no reason, stealing kisses every few steps just because you can. By the time Leo and I start meandering back to camp, I am distinctly aware that we are insufferable, but not aware enough to know if five minutes have passed or five hours.

"Want to make a pit stop?" Leo asks at one point, turning his head toward a clearing up ahead.

I nod, but mostly because he could ask me if I wanted to swim in a cage with an unfed shark right now and I'd probably do the same. I'm so wrapped up in us and this weird bubble of things we're allowed to do—for some reason I've been touching his forearm constantly, like that's a totally normal thing—that I don't notice where he's taking me until we're directly in front of Make Out Rock.

And its current status is very much occupied.

"Oh shit," I blurt first, without a shred of decorum.

Savvy's ponytail is not even ponytail reminiscent anymore, and Mickey's shirt is so askew that I can spot a temporary Flounder tattoo peeking out from the Ariel on her shoulder.

"Hey," Mickey squeaks, spotting us first.

Savvy whips around, mouth open like she's poised for damage control. Victoria's rules about staff romance are probably something along the lines of "don't." When she sees it's me, her eyes go wide.

"Well, look at *you*," she says, and it occurs to me that my face must be every bit as red as it feels. That, or I'm being extremely unsubtle about my newfound talent of glomming on to Leo, which has manifested in my good arm roping around his torso and his around my shoulder.

"Excuse us," says Leo, "we didn't realize this spot was already, uh, taken."

"That's the glory of becoming an unrepentant summer camp cliché," says Mickey, gesturing for us to take their place. "The ability to pass the torch to the next. Go on, my children."

"Nah. I gotta get this one back to camp," says Leo, his grip tightening on me. I sink into it, and Savvy catches my eye, the both of us looking a little delirious.

"And I need to get you *both* to camp before the head chef calls out a prelunch search party," says Savvy, eyeing Mickey and Leo.

Mickey glances at her watch. "Oh, yeah, it's five past We're Definitely Getting Lectured o'clock," she says, her eyebrows shooting into her hair. She turns to Savvy, lifting herself on her tiptoes to kiss her again. Savvy leans in, more shy than I might have expected, but Mickey ends the kiss by tugging the dangling hair tie from the remains of her ponytail and snapping it in the air.

"Thanks, babe," she says, pulling it into her own hair and making a messy bun.

"*Hey.*"

Mickey arches up a little to mess up Savvy's hair. "See you after lunch?"

"What color should I make the Gcal invite?"

"Too soon!" Mickey calls, already dragging Leo by the arm up the path. He stops long enough to kiss me, half mouth and half cheek, the gesture fast but the big sloppy smile on our faces lasting way longer than they probably should.

Savvy knocks her shoulder into mine. "So . . ."

I clear my throat, meeting her eye. "So."

"I'm proud of us," says Savvy.

"Yeah. We waited six full minutes after solving our parents' drama to stick our tongues down Mickey's and Leo's throats." Savvy doesn't say anything right away, and there's this twinge that sneaks its way through the bubble, a reminder of what's beyond the thick of these trees and the morning haze. "*If* we solved our parents' drama."

Savvy slows her pace, watching Leo and Mickey and deliberately putting space between us and them. When I look over at her, there's a lightness in her expression, a gleam in her eyes—I think of that first day we met, of Queen Quack and the brief hint of this girl I saw then that I am starting to see more of every day.

"We did a better job than you think."

I smile back, mostly because I don't know how to stop. "Yeah?" It's a nice thought. One that I could spend an hour poking holes in, except I'm happy right now. Happy enough to hope. "Do you think they'll ever . . . I don't know . . . talk again?"

"Well, they're going to have to talk logistics, at least," she says matter-of-factly. Her words are all business, but her tone is light.

I peer at her. "You mean with us?"

"That," says Savvy. "And, well—my dad called this morning."

The grin on her face is brimming, threatening to burst. Before she even says anything I can feel it flowing through me— the feeling of knowing the magnitude of something without knowing the shape of it, of catching someone else's joy before you even know why.

"He and my mom bought Bean Well."

I don't think she's even fully finished the sentence before I let out the kind of squeal that would make Rufus howl, launching myself at her. The two of us hug each other so tightly that we almost add some broken ribs into the mix. We pull apart just as fast, just as breathlessly, like we need to look at each other to believe it. Our eyes meet and the moment stamps itself to my heart, taking up a permanent place in me before it's over, and I hear Poppy's voice in my head—*If you learn to capture a feeling, it'll always be louder than words.*

I don't know if I'll ever feel one louder than this.

one year later

I'm late, but knowing Savvy, I'm early—because knowing Savvy, she told me the meeting was at half past noon when it's at one. Sure enough, when I stumble into Magpie, the bell jangling so loudly that Ellie the barista looks up in alarm and one of the writer types who hangs out by the window nearly drops her latte, I see her and Mickey camped out in our usual spot in the back, without the other dozen people in our budding little Instagram community.

"Mickey, that's enough emojis to make someone black out," I can hear Savvy say, kneeling on the couch so she can look at whatever Mickey is typing into her phone over her shoulder.

"I'm not an influencer, I can afford to break a brain or two."

"Yes, but do you need six rainbows *and* a knife?"

"It's my Tuesday mood."

Before I announce myself I wave over at Ellie, and she starts making me the hot chocolate I always order and pulling one of Leo's legendary Nutella-stuffed, parmesan-topped ensaymadas out of the display case—one of the many creations of his that have been rotating in and out of Magpie's seasonal offerings, whenever he's home for a few days and wants to test something outside the confines of culinary school. I wonder who he taught to make them, since he's not supposed to be back from his family's trip to the Philippines for another few days.

"My stars," says Mickey, clutching a hand to an invisible string of pearls. "Is it—can it be? In the flesh? Star photographer Abigail Day, gracing us with her esteemed presence—"

"Hey, you," says Savvy, getting up and squeezing me into a hug. "Long time, no see."

It really has been—well, long for us, at least. These days Savvy and I see each other a few times a week, between meet-ups for this Instagram community (fittingly called "Savvy About Instagram"), study sessions when she sneaks me and Connie into the University of Washington's ridiculously beautiful undergraduate library, and the occasional times she's babysat for my brothers. (Unlike me, they took the whole "surprise sister" thing in stride—and also unlike me, decided to blow up my parents' spots by immediately telling their teachers, most of our neighbors, and the woman who writes "Happy Birthday" on the cakes at the grocery store, so the cat's extremely out of the bag.)

But I've been in Alaska for the last three weeks, stalking moose and whales and bears, taking the terrifying winding bus through the thin mountain roads of Denali and kayaking in the endless summer sunlight. I have so many photos that trying to choose the ones to highlight for the ambassador program feels like choosing which of my organs to keep. But even with the hum of the adventure still in my bones, it's a relief to be back.

Before I can ask what they've been up to, Mickey hands me a flower—a red rose, identical to the one Savvy has tucked behind her ear.

"Oh—uh—thank you?" I say, pleased and confused.

"It's from Leo," she says. "It's our one-year anniversary, you know. Yours and Leo's, too. If we're counting from the day we all started making out."

I blink at her. "It's been a whole year?"

"Yeah. Anyway, since Leo isn't back yet, I told him I'd chuck a flower at you in his stead."

"I believe you called it 'Tuxedo Masking,'" Savvy chimes in, grazing the petals of her own flower with her fingers.

"To possess even one *iota* of his dramatic flair," says Mickey, flinging herself on the plush pink couch.

I hold the rose up to my face, feeling the flutter of it against my skin. There's that same dopey, happy lift in my heart that I'm not quite used to—the little ways that I'm still surprised by the Leo I knew then versus the Leo I know now. The Leo I grew up with versus the one who tucks my hair behind my ear, who falls asleep on movie nights with his head in my lap, who sometimes tugs me by the hand while we're walking for a sneaky kiss. It's the same Leo as before, but it's as if I've tapped into some other dimension of him, one that I must have known somewhere deep down was there even when I wasn't capable of seeing it on my own.

Or maybe it's not Leo who changed, but me. I feel like in the last year a part of me has opened up, as if it was just waiting until there was someone worth making space for. A lot of it is Leo, but there was more room to fill than I ever realized—room for Savvy and Pietra and Dale. For Mickey and Finn. For the parents I thought I knew but understand so much more of now.

"Speaking of dramatic flair, is this supposed to be a unicorn cow? Or just a cow that is dressed up as a unicorn?" I ask, squinting at one of the new fixtures by the couch.

"Its origins remain a mystery, as do all of its fellow ceramic cow brethren," says Mickey, gesturing to the rest of the space.

I glance around and see what else changed in the two weeks I've been gone—the local art on display sells and rotates so quickly that the place is essentially transformed from one day to the next. One week will be splashy slashes of primary colors on giant canvas, the next will be delicate pastel watercolors of views of the Puget Sound, and right now the place is cows on cows on cows—a doctor cow by the window, an astronaut cow on the barista station, a cow in a Seahawks jersey by the window. The only constants are the big, plush, cozy couches and chairs, the giant framed photos I've taken all over Shoreline and Seattle (including my favorite, one of a very haughty-looking duck on Green Lake labeled "Queen Quack"), and a table from the original Bean Well with Poppy's and Gammy's names inscribed in the wood.

"So?" says Savvy. "I got bare-bones details, but I gotta hear about the rest of your trip. Did you see anything cool?"

"Did anything try to eat you?" Mickey cuts in, leaning forward. On the inside of her wrist is the newest of her tattoos, the first one in permanent ink—a miniheart that says *Mick + Sav* on the inside, identical to the one on the tree back at Camp Reynolds. It's the first year none of their little crew will be spending the summer there, but with Mickey starting a bachelor's in education in the fall, it will probably only be a matter of time before she's back.

I set the rose down on the table, leaning in. "Actually, at one point, right after we got on, a bear wandered *right up* to the bus—"

"Uh, this is the first time I'm hearing *that* story." It's my mom, coming out from the back room, where we hold classes and let meetup groups rent the space. I hadn't realized she was here.

"Did I say a bear? I meant a deer. A tiny baby one about yea high."

My mom shoots me a *don't think I won't be bringing this up later* look, right as Pietra wanders out behind her, her face streaked with paint. "I'm ninety-eight percent sure I cleaned up the last of the finger paint from the Mommy and Me group, but the lot of you should watch your butts just in case," she informs us, giving my shoulder a quick squeeze in greeting. "Maggie sent me some of the pictures from your trip. Stunning as usual."

I flush.

"We're gonna have to open a second shop to display them all," says my mom.

This is only half a joke, especially now that my mom is so involved. She's shifted from full-time lawyering to part-time, and every hour she isn't working or wrangling my three brothers in line is spent here. She's either meeting with families who come here for legal help pro bono, just as she envisioned for the original Magpie, or helping Pietra run the business—which is ridiculously booming. We got a few write-ups in newspapers and artist blogs that led to us getting put into a "13 Underrated Gems in the Seattle Area" article that went viral last year, and the word-of-mouth from the meetup groups that come here has certainly helped. The place is usually so packed that it's hard to find a seat. I heard murmurs of her and Pietra looking into a second location, one closer to Shoreline. Savvy and I have already been brainstorming coordinating color schemes.

"Hi hi hi," comes a voice from the front, and in comes Connie, beelining for me and squishing me into a hug. We've been in near constant touch even during my Alaska trip so we can coordinate our apartment in the U District we're moving into next month—Connie's starting at the UW, and I'll be taking classes at the community college while I throw more time into my photography and the whopping hundred thousand followers on the @savingtheabbyday Instagram account.

"Did I miss it?" she asks, her eyes wide. "Have you already spilled all the beans about your trip?"

"Just the terrifying ones," says my mom wryly, making her way to the kitchen.

"Sorry I'm late," says Connie, directing it at Savvy and Mickey. "I was using that Pomodoro Technique for productivity you were telling me about, breaking up tasks into twenty-five minutes, and—"

"Yes!" Savvy exclaims. "And you love it, right?"

"I love it so much I got obsessed with like, *little* time but forgot about big, actual time— I got *so* much done today, though—"

"I told you! It's one of my favorites. A lifesaver during finals week."

While Savvy has eased up a lot in the last year—her Insta, @howtostaysavvy, now regularly features frizzy post-rain hair, the unspeakably ugly highlighted study guides Savvy makes for her classes, goofy selfies with Mickey, and even my grimy brothers on a few occasions—she is still the kind of productive that puts mere mortals to shame. And in a not-so-plot-twist that anyone in the world could have seen coming, putting Connie and her in the same room together is dangerous enough that they've come up with designs for entire full-blown business concepts while I was peeing.

"Think you can spare one of your precious Pomo-whatsit minutes to help us set up in there?" Mickey asks, helping me drag the two of them over to the barista station so we can stock up on treats for the group.

As we're setting up, people start spilling in. First it's Jemmy and Izzy, who carpooled; then Finn and Cam, who have been pseudoflirting with each other so bashfully for so long that the rest of us have bets on when they'll finally make it Instagram official; then a few other people trickling in around or slightly after the official start time, giving a loose feeling to the whole thing. To be fair, in the last few months the group has become less about Instagram strategies and more about eating dessert and filling everyone in on each other's lives.

"Hey, Bubbles." Finn reaches out and plucks the rose from my hand. "What's this for?" he asks, holding it upside down to examine it.

I pry it out of his hands. "Leo sent it."

Finn frowns, looking back at the parking lot. "But why would he bother sending it if he's—"

Cam dives forward and claps a hand over Finn's mouth. His eyes bulge, whatever he was going to say muffled incomprehensibly into Cam's palm until she pulls it away, cackling. "Did you just *lick* me?"

The door opens again, the bell jangling. My heart leaps before the rest of me does—there in the doorway is Leo, grinning broadly, a backpack slung over his shoulder and a bouquet of roses in his hand. He has to abruptly deposit them both on the empty table by the window, though, when I start running for him with the kind of speed that would incite terror in anyone else.

I collide with him so forcefully that he ends up lifting me up from the ground and spinning me to absorb it, my legs wrapping around his torso and my arms so tight around his shoulders that I'm probably about to suffocate him. I lean back, grinning into his grin—the kiss tastes like cinnamon and warmth and *Leo*.

He sets me down, his hands on my shoulders, my whole body dizzy with joy.

"You're *here*," I say, grabbing his face between my hands to anchor myself. I kiss him again, ignoring the catcalls from Jemmy and Izzy and the throat clearing that sounds suspiciously like my mom. "How are you here? I thought—"

"We ended up shifting everything a week earlier so Carla could get back in time for cheer conditioning," he says, his hands moving down to my waist. "We got in this morning."

He pulls me in closer, and I rest my head against his chest, hiding the most ridiculous smile I've ever had. It isn't the first time we've surprised each other like this, with him coming home for an unexpected weekend or me flying out to New York for spring break, but somehow the thrill of it never wears off.

"Happy one-year anniversary, you dweebs," says Connie, pulling me and Leo into another hug, one just as sloppy and silly as the hugs we were giving each other ten years before.

When we pull away I look around the room, and I feel the full force of what happened a year ago, and a staggering appreciation for everything that has happened since. For the way my days then look almost nothing like my days now; for the little things that snowballed into big things that gave me the life I have today.

It's been a year of wandering all over Seattle with Leo on the weekends he comes to visit and cinnamon-soaked kisses in the rain. A year of our parents leaving me and Savvy to babysit my brothers during their monthly double-date nights, and my brothers essentially declaring shared custody of Rufus. A year of watching this place slowly come to life, shifting from Bean Well to Magpie with every new installation, every new couch one of us found at a thrift shop, every light fixture Mom and Pietra chose. A year of hearing all these stories spill out of my parents—from my dad's illness to law school mishaps, from the years they were inseparable from Dale and Pietra to the new memories they're making with them now.

A year of making memories of my own—the thousands I have saved in my camera roll, and more stamped into my heart than I could ever count. I glance around the room, drinking in the sight of my friends, old and new, gathered around the table; my sister, catching my eye with a smile; the sound of my mom and Pietra, cackling about something on their phones across the café; the velvety petal of Leo's rose between my thumb and my finger. I close my eyes, breathe it in, and make one more.

acknowledgments

First of all, thank you to my little sisters, Maddie and Lily, the Blossom and Buttercup to my Bubbles, the keepers of my heart. I've loved getting older and seeing all the magical ways being a sister changes with time. I've gone from bossing the two of you around like it's my job to learning more from the two of you than I'll ever learn from anybody else. It is a unique privilege to have sisters, and I am endlessly grateful to be yours.

Thank you also to our big brother, Evan, who is the best brother of them all (and you can fight three of his sisters and also two Shih Tzus on that).

This book was written before the pandemic, but all of the efforts to bring it into the world were made during it. Even as I'm writing these acknowledgments we're still living in it, and like everyone else, I have no idea what the world is going to look like in the next few months and years, let alone when *You Have a Match* is out. But one thing I never had to worry about was what would happen with it—everyone at Wednesday Books has worked so tirelessly and creatively to bring stories to life during these uncertain times and kept us a part of the process every step of the way, and for that I don't know if a "thank you" will ever cut it. So while I can't adequately express my gratitude for something that big, I will aggressively thank everyone there for the things I can. Thank you to Alex and Vicki for your support and the kind of edits that made me go "GALAXY BRAIN!!" a hundred times over. Thank you to Mara, for keeping my human self on track, and to Meghan and DJ for shouting "Book!" from the mountaintops. I am the luckiest human to get to work with y'all.

Thank you to Janna. It is the world's biggest understatement to say none of this would have happened without you, but if I correctly state it, it will come out in multiple sentences of caps lock, and people will be alarmed.

Thank you to my niece, Marcella, for being born. I got to chill with your parents for a few of the coolest days of my life doing research for this book, and then you were cooking at the same time I was writing it. You came out much cuter! Flawless first draft! Your little baby smiles are my new favorite thing. You will be over a year old by the time this book comes out and it feels illegal that we're letting you grow up so fast.

Thank you to the Barbee family for all of the Vashon adventures. Those memories are stamped into my heart forever, and so many of them made it into this book.

Thank you to 23andMe for telling me about my unibrow. Rest assured, I already knew.

Thank you to my vast writer-y squad. To Suzie and Kadeen, the kind of friends who don't flinch when you yell in an otherwise dead silent cabin, "I'M GOING TO CONTROL-F + REPLACE-ALL TWO OF THESE CHARACTERS' NAMES, IT TURNS OUT I HATE THEM!" when you're 310 pages into a draft. To Gaby and Erin and Cristina, for endless conversations commiserating over books and writerly woes and always having the best advice—y'all are the most ~marquee~ friends a girl could ask for. To my soul twin, JQ, who now knows the publishing industry inside out because she has heard every trial and tribulation in exhaustive detail, and is the kind of brave I want both my human self and my characters to be. To my fellow Wednesday authors, who I'd die/kill for despite being a Hufflepuff down to the marrow of my bones.

Extremely bless everyone at AfterWork Theater. I'd be lost without you guys, and I mean that both emotionally and also literally because I'm a delinquent and watch y'all for all our dance cues. Cheesus only knows what I'd do without jazz hands and post-rehearsal Bud Lights and ridiculous ensemble backstories. It's an honor being everyone's Weird Dad TM.

And as always, thank you to my mom and dad. You didn't just give me an awesome life, but the three best humans to guide me through it. I could write a bajillion stories and not come close to the magic of what you guys made for us.